"*The Things We Wish Were True* is a brilliant glimpse into the realities of suburban life. Startling. Compelling. Redemptive. It's the kind of story that makes us wonder how well we really know ourselves—much less our neighbors. Marybeth Whalen has a gift for turning over the pretty surfaces of life, finding the hidden things beneath, and then exposing them to the light. I found myself drawn in, unable to look away from these characters and their dark, tender, familiar lives. I utterly loved this novel."

—Ariel Lawhon, author of *The Wife, the Maid, and the Mistress* and *Flight of Dreams*

"Marybeth Whalen has a gift for illuminating the dark corners of suburban life. The neighbor you think you know . . . but do you really? The couple with the seemingly perfect marriage . . . until the blinds are drawn. *The Things We Wish Were True* is a novel that explores the nuances of community and belonging, showing us the hope, pain, disappointments, and joy that exist behind the facades of a typical American subdivision. The characters are relatable and engaging, and you'll find yourself pulling for them all, from the overwhelmed single dad to the hyperresponsible young girl to the lonely empty nester or the divorcee forced to return home and face the past she'd vowed to outrun. Perceptive, astute, and oh-so-relatable, *The Things We Wish Were True* is a winner!"

—Kim Wright, author of *The Unexpected Waltz* and *The Canterbury Sisters*

"With skill and compassion, Marybeth Whalen digs beneath the surface of a quiet suburban neighborhood to reveal its darker secret side. Full of unexpected twists and sympathetic, relatable characters, *The Things We Wish Were True* is both surprising and heartwarming, and it's sure to have you examining your own peaceful neighborhood with new eyes."

—Diane Chamberlain, *USA Today* bestselling author of *Pretending to Dance*

"The characters in *The Things We Wish Were True* may live in a small town, but their hearts are as big as all outdoors. Marybeth Whalen has created an ensemble cast whose lives intertwine and touch one another in moving and surprising ways. A generous, compassionate novel that will leave a warm glow long after the last page has been turned."

—Yona Zeldis McDonough, author of *The House on Primrose Pond*

"*The Things We Wish Were True* masterfully blends dark, twisted secrets with a redemptive story about the power of community. As the families of Sycamore Glen, North Carolina, kick off summer at their neighborhood pool, Marybeth Mayhew Whalen peels back the layers of their past and present lives to reveal the underbelly of suburbia. A fabulous page-turner with the ending you want."

—Barbara Claypole White, bestselling author of *The Perfect Son*

"*The Things We Wish Were True* is a story of startling truth revealed through the intricate lives of those we *think* we know. Profound. Perceptive. Marybeth Whalen knows how to braid together the seen and the unseen in a profound story that startles and enlightens. Readers will eagerly turn every page."

—Patti Callahan Henry, *New York Times* bestselling author

"In *The Things We Wish Were True*, Marybeth Whalen has pulled off an impressive feat, an ever-shifting narrative through a neighborhood full of secrets. Each of these characters is compelling and fully realized, and the final twists and reveals left me breathless and, ultimately, at peace. An impressive achievement that you'll want to put at the top of your to-read list."

—Catherine McKenzie, bestselling author of *Hidden* and *Fractured*

THE THINGS WE WISH WERE TRUE

THE THINGS WE WISH WERE TRUE

Marybeth Mayhew Whalen

LAKE UNION
PUBLISHING

Text copyright © 2016 by Marybeth Mayhew Whalen
All rights reserved.

Published by Lake Union Publishing, Seattle

www.apub.com

Amazon, the Amazon logo, and Lake Union Publishing are trademarks of Amazon.com, Inc., or its affiliates.

ISBN-13: 9781503936072
ISBN-10: 1503936074

Cover design by Janet Perr

Printed in the United States of America

For the Caileys of the world. May you find a place to belong.

MEMORIAL DAY WEEKEND, 2014

Sycamore Glen
Neighborhood Pool
Matthews, North Carolina

CAILEY

Cutter and I were there when they opened the Sycamore Glen pool for the summer. So I actually saw, with my own eyes, the spider web that was woven across the gate, keeping all the people from just walking right on in like they'd done every year. Our new neighbors shuffled their feet and sighed real loud as they waited for the lifeguards to figure out what to do. They held their towels and coolers and floats and bags and stared at the web, as if they could burn it down with their eyes like superheroes.

We all took in the large spider, round and yellow with black stripes, sitting smack-dab in the middle of that web. It seemed to be waiting for us, as if it had a message to deliver before the summer could begin, like that spider in *Charlotte's Web*. But no one wanted to hear that spider's message. All they could think of was how to get it out of the way so they could get on with their fun.

Some of the boys grabbed sticks and tried to poke at the spider, the desire to destroy wound up in their DNA like we'd learned about in science class. They brandished the sticks like swords, content to fence with them when their mothers wouldn't let them kill the spider.

I could feel Cutter beside me, wanting to join in with them yet knowing he couldn't. His body was tense, his inner self trying to get over to those boys even as his arms and legs stayed still. I didn't say a word to him or make a move. I didn't have to. Cutter knew how it was without my ever having to tell him. Much as he wanted to be, Cutter wasn't like those boys.

Meanwhile, the girls huddled in fear, clutching at each other with more drama than necessary, shrieking so loudly that one of the lifeguards covered his ears, and the parents rolled their eyes and told the girls to be quiet. I didn't shriek, of course. I wasn't like those girls any more than Cutter was like those boys. So I just watched that spider, feeling bad that all its hard work was being knocked down. I hoped that no one would hurt it, that someone would stop those boys from killing the poor thing when the mothers weren't watching anymore. Cutter and I stood, the two of us, off to the side, apart from the crowd.

One of the lifeguards got a stick and used it to gently move the spider from its web, then let it down into the grass without causing it harm. A couple of the boys pretended to find it and stomp on it after he'd let it go. Then the other lifeguard used another stick to knock down the web, allowing the crowd that had gathered to get into the pool area. The web was quickly forgotten, and they ambled in as if nothing had happened. They slathered on sunscreen, cracked open beers, and pretty much ignored their kids while they caught up on all that had happened in the past nine months. That pool brought this neighborhood together, but only in the summer.

It rained that afternoon, and everyone had to run for their cars in the downpour, grumbling about a day cut short, calling out to each other that this was a bad beginning to the summer season. They ran out the same gate through which they'd entered, forgetting that spider ever existed. Later I would think about that spider, wondering what its message to us might have been and how it might have made a difference if we had all paid attention.

ZELL

Zell Boyette made her way gingerly down the stairs, gripping the handrail, grateful for it. She used to just fly down those steps, her feet barely lighting on them as she rushed from one activity to the next—book club, church, neighborhood board meetings, lunch dates with friends. John used to scold her, "You're gonna hurt yourself!" She *had* hurt herself, but that was not how she'd done it.

She did her best to walk normally as she entered the kitchen, where John was having his coffee at the table and peering at his computer screen, looking confused. He glanced up and saw her there. "Mornin'," he said.

She poured herself a cup of coffee and joined him at the table, laying her hand on his. "You hungry?" she asked. They'd had some form of this exact conversation for the last thirty years.

He shrugged. "I'll eat something if you make it." This was his standard answer.

She hobbled over to the pantry. She could feel his eyes watching her and knew what he wasn't saying just as surely as if he'd said it out loud. John was worried about her knee, always bugging her to see a doctor. When he'd asked her what she'd done to it after it first happened, she'd told him she'd hurt it running. That was close enough to the truth for it not to be a lie.

She set about making them some granola and yogurt parfaits with blueberries, but a knock on the door interrupted her. The knock was light and hesitant and one she'd become accustomed to hearing at least once a day. She opened the back door to reveal little Alec from the house next door. He looked up at her from under bangs that needed trimming. She should offer her grooming services to his father, tell him how she used to trim her own boys' hair when they were Alec's age.

Lance would say no, wave his hands as if he were putting the final flourish on a magic trick that would make it all go away. He would assure her that everything was fine, that he'd been meaning to take Alec and Lilah for haircuts. Then he'd get that anxious look that made her worry for him. The man was going to have a heart attack before age forty.

"Hi, Mrs. Boyette," Alec said. He attempted in vain to push his bangs from his eyes. "My dad said ta ask you if you had any milk." The boy shook his head and looked at the ground as if his father's ineptness was too much to bear. "He forgot to get some at the store again." Alec had been on her doorstep just yesterday asking for the exact same thing. She'd handed over her remaining milk, which wasn't much, then limped to the grocery store to fetch more. Part of her wanted to say that she couldn't keep supplying them with milk and other items. But the other part—the bigger part—knew that of course she would.

"Of course I do, Alec," she said, giving the boy a smile to put him at ease. She retrieved the milk from the fridge and handed him the full gallon. Alec accepted the milk with a little *oof* sound, then cradled the gallon like a small child he had to protect with his life, the condensation from the carton wetting the front of his T-shirt, which already had a chocolate syrup stain down the center.

"Enjoy your cereal," she told him. She knew those children were eating terribly. She didn't approve of Lance giving them sugary cereals, but he hadn't asked her opinion, and she suspected that, while he appreciated her help, he couldn't care less what she thought. But that didn't stop her from wondering what Debra would think if she could see her children with their unkempt hair and dirty fingernails, their sallow complexions and the little rolls of fat accumulating around their bellies. She fingered the belt on her robe. Not unlike her own stomach. They'd all changed since last fall.

She waved goodbye, but Alec couldn't return the gesture with his hands full of milk. "Thanks, Mrs. Boyette," he said instead, then turned to head home.

And then, because she cared about the family next door—perhaps a little too much, if truth be told—and because of something in the way Alec's little shoulders slumped forward, as if the weight of the world were contained in that gallon of milk, she called after him, halting his steps.

"Will you guys be heading to the pool today for the opening?" She pictured Debra that first year after Alec was born, floating him around in the pool in one of those little baby boats. He'd worn a sun hat with a brim that kept flopping in his eyes, and he'd laughed a delicious baby laugh. Debra had tipped her head back and laughed with him.

Alec shook his head slowly, sadly. "My dad says he has ta work."

The words were out of her mouth before she could stop herself. "Well, you tell him I can take you two. You tell him to come over here just as soon as he gets a chance, and we'll get it worked out."

He gave her an "are you serious?" look, and she nodded in affirmation. "Go on! Go tell him!" She prompted him toward his house with her hands.

She turned back to find John watching her, his face telling her all she needed to know. "What did Oliver Twist want now?" he asked. John pretended to be gruff, but he was an old softie.

"Be nice," she chided. She set his parfait down in front of him.

He raised his eyebrows. "Did you just offer to tote those kids to the pool today?"

She shrugged. "They wouldn't have gotten to go otherwise. Lord knows Lance doesn't have the time to take them."

He crossed his arms over his chest, gave her an impervious look. "You better watch out, or they're going to suck you right in."

She waved his words away. "Oh, they are not. Eat your parfait."

"I like my parfaits to involve pudding," he groused, but he began to eat.

After a few minutes of silence, John took a drink of his coffee and said, "So I was talking to Clay Robinson. Seems they're in the same boat as us. Kids gone, nothing planned for the summer . . ." She looked over at him, feeling where the conversation was going but not liking it. He ignored her panicked look and continued. "We talked about maybe going on a little couples' getaway."

Zell didn't want to go on a couples' getaway. She wanted to go on a family vacation like they used to—rent a house on the beach or a cabin in the mountains by a stream, or stay in a hotel near an amusement park. She wanted to pick up wet towels and soothe sunburned skin and sweep up sand. She wanted to go fishing and camping and ride roller coasters and make s'mores and play board games. She wanted the summers of the past. She wanted to do it all again.

But she could not say that to John, who still loved her, still wanted her, still held her hand when they drove somewhere in the car. This was, she knew, something. She lowered her hands to his forearms. He had such strong forearms; even now she admired the way the muscles rippled underneath his skin. "What did you have in mind?" she asked.

"I was thinking Lake Lure?" he asked. "Somewhere quiet and peaceful like that? Maybe a little cabin by the lake." He grinned, proud of himself for thinking up this plan. "With a screened-in porch." She was a sucker for a screened-in porch, and he knew it. They'd been talking about adding one to the house for years, but with three kids to get through college, the cost had been prohibitive. Maybe now they could do it.

"Clay and I could golf. You and Althea could poke around in the shops." Clay and John had been work buddies for a long time. She tolerated Althea, but she would never elect to vacation with her. The woman had the most alarming breasts. They looked like when her son stuck water balloons down his shirt to be funny; they hung absurdly low and moved independently from the rest of her. Althea also thought her only son looked exactly like Tom Cruise and used every opportunity to whip out her photos of him. This also disturbed Zell; she'd stood by once too often as Althea accosted some poor soul with photos while they nodded and agreed politely.

"That sounds nice. I'll give Althea a call about it as soon as I get a chance," she said agreeably. She'd think of a way out of it later.

Satisfied, John put down his coffee. "You know, I don't have to get to work *right* away," he said.

She laughed. "I haven't even brushed my teeth yet."

"It's not your teeth I'm interested in." He flashed his most charming smile, rose from his chair, and carried his dishes to the sink. He turned back and raised his eyebrows in invitation. She giggled and waved him away. He shrugged, then shuffled off to shower and get ready for his day.

She went to the sink and busied herself with washing the coffee mugs and dishes from breakfast, half thinking of going upstairs to join John in the shower. Wasn't this the kind of freedom they once dreamed of having? Outside the window over the sink, something caught her eye, distracting her from her thoughts. A blue Mylar balloon shaped like a heart floated on the breeze, carried down their street as if an invisible child's hand were tugging it along. She stopped washing dishes and watched as it floated away.

BRYTE

The moment her eyes opened, she went into planning mode, listing the responsibilities of the day ahead. Opening weekend at the pool meant making sure the bags were packed, the lunches made, the meeting time confirmed with friends, the ample supply of sunscreen readily on hand. She lay in her bed going over it all, ticking off the mental bullet points.

In the next room she could hear Everett talking with Christopher about dinosaurs, going over the different kinds again, answering the same questions he'd answered dozens of times before. Christopher couldn't wrap his tongue around all the syllables in the long dinosaur names yet, and his mispronunciations were legendary. She could hear Ev laughing over Christopher's butchering of the word *velociraptor*. Then she heard the unmistakable screech of his impression of one. The sound of the two of them pulled her from the cocoon of her bed, pushed her toward her son and her husband, the nucleus of their family, her very center.

"Mommy's up!" Everett told Christopher. He gave her a grin over the top of the little boy's head. Their hair was the exact same shade of brown, their eyes, though shaped differently, almost an identical blue. *My boys,* she thought, and her heart contracted with love.

"Tell Mommy where we went this morning while she was sleeping," Ev prompted.

Christopher thought about it, his eyes lighting up when he seized on the right answer. "Krispy Kreme!" From him it sounded like "Kwispy Kweme."

"And what kind of donut did you pick out for Mommy?" Everett coached.

"Chocolate with sprinkles!"

Bryte laughed along with Everett. She knew that "her" donut would be quickly devoured by a certain almost-three-year-old boy with laughing eyes and a love for dinosaurs. She scooped him up and pressed him to her, inhaling his early-morning smell the same as she had done since he was born. He was her precious, long-awaited baby, the child she'd feared they might never have.

"Hey, buddy," she said. "What letter do *donut* and *dinosaur* start with?"

Christopher scrunched up his face, thinking hard. He was so smart, already linking sounds to letters, recognizing their distinct shapes. Behind them, Everett whispered, sotto voce, "D." Bryte swatted at him as Christopher shouted out the answer as if he'd thought of it on his own.

"D!" he crowed, then laughed, looking around in victory as his parents joined in with him.

"I told everyone we'd meet them up at the pool around eleven," Bryte said to Everett. "That'll give us a few hours before *n-a-p* time. But one of us will need to go over and walk Rigby before we go."

Everett nodded in agreement and motioned her into the kitchen, where a donut and freshly made coffee with cream awaited her. He'd made a big deal on Mother's Day just a few weeks before, and Christopher had latched on to the concept of fussing over Mommy's breakfasts ever since. She wasn't complaining. But the thought of eating the sugary-sweet donut nauseated her.

She recalled those early-morning sprints to the bathroom while pregnant with Christopher, how she'd both loved and hated throwing up—loved that it meant that the baby was growing, hated that her life had been taken over. *There is no turning back,* she'd thought every time she crouched over the toilet and lost her breakfast. *This is happening,* she'd thought then.

But she knew it wasn't happening now. She thought of the conversations she'd had with Everett lately about Christopher getting bigger, how he felt they should start trying again. "Remember how long it took?" Everett had pressed last week. As if she could forget.

How could she tell her husband she couldn't do it again? That she wanted Christopher to be their only child? Could he ever understand or accept that? Would he still love her if she just said a firm, nonnegotiable no?

As if reading her thoughts, Everett asked, "You're thinking about what we talked about, aren't you?" He gave her that enticing grin, the one that could coax her into just about anything. It had been that way since they were in ninth grade and he'd talked her into making out that one time during night games in someone's front yard, the other kids playing freeze tag and hide-and-seek in the dark, their disembodied voices calling out from the darkness.

She'd strolled by that very spot just yesterday, now pushing their son in his stroller as she walked their elderly neighbor's dog. Another family lived in that house now, one of a string of families occupying and abandoning the house everyone called "the eyesore." But she could still remember the way the house looked before the renters began destroying it. She could remember a lot about this neighborhood she'd called home all her life.

She had not gone far, geographically speaking, yet she'd gone to lengths she'd never thought herself capable of. She thought of her solitary visit to the doctor's office, of the things she'd had to do after. She would never do those things again. Another child wasn't in the cards for them, and that was all there was to it. Now she only had to make her husband understand her resistance without explaining just how deep it ran.

Everett was looking at her, watching in his wary way. "What do I have to do to convince you that this"—he gestured to Christopher sitting in his little booster seat, a ring of chocolate coating his mouth—"is a very good idea? We can't have too much of this."

The bite of donut she'd forced herself to take turned to glue in her mouth. She took a gulp of her coffee, feeling the mass lodge in her throat, making it hard to speak. "Christopher was a very good idea." She glanced at her son as she said it, ready to give him a wink. But he wasn't listening, engrossed in driving a toy car through the sprinkles that had fallen off his donut. She continued, "But one's a gracious plenty right now. I mean, we've also talked about that e-mail from work wanting me to come back, and with him starting preschool in the fall . . ." She picked at what remained on her plate, scattering more sprinkles onto the table as she did. She could not look Everett in the eye.

"Mommy, you are making a mess," her son observed. He pointed at the colorful sprinkles now scattered across the table and began attempting to get out of his booster seat, ostensibly to clean up her mess. She watched as Everett stopped him, settling him with soothing words and promises that Mommy would take care of it. She met Everett's eyes and blinked back her understanding. Taking care of things was her job.

JENCEY

Jencey swung into the McDonald's parking lot and navigated the huge SUV into a narrow parking space, throwing the vehicle into park with a flourish, projecting a confidence she didn't possess. She turned around to find two pairs of wide eyes blinking back at her, the looks on her children's faces akin to the time she took them to the circus—incredulity with a trace of fear. "You guys hungry?" she asked.

"We're . . . eating *here*?" Pilar, her older daughter, asked.

"Sure!" she said. She tried to keep her voice light, breezy. "Let's go see what they have."

Pilar rolled her eyes, trying out her newfound tween attitude. "Mom, it's McDonald's. They have burgers."

"And french fries!" Zara, her younger daughter, added. She leaned forward, lowering her voice as if she were going to tell a secret. "Can we get french fries?"

"Sure!" Jencey replied. She opened her door, throwing the interior light on as she did, the glow of it emphasizing her daughters' faces in contrast to the oncoming night. *Everything that's precious to me is in this car,* she thought. "We can even get milk shakes!" She waved at them to follow her and climbed out of the car.

Pilar opened her door just a crack and gave Jencey a look that reminded her so much of Arch she had to look away. She fiddled with stowing her keys in her purse, right beside the roll of money Arch had hidden for her. She would have to use some of it to pay for this dinner. It was all the money she had left in the world. "Mom," she heard Pilar say, her tone parental, "you never let us have McDonald's."

She turned back. "Well, there's a first time for everything, now isn't there?" She began walking, trusting that the girls would follow her. They did.

Inside, they took their places in line. She scanned the menu, tried to remember what she used to get at McDonald's back when she and Bryte considered it a treat to go there. They used to get the hot fudge sundaes, she recalled. With nuts. She scanned the board and found that they still served them. This brought her an inordinate amount of comfort. Some things didn't change. She wondered if Sycamore Glen had.

Zara tugged at Jencey's elbow to get her attention. She looked down. "Yes?"

"Were you serious about the milk shake?" she whispered.

Jencey laughed. "I was totally serious," she whispered back. She tried to catch Pilar's eye, but her daughter was ignoring her. She was angry about having to leave her home, her friends, her life behind. Jencey didn't blame her. She was angry, too. Angry and sad.

She thought of Arch behind the glass partition that had separated them, his mouth moving as his voice came through the phone. "You have no idea," he'd said. "No idea at all what it took to keep all of it up." His spittle had hit the glass, leaving a pattern, a constellation. "I did it for you!" he'd added, as if she were somehow complicit in his crimes. She'd turned then, hung up the phone that connected them, and walked away. If he'd said anything else, she hadn't heard it.

Zara ordered a chocolate milk shake, and Jencey added, "Make that three!" her voice full of false cheer. Pilar started to argue about the milk shake, but she gave her a look to silence her. *We need this,* she wordlessly implored her oldest. *Play along.*

The cashier rang up their total, and she counted out the money to pay for it. A penny got away from her and rolled lazily along the counter until it fell to the sticky floor at the cashier's feet. The girl blinked at her from underneath a brown visor, managing to look both bored and busy as she waited for that last cent. Jencey handed over another penny. Her life before hadn't included pennies.

After their so-called dinner and a quick stop at a nearby station for gas, they got back on the road. She intended to drive straight through to her parents' house as the girls slept, the highway numbers changing from 95 to 40 to 85. She used to know how the highways were numbered, and now she tried to remember. Were the odd numbers for east to west or north to south? It had to be odd for north to south. Fitting: odd numbers for this odd journey from one former home to another. She thought of the home she'd left behind, the yellow crime-scene tape barring her from ever having access to it again.

JUNE 2014

ZELL

Somehow that one impromptu offer to Alec Bryson on Memorial Day weekend had turned into a standing obligation. (John had been right about her getting sucked in, though Zell was loath to admit it.) Three weeks later she was schlepping up to the pool almost every day with Alec and Lilah in tow, seeing to their sunscreen and snacks, hollering at them not to run, keeping an eye on them when it seemed the lifeguards weren't doing an adequate job.

She scanned the circumference of the pool, hoping to spot a friendly face like she used to find whenever she came here with her own kids. Back then she'd had friends, peers in the same boat as she was. They'd share sunscreen, slathering it on one another's kids without even noticing which child they were tending to. They'd make enough food to share, too, passing out peanut butter-and-jelly sandwiches that had fermented in the heat. On Fridays they'd bring cans of beer and toast the weekend, sharing recipes for marinades and macaroni salad, the foods of summer.

They'd sit together for hours on end, griping about money and children and, always, husbands. But it was the kind of griping that brought comfort, that told her she was part of something bigger. In those end-less days at home when she felt isolated and forgotten, she'd think of her pool friends doing the same thing in their respective houses and feel less alone. In the winter she'd find herself counting the days until the pool reopened. They just didn't keep up with one another during the school year like they did in the summer. They were their own little summer society.

This summer she found herself lured back into the world of mothers and children, sitting on a lounge chair in the vicinity of these younger women (for it was mostly women, still, in spite of all the advancements society had made) because that was where Alec and Lilah wanted to be. Well, Lilah did, at least. Alec kept to himself mostly. She worried about him, wondered what kind of damage he'd sustained in all that had happened.

She felt a presence and opened her eyes, squinting from the glare of the sunlight reflecting off the pool. Alec stood over her as if she'd conjured him up. He was still dry, and the intensity of his expression was so much like his mother's she had to look away. He'd refused to get into the pool today, sitting off to the side and watching instead. "When are we going to leave?" he asked.

"Well, Alec, we just got here," she responded. She pointed to a group of kids in the pool, all playing some sort of strange game that involved swimming from one side to the other very fast. "Why don't you go play with the other children? They seem to be having a good time."

Alec glanced in the direction she was pointing, then shook his head. "Don't wanna."

Zell spotted a young woman in the pool playing with her little boy, and wondered if that was why Alec wanted to leave. "Well, we just got your sunscreen on, and we haven't had the nice snacks I packed for us, and your sister seems to be having a good time. So we'll have to stay for a little while."

Alec sighed deeply. "OK," he said, then started to shuffle away. He stopped short and shuffled back. "Can I go over to the playground?" A note of hope had returned to his voice.

They'd replaced the playground since her children were little. The old playground had been deemed "unsafe," though Lord knew her kids had played there for countless hours and never been hurt. But parents these days worried about every living thing under the sun. It made her thankful that her children hadn't had their own children yet. She wasn't sure she was ready for all their rules and regulations when she kept her grandchildren. She'd heard stories about the special formula shipped on dry ice that cost as much as gold, the car seats that could practically drive themselves, the allergies and sensitivities and diagnoses, everything with a fancy name to it. This new generation of parents just had too much information, if you asked her. It was that Internet, fueling their neuroses, empowering them. And don't get her started on all their devices, their heads bent down over their phones so much they could barely be sociable.

"Can I?" Alec repeated.

She glanced over at the play structure, a large wooden thing with all kinds of complicated platforms and ladders but just two little swings, located over the fence from the pool and adjacent to the neighborhood lake, which was really just a glorified pond.

"I suppose so. Does your—" She caught herself. She'd almost said "mom." "Does your dad let you go over there?"

Alec nodded vigorously. "I'll be careful," he said. Lance had at least gotten Alec's bangs cut, so now she could see his huge, brown puppy-dog eyes.

"OK, just listen out for when I call you," she instructed. He gave an absentminded nod and walked quickly away. She wondered if perhaps he was putting one over on her, if this was something that Debra would've allowed. She sighed and threw her arm over her eyes. Debra had left, and Zell was here. So what Debra wanted didn't matter anymore. It was Zell who was making sure their skin didn't burn and that they got fresh air and had milk for breakfast. It was Zell who was worrying about Debra's husband and making her own husband cut their grass so poor, overloaded Lance didn't have to. It was Zell who was keeping one eye on Debra's son on the playground and one on her daughter in the pool. It was Zell who was responsible. Sometimes she thought of just telling Lance the truth about Debra, but instead she focused on helping with the children. She told herself that was enough. Because telling Lance the truth about Debra would be telling the truth about herself.

The lifeguard blew his whistle. "Adult swim," he hollered, then climbed down out of the lifeguard stand with a relieved look on his face. In unison, the kids all groaned loudly and exited the pool, making their way over to where the parents were congregated, the lounge chairs clustered in odd arrangements that were far from the nice rows they started out in every day.

Lilah and two of her little friends came over to Zell. "Can I have a Popsicle?" she asked, her voice sweeter than normal. Ten years old and she already knew how to manipulate. Her little friends hung back, wary, their bathing suits dripping steadily onto the cement.

"We didn't bring any Popsicles, dear," Zell answered.

"My friends did, though." She gestured to the two girls with her, who tittered in response. "They said I could."

"Well, I guess if their mother says it's OK, then that's fine," she said. She reached into her pool bag and pulled out a bright-orange visor with the name of some drug written across it, a leftover from one of John's many pharmaceutical conventions. She popped it onto her head. The sun was brutal. But her skin was getting tanner, and that made it all sort of worth it. She would have tan fat at least. She looked down at the expanse of her stomach housed in blue Lycra. Too bad John's company never made a drug that made people lose weight without killing them in the process.

The girls squealed with glee, their voices nearly piercing her ear-drums, and ran toward where the mother of the other two sat. She looked as uncertain and out of place as Zell felt.

Two chairs over from where Zell sat, a young mother walked back to a chair with a little boy, who was dripping wet and crying softly. "This is adult swim," the girl patiently explained. "That means the mommies and daddies get to swim with no kids in the water." She pointed to the empty lifeguard stand. "See? There's no lifeguard to protect the little children."

The little boy was not placated by this explanation. "But I want to swim," he whined, his voice teetering on a tantrum. Zell recognized the warning sound.

"Well, right now we're going to have a juice box and some straw-berries. And by the time we're done eating, it'll be time to go back in the water." The girl's voice was singsongy, as if she was attempting to sound kind, but bordering on losing it. Zell recognized that as well. Parenting might've changed since she'd done it, but some things were still the same.

"Excuse me," a voice interrupted her eavesdropping, and she looked up to find a nicely manicured hand hovering in the air between them. Reflexively, she reached up to take it.

"Yes?" she asked as her hand was pumped up and down a few times. There was something familiar in the face that belonged to the hand, but she couldn't place it.

"My girls are Pilar and Zara?" She pointed at the two little girls Lilah had run off with. The three of them were wrapped in towels in a circle, eating red, white, and blue Bomb Pops. "Are you Lilah's . . ." She let her voice trail off, uncertain just who Zell was to Lilah.

"Neighbor. I'm her next-door neighbor. Her dad was busy today, so I said I'd take the kids off his hands."

"Oh, well, that's . . . nice." She glanced over at the girls and back at Zell. "I think that Lilah had invited the girls over to play, and I had said yes, but then I thought I better find out whether you would approve, but now I see that . . . that's probably not possible."

"Yes, I doubt Lance—that's her dad—would want extra kids over. He's working from home these days, and well, it's a bit of a difficult situation."

The woman gave a cynical laugh. "Oh, I understand that," she said, then more to herself, added, "All too well." The little boy a few chairs away delivered a belly laugh as if on cue.

"What did you say your name was?"

"Oh, sorry, where are my manners? Jencey Wells."

Zell squinted at her, trying to make sense of the different last name and the grown-up face. She had known a Jencey once, a girl the same age as her son Ty. That girl had been the little queen bee of the neighborhood, calling all the shots and determined to take the world by storm. All the boys had crushes on her, including her own son, though he would never admit it. Then all that unpleasantness had occurred, and she'd been spirited away in the night by her parents, hidden away in some college up north. Zell heard she'd turned into a Yankee, married some man up there with tons of money, and hardly came home to visit. Folks said her mother, Zell's old friend Lois Cabot, barely knew her own grandchildren. Jencey Cabot was a cautionary tale passed around among the grandmother set.

"You're not . . ." Zell started to ask.

Jencey gave her a wide, false grin and said, a little too loudly, "Yep, it's me! Jencey Cabot."

"Well, Jencey, how nice. You here visiting?" she asked. "I'm sure your mama is just tickled!"

"Yes," Jencey said. "We, um, came to visit."

"I'm Zell Boyette. You knew my sons, John Junior and Ty?" She almost said, "I think Ty had a crush on you," but held her tongue. No one cared about that now.

"Oh sure, Mrs. Boyette, how are they?"

"They're fine, doing fine. JJ's married to a lovely girl. They're both building their careers and absolutely refusing to have any grandchildren for me." She didn't mention Ty, and thankfully, Jencey didn't ask after him. Ty wasn't as . . . upwardly mobile as his brother.

"Well, please tell them I said hi," Jencey said. She glanced over toward the bathrooms with a grimace and took a step in that direction. Her girls were coming out, laughing and jostling each other. One of them turned on the outside shower and stuck her head under it, being silly.

"Jencey?" Zell heard the young woman with the little boy say, stopping Jencey before she could make her exit. The girl was up off her chair and over to where Jencey and Zell were in no time. She wrapped her arms around the startled Jencey, then stepped back to give her a good look. "I can't believe it's you! You're here! You're back!" she marveled.

"Bryte?" Jencey asked, looking as stunned as her friend. Zell was witnessing a reunion. "Bryte Bennett? I can't believe it!" Jencey reached out and gave her friend another hug then pulled back to give her a good look. "You're all grown up."

The other young woman, another child whose mother had once been one of the women Zell whiled away her summer days with, laughed and said, "So are you!" Zell couldn't believe she hadn't recognized her, either. But now that she heard the name, she thought, *Of course.*

"You look just great!" Jencey said to Bryte. "I mean, really beautiful." There was a note of incredulity in her voice, overshadowing the compliment, if you asked Zell. But both young women had all but forgotten she was there.

Bryte colored. "Um, thanks." She looked down at the little boy hovering at her knee, taking the chance to veer the conversation away from the uncomfortable fact of her beauty. Zell remembered this girl as being sort of plain as a child. She'd certainly grown into the name; light emanated from her now.

"This is my son, Christopher," Bryte said. "He's almost three. And you? I heard you have kids?"

Zell started to speak, to point out something that would loop her back into the conversation, to make her presence in their midst necessary. But she thought better of it. She listened to the two younger women talk, feeling superfluous not unlike the discarded towels, the crumpled juice boxes, the wet footprints that appeared on the concrete, then just as quickly faded away.

JENCEY

The girls were coming out of that dirty bathroom sans flip-flops, and she'd been about to go warn them (again) about the dangers of foot fungi when someone called out to her. She turned to take in this person who knew her name, her brain taking a few seconds to register just who she was seeing. She hadn't expected to run into Bryte here, though now she realized it had always been a likely encounter. Bryte had never intended to go far.

Deep down she'd known that this moment—or one close to it— would come. She couldn't wind up back in her childhood neighborhood and not run headlong into the people *from* that childhood. In hindsight, taking the girls up to the pool might not have been the smartest move. But she'd been desperate to take their minds off things. When they were playing in the pool and making new friends, they weren't asking her what would happen next. And at the pool she wasn't under her mother's watchful, concerned eye.

Bryte had married Everett. Of course she'd known that. Her parents had gone to the wedding, urged her to come, too. "Bring Arch," they'd said, as if Arch's presence would alleviate the awkwardness. But she'd been nursing Zara and begged off, saying it was just too hard to travel with a nursing baby. It had been a lie that no one could argue with. She'd sent the happy couple an expensive silver tray.

She examined the little boy holding on to Bryte's hand—Bryte and Everett's child, how strange it all was—and looked for a trace of Everett. The hair and eye colors were the same. But mostly he just looked like Bryte. This heartened her some, gave her the courage to keep standing there making small talk with the girl she had once both loved and betrayed, and who had ultimately betrayed her right back. But could it really be called betrayal? Now that they were older, she wasn't as certain that's what it had been.

She knew what real betrayal was now. An image entered her mind: Arch behind the glass in prison.

The lifeguard blew the whistle, and she watched as the girls and their new friend dove back into the pool. Bryte urged her to come with her into the pool to appease the little boy and continue their conversation. They gave the older woman they were awkwardly standing near a wave as they followed the little boy—she'd already forgotten his name, or maybe she'd blocked it out on purpose—over to the shallow area. She'd been thinking of getting in anyway; it was so hot, and it was only June. She'd forgotten the heat and humidity of a southern summer. But she'd also forgotten her mother's tomato sandwiches (white bread, peeled and sliced tomatoes, Duke's mayonnaise, liberal salt and pepper), the way peaches fresh off the tree tasted, and chasing lightning bugs at dusk, the air at night as warm as midday in Connecticut. The home of her childhood could still offer the comforts of that childhood, comforts she welcomed.

"This is so great!" Bryte said. She looked at the boy. "Christopher." Her voice dripped with the kind of gentleness only a first-time mother can muster. "This is one of Mommy's oldest friends. We grew up together." She looked over at Jencey, seeking validation that her claim was true.

Jencey nodded and looked away, pretending to look for her girls even though she knew precisely where they were: on the little diving board. At their club back home, they had a high dive, a curving slide, a snack bar with waiters to deliver drinks to your chaise. She and her friends practically just held out their hands and the drinks appeared like magic. She wondered if Bryte knew the truth about why she was back. She had yet to hear that unmistakable note of pity she'd heard in the voices of her former friends in Connecticut the unfortunate times she'd run into any of them before she'd left.

She hadn't wanted to tell anyone what had happened to Arch, including her parents. But when it became apparent that she might end up needing her folks' help, she'd filled them in on all the gory details. Her father, good man that he was, had asked if he should come up there and kick Arch's ass. She'd laughed in spite of herself and assured him that, no, his ass-kicking services would not be needed. The federal government was doing a fine and dandy job of that, thank you very much.

"Just know we're here if you need us," he'd said. The kindness in his voice had brought tears to her eyes. It had made her remember the support he'd offered before, back when the hearts had started showing up everywhere and she'd had no choice but to go somewhere that her "admirer" couldn't find her anymore. It was her father who'd driven her up north, to a college they'd told no one about, since no one could figure out who'd been stalking her. They couldn't afford for the wrong person to know, the wrong person to find her. That had been a long, quiet ride, the radio on low, the mood in the car pensive, not unlike her ride back all these years later.

"I can't believe my mom didn't tell me you were here!" Bryte said, her focus intent on Christopher instead of Jencey, which was a good thing.

"She probably didn't know," Jencey said.

"Didn't know?" Bryte repeated as a question. She looked up at a plane making its way across the wide blue sky and nodded an answer to Christopher's (incessant) questions.

"I sort of asked them to keep it quiet. That I was here."

"Oh no, did something happen?" Bryte's face registered legitimate concern, but in spite of that, Jencey couldn't tell her. She could tell Bryte was trying to be her friend, but things weren't the same between them for a lot of reasons.

She waved her arm in the air and forced a smile. "Just didn't want a big to-do. You know, after all this time."

"It has been a long time, Jencey." Bryte's voice got quieter. "I never thought you'd stay gone so long."

Though she tried to hide it, Jencey picked up on the hurt in Bryte's voice and attempted to lighten the mood with a joke.

"Well, you know, I met this man, and I got pregnant—oops!" Jencey grinned, expecting Bryte to laugh, but Bryte didn't even smile over her standard joke, which usually got a better response. She continued talking, her words tumbling over themselves. "So we got married and had the kids, and things were crazy. We made a few quick trips back, but we never stayed very long. It was easier to have my parents come to us." She took a breath. "So what about you guys? How'd you end up back here?"

Bryte watched as Christopher barely put his face into the water, then she applauded as if he'd just swum the length of the pool. "We bought a house here when I got pregnant with Christopher. Wanted him to have the same kind of childhood we both did. You know . . ." Bryte's words died on her tongue as she realized what she was saying. This wasn't a place full of happy memories for Jencey. For her, this was a place to run from, not to.

Bryte recovered quickly, her voice confident. "I mean, we love it here."

"Of course," Jencey found herself saying. "It's nice." She looked around at the handsome lifeguard on the stand in his *Risky Business* sunglasses, the rippling water, the assortment of children playing together, and the older woman who'd been so nice—JJ's mom. If she tried to recall some happy memories of this place, she might come upon them. She might see things differently.

"Look, Mom!" she heard Zara call, and turned to see her youngest, most cautious child standing on the diving board. Back home Zara never went near the high dive or the slide, hanging out in the splash pool for babies instead and insisting that was all she wanted. Maybe this short diving board was more her speed. "Watch this!"

"I'm watching!" she called back brightly.

Zara sprang into the air and gathered her feet to her, forming herself into a compact little ball just before coming down with a loud splash into the water. All the other kids clapped as Zara popped back up to the surface, blinking to clear her vision so that she could make sure Jencey was still watching.

BRYTE

On the way back to her chair, Bryte stepped on a discarded juice box, and the remaining contents squirted her foot. She grimaced and sat down to wipe it off with her towel. Her friend Karen had arrived with her daughter, Sarah, while she was catching up with Jencey. Karen sprayed the child with SPF 100, coating the air more than the kid. Bryte waved the mist away and handed a cup of water to Christopher, who was already whining that he wanted to go back in the water.

"We need to say hi to our friends," she coaxed. She looked at Karen and sighed with exhaustion. "Hi," she said.

Karen laughed and pointed over at Jencey. "Who was that?"

Bryte smirked at her. How to explain who Jencey was? She didn't have the energy to go into it now, so she gave as brief an explanation as possible. "That was someone I grew up with. She's in town with her girls for a visit." She made her voice sound light and carefree as she said it.

Karen checked Jencey out surreptitiously from behind her dark glasses. "She's pretty," she said. "Really pretty."

Bryte flopped back on the chaise. "She always was," she said. "And besides, her kids are older. She has more time to spend on herself."

Karen pointed at herself. "Don't I know it—this bathing suit?" She gestured to the plain black tankini she wore. "When I put this on today, it was the first time I'd been out of sweats in two days! When Kevin wants to have sex, I'm like, 'Dude? Have you looked at me? Have you smelled me?'"

Bryte laughed. "Preach, sister," she said.

Karen began the arduous process of pulling the floaties onto her daughter's arm as Sarah twisted and whined. "You can't go in unless you have these on," she said. "You know the rules." She gave up when the floaties were just above the elbows instead of at the biceps where they belonged. She waved Sarah toward the pool. "Let's go," she said.

She motioned for Bryte to get up, and Bryte moaned good-naturedly. "I will pay you one hundred dollars to take both kids in the pool for one hour."

Karen shook her head vigorously. "If I go, you go. It's the mother-hood code. And besides, I'm the one who's pregnant. I should be the one who gets to lounge." Bryte didn't need reminding of her friend's current state. It was Karen and Kevin's announcement that had started Everett on his quest to add to their family. Ironically or not, Karen and Kevin's last name was Jones. And Everett was committed to keeping up with them.

They passed the time in the water, talking about the latest neighborhood happenings, revisiting the same subjects they always covered. Should they resume bunco game nights in the fall? Who was bringing what to the Fourth of July potluck? Would the women of the neighborhood respond to the idea of doing a painting class in the clubhouse once a month? And what books should they select for this year's book club when it started again in September? Karen was the Energizer Bunny of the WOSG (Women of Sycamore Glen).

"You think your friend over there would want to come to book club?" Karen gestured at Jencey, who was, in fact, reading a book.

"Oh, she's just visiting."

"Got it," Karen said, but she gave Bryte a look that told her she'd responded just a little too passionately. Karen could smell a good story from fifty paces, and if Bryte wasn't careful, she'd sniff this one out, too. Bryte didn't need to share their complicated relationship with anyone.

Bryte glanced at the clock on the clubhouse wall. "Ugh. I gotta go."

"But I just got here!" Karen said. "You can't leave me!" She made a dramatic, desperate face and playfully tugged on her arm.

"I'd stay—believe me—but I promised Myrtle Honeycutt I'd walk Rigby."

"It's too hot to walk that dog!" Karen argued, looking legitimately horrified.

"We'll drink lots of water, and we won't go far, Mom." Bryte smirked at her. "Besides, if I don't take him, she will try to." She shrugged. "It's become part of our routine."

Karen poked her in the shoulder. "You, my dear, are too nice."

Bryte waved goodbye and pulled Christopher from the pool. As she collected her things, she glanced at Jencey one more time, catching her eye and waving goodbye, wishing she could ask her so many questions, wishing the years hadn't turned them into strangers.

CAILEY

We had a summer routine, Cutter and me. We got up, and I made Cutter some breakfast. Usually it was just cereal, because Mom didn't like me using the stove when she was at work. But sometimes I made him toast because I was allowed to use the toaster. When Mom got paid, she bought us Pop-Tarts, even though they are very bad for you and you should not eat them. It was only once a month, so she said it was OK.

After breakfast, we did our chores. I cleaned the dishes, and Cutter swept the floor, though mostly he just hit the floor with the broom until I told him to stop. Then we vacuumed or cleaned the bathroom or did something to make the house look nice inside. When we first moved in, I went outside and looked around for something I could do to make the outside of the house look nice, but I didn't have any money for paint or flowers or anything like that, so I decided to stick to the inside. I learned to just walk really fast inside the house so I didn't have to see how ugly it was on the outside.

I knew what people said about our house. I listened to the conversations at the pool when they thought I wasn't listening. They called it "the eyesore," and they talked about how *that* house should not be in *their* neighborhood. Truth be told, I'd had the same thought the first time I saw it. Driving past all the pretty houses had filled me with hope that maybe this time things would be different and we'd have the better life that Mom was always dreaming about. But that wasn't to be. Instead, we had to walk into that house, the one people looked at like a black tooth in the middle of a mouthful of pearly whites.

Our house probably used to be gray, but it looked kind of white now since most of the paint was gone. It was basically no color at all. The bushes (if you could call them that—they were more like trees by then) had grown up so high they covered half the windows in the front of the house. Other than the overgrown bushes, there were no trees in the front yard, just scrubby grass, where there was any grass at all. And to top it all off, there were some shutters missing, and the mailbox leaned like it was thinking about falling over any second.

The neighbors hated that house; they wanted to knock it down. And they weren't too happy about us living in it, either, on account of how they *could* knock it down if folks would just stop renting it. The people at the pool said stuff about the kind of people who would rent a house like that. They said that we were white trash and how they'd heard me and Cutter's daddy was in prison. (But they were wrong about that. Cutter's daddy was in prison. I don't have a daddy. At least, not one I've ever seen.) Our new neighbors didn't like us even though they'd never met us, never came over and brought us a casserole and introduced themselves like people do on TV. The sign on the entrance to the pool said WE'RE ALL FAMILY HERE. But that was just not true.

I tried to tell Mom what people were saying, but Mom said it was a better life for us and that we'd just have to learn how to get along. She told me to stop eavesdropping if it was going to upset me so much. "My little snoop," she said, ruffling my hair. "This is a good place." But she also said to keep the door locked and reminded me about a hundred times not to talk to strangers. A girl disappeared from nearby right before we moved in, and my mom was all freaked out about it.

So, since all our neighbors were strangers, and that didn't seem like it would ever change, we didn't talk to anyone at all.

After we finished our chores, we did our reading. I made a rule: we had to read for thirty minutes every day. Mom took us to the library when she could so we would have books to choose from. I would get as many as my arms could hold, and Mom would say it was too many, but I would promise to read them all. And I did. Cutter always got picture books, and I told him he should get harder books, but Cutter didn't like to read. Sometimes when it was reading time, he would argue with me and say he wouldn't do it. I told him that if he didn't, he wouldn't get TV time. And he knew I meant it. So he usually went in his room and looked at the pictures, which made me happy because I got to be alone in my room with no Cutter to pester me for thirty whole minutes.

A good thing about the new house: we each had our own room. At our old apartment, Cutter and I slept in the bedroom, and Mom slept on a pull-out sofa in the den. Sometimes her boyfriend, Joe, slept with her on the pull-out sofa, and if I needed something from the kitchen, I had to walk past his sleeping self. I didn't like the way he smelled up our den with his oily man smell. I was glad when Joe went away. The best part about the house in Sycamore Glen—eyesore or not—was there was no Joe.

After reading time was over, we turned on the TV. We alternated days of who got to pick what we watched. Cutter liked animal shows, and I liked reality TV. We were both happy with animal reality TV, like the ones where they catch wild animals that get in people's houses or the ones where they wrestle alligators. Sometimes we'd just watch cartoons. The TV company made a mistake and gave us more channels than we signed up for, so there was a lot to choose from, more than we'd ever had before. I told Mom we should probably tell them they made a mistake, but Mom said what they didn't know wouldn't hurt them and that sometimes life just works out. That had not been my experience, though. When I told her that, she laughed and laughed. I liked it when my mother laughed.

After TV time, it was time to eat again. Mom said Cutter and I were eating machines, so I tried not to eat too much. But Cutter didn't give it a second thought. He scarfed down food, and he usually didn't care what kind. Mom said he had a hollow leg. At lunch, I made him eat some fruit, even if it was just canned fruit cocktail. Sometimes we had chips to go with our sandwiches, and once in a while, we had cookies. I like homemade chocolate-chip cookies, but we only had those if Mom was in the mood to bake, which was hardly ever because she was always so tired from working. Mom worked one job during the weekdays and one on the weekends, so she was at work pretty much all the time. She had to do that, she said, so we could have the kind of life we had. Sometimes when I saw people with their fancy cars and their nice houses, I wondered how many jobs they must have had to work to have *that* kind of life.

After lunch, it was finally time to go to the pool. Cutter was not a very good swimmer, so I made him wait as long as I could to go to the pool, even though he started begging to go as soon as his eyes popped open in the morning. He made me nervous in the water, and it was hard to watch him all the time. I knew there was a lifeguard there who could save him if he started to drown, but Cutter was my responsibility. That's what Mom said every night when she kissed me good night. She said the same thing: "I'll be gone when you get up. Be good, be smart, and watch out for your brother." Then she said, "I love you more than life itself." And even though she couldn't be home as much as I wanted her to be, I knew she meant it.

I didn't like it when people said bad things about my mother. Her old boyfriend, Joe, said a lot of mean things about her, and about Cutter and me, too. He was not very nice to her, and that night after he'd said the worst things ever, I gave her a hug and told her not to listen to him. I felt bad because he'd caught me snooping in his wallet, and that's what caused their fight. But she said it wasn't my fault, even though I shouldn't snoop in people's stuff. (I was still working on that.) Then she hugged me and made me promise I'd grow up and have a better life than she did. She wouldn't stop crying until I pinkie-swore I would. The trouble was, I wasn't real sure how to get a better life or even what she had in mind.

At the pool, the moms and dads didn't talk to me and Cutter. I didn't really expect them to. They were parents, and parents usually don't talk to kids unless it's to their own. But it was more than that. They looked at us as if we were sand that got in their bathing suits. When I told Mom about it, she said, "Well, then, just don't go up there, Cailey." She had her tired voice when she said it, the one that told me I should just drop it.

But even though Cutter couldn't swim very well and the people ignored us, I liked being there. I liked the water and the sunshine and the sound of people laughing. Even though we didn't talk to each other, we—Cutter and I and all the moms and kids—were all there together. It was *our* pool. And so Cutter and I went up there every day after lunch. We walked a long way to get there, we swam, and we walked a long way back home. And then we did it all over again the next day. And that was, I expected, the way we'd spend that whole summer of my eleventh year and Cutter's sixth. I was, of course, as wrong as could be.

JENCEY

Their days had settled into a routine, every day much the same as the one before it. Jencey had taken to going on walks after dinner, leaving the girls to play cards with her mother on the screened-in porch as the day ended and the first lightning bugs began to emerge. The girls loved the time with her mother. She watched the three of them, hunched over their cards at the rickety little table they'd set up on the porch. Pilar liked winning. Zara liked being included. Her mother, for her part, just seemed ecstatic to have the girls with her in any capacity and patiently reexplained the rules of rummy and spades and crazy eights night after night.

Every night Jencey told herself she'd stay and play with them, yet every night by the time dinner was over and another day was gotten through, she felt the pull to escape the confines of home and family, the magnet in her chest tugging her back to the streets of her youth. She wandered those streets looking for the childhood she'd forgotten, the good parts from before the hearts started showing up.

She'd been desperate to forget this place when she'd left at eighteen. Now she forced herself to remember, if only in an effort to forget the more recent past. She quizzed herself as she walked: Didn't that house used to be gray? Was that the house that always smelled like curry? What was the name of the girl who lived in that yellow house, the one who was so crazy about horses? Was that the house that was always decorated so outlandishly for Halloween? She wondered if the same people still lived there, if the woman still sat on the porch dressed as a witch, scaring kids.

She would find out in October if she was still there. But she couldn't still be here by then. She would dry up and blow away like the leaves, crunchy and brown and lifeless. She had to find a way out. She'd told herself this was just a visit, a stopping-off place en route to somewhere else. But where? She had no idea. For the first time in her life, she didn't have a plan. Even when she'd run from here, she'd had a plan of what to do, forming it as she and her father drove north.

It took her more than a week to work up the courage to find out if the hideaway was still there. She took the path around the neighborhood lake, telling herself she didn't have to veer from it, coaxing herself along with internal promises that chances were the little offshoot path wouldn't be there any longer. It had been so long ago. Things had changed; progress had happened even there, in the neighborhood that time seemed to have forgotten. Her path along the lake was nothing more than a walk like any other night, she reasoned. And yet her eyes were already betraying her, scanning the landscape for the path with a kind of hope. She needed, she realized, to get back to it.

Walking along, she felt like a time traveler. With each step, she was closer to the young girl she'd once been. It came back to her a little more, the feeling that the future was something to be run toward, that good things were possible. There, on that dirt path, she was younger, brighter, more innocent. She didn't know that life could end with the arrival of black SUVs containing agents in dark suits and sunglasses, that someone you loved could lie to you so completely, that everything you worked for could go up in smoke as surely as if someone had struck a match and set it all on fire.

As she stepped off the beaten path onto the less-traveled one that was right where she remembered, she felt special again. She was the girl who could do anything. She was the sophomore nominated to homecoming court, then improbably elected queen. The girl who still didn't know that the next day the hearts would start arriving. This path was her looking glass, her wardrobe, her yellow brick road.

She pushed through brush and brambles, her shins and ankles brushing up against prickles with barely registered pain. She kept her eyes peeled around every corner as she wound her way deeper into the woods. When doubts about her safety began playing in her mind, she banished them, letting herself enter fully into her memories of past visits, of what it was to be here, of whom she used to meet there and the things they used to say to each other. There were the dreams and the whispers, the fights and the surrenders, the truths and the lies. She had been herself then, with him, but was that self a shadow of her actual self or the more realized version? Did life add to or take away from who we are at sixteen?

The path took her to the little ring of trees waiting there for her like old friends, their branches waving her over as if they'd been waiting all these years for her inevitable return. The breeze through their branches sounded like a sigh of relief. She slipped through the leaves to enter into a world apart, the place of shelter she'd run to so many times before. Their world, they claimed, hers and Everett's. It existed just for them, and no matter what happened, they could always get back to it, hide inside it. She turned around, hugging herself as she looked up at the bit of sky visible from the center, the leaves otherwise blocking the visibility out or in.

That is what they'd loved about it, how utterly hidden they'd felt. At a time when they'd had no space of their own, this had been exactly what they needed: a place to slip from sight, to hole up and disappear together. In that space they could—and did—do anything they wanted. She'd lied to her parents so many times. She was going to Bryte's, to the movies, to a party, to the library. But she came here. This place was the one place she'd always, always felt safe. Until she didn't feel safe anywhere.

She shivered in the gathering dark, sensibility returning as she reached for her phone in her pocket just to be sure. She held it up to check the reception and thought of the news report she'd seen on the television her mother kept on in the kitchen all day. There was an interview with the lead detective on the case of a young girl who'd disappeared nearby. She'd started watching it with the concern of a parent before realizing the girls were there, both watching the same thing, their eyes round with horror. Pilar had looked at her as though she was uncertain why their mother had brought them to a place where little girls could disappear. She'd snapped the TV off despite her mother's protests that the weather report was up next.

Now standing in the woods with darkness coming on fast, she thought about how far she'd ventured from earshot. No one could hear her if she screamed. Anyone could be in these woods. She wrapped her arms around herself and listened for danger. But all she could hear was wind, birds, and the rustle of the branches. What had happened before was over; she had nothing to be afraid of anymore. She forced herself to stand there a few seconds longer, and then she let herself leave, her steps out of the woods quicker than her steps in.

She returned home to find her mother alone on the porch, waiting for her but trying not to look like she was. Jencey folded her arms across her chest and waited for whatever she was going to say. She saw the concern her mother was unable to mask. Jencey held back from saying what she wanted to say, which was, *I love you, and I'm sorry I stayed gone so long.*

"Are you OK?" her mother asked. In the light from the bare bulb hanging from the rickety ceiling fan, she could see that her mother's eyes had filled with tears. She blinked them away, but it was too late.

Jencey waved her hand in the air, reassuringly. "We're OK."

"Well, you know you're welcome to stay here as long as you need. The girls could even enroll in school." She smiled. "I hear the schools around here are good." The sentence seemed to have a question mark attached to the end of it, as if she were asking Jencey if what she'd heard was accurate. "I don't know much about the schools anymore, now that I don't have kids that age. Of course I guess they could've gone downhill. They're always changing things around. Seems like something's in the news every day about it."

"I'm sure the schools are fine, Mom. Bryte wouldn't have moved here if they weren't top-notch." She thought of the way Bryte looked at her son, like she was watching a continual miracle. "Trust me," she added with a laugh.

"So you've seen Bryte?" her mom asked, trying—and failing—to sound casual.

"Yep," she answered.

"That must be nice for you girls, together again," her mom pressed.

"Sure," she said. "We've talked some, at the pool." Anxious to change the subject, she added, "The girls sure do enjoy having the pool. It's made these three weeks go by fast."

Her mother ignored Jencey's attempt at a segue. "And it isn't strange? With her married to Everett now?" Jencey thought of serious, intent Everett, begging her not to leave as if he could change anything that had happened, as if her father wasn't already at the wheel of the car and her things weren't already packed. For a while, even Everett hadn't known where she'd gone, because he could have inadvertently let on where she was to the wrong person, a person who'd been growing increasingly bold and dangerous. She'd only had to look at Everett to confirm that.

"It's fine, Mom. We've all grown up. Things change." The way she said it, it sounded so simple.

Her mother was silent, thinking this over. Jencey rested her head against the knotty wood and listened to the crickets, cicadas, and tree frogs croaking out a summer serenade. In their previous neighborhood, there hadn't been the sounds of nature, at least not that she could recall. They'd drowned out those noises with their sound system, their waterfall, their man-made ambience. Standing there listening, she thought that perhaps in attempting to give them everything, she and Arch had cheated their girls. She heard a shriek from inside the house, followed by a belly laugh.

"They seem good," her mom said.

"They are," she replied a little too quickly. "We all are."

Her mother sniffed the air, and Jencey wondered what scent she was detecting. Her father's pipe smoke? The charcoal grill down the street? The jasmine in the hanging basket or the magnolia tree in the yard or the gardenias in her garden? Maybe it was the baby shampoo her youngest daughter still used, innocence bottled. She didn't ask, though.

"I don't think you're going to have any trouble here now," her mother said.

"No, no, I don't think so," Jencey agreed.

"I'm glad you came back here," her mother added, her voice tentative, almost cautious. "I think it was time." Jencey sensed her mother's discomfort around her; she felt it, too. They were relearning each other, having become basically strangers in their years apart. They no longer knew how to be around each other, so their conversations were awkward, infused with a strange tension that Jencey hoped would go away with time.

Her mother stood and began gathering the playing cards, still strewn about on the table. Jencey moved to help her, her hand falling on the ace of spades. Her mother rested her own hand on Jencey's. There were age spots on the back of her mother's hand that hadn't been there when she'd left.

They stood there for just a moment like that, not speaking, their eyes locked in what Jencey assumed was her mother's version of a promise. She would keep her safe. They would be OK. All the things a parent tells a child. Jencey knew this because she was a parent now. She knew the urge to protect, and she also knew that even when you couldn't protect your child, you would still vow that you would.

LANCE

Lance needed to find a babysitter or he was going to lose his job. He had to stop depending on that neighbor lady, Zell. She was like a fairy godmother, showing up just when he was about to explode, taking the kids to the pool so he could work for a few hours without interruption.

He grabbed the bag that held the kids' pool things—sunscreen and towels neatly rolled, a box of snack crackers, some change for the drink machine. He had not put this bag together; Zell had. He wondered if he could hire her to come over and create this same degree of organization in every aspect of his life. Maybe this was why Debra had liked her. Now that she was gone, he remembered how often Debra used to mention Zell, back when he didn't pay attention because he took everything for granted. He'd barely listened to his wife then. He wasn't sure what role Zell had played in Debra's life, and of course, he couldn't ask Debra now.

"Lilah," he called, "let's go!" He wanted the kids gone. He wanted the house quiet. He'd promised himself he would not work today. He would take a true break. Watch sports—it didn't matter which sport, anything on ESPN would do—drink beer, sit around in his boxers. He would not be Dad today. He would not hop up to solve anyone's problems. He would sit for longer than a five-minute stretch. At lunch, he would make a big, messy hoagie sandwich and devour it on the couch. He would not use a plate. He would burp and fart and not have to apologize for it because he would be no one's role model for a good couple of hours. He had fantasized about this time nearly as much as he used to fantasize about sex.

Who was he kidding? He still fantasized about sex. When he wasn't too damn tired to do so. But he did not fantasize about Debra. He couldn't bring himself to do that. It just seemed wrong. The women he fantasized about now were always faceless.

The kids materialized from wherever they'd been keeping themselves, their faces as drawn as if he were sending them off to do math problems all day. "You guys ready?" he asked, clapping his hands together, ignoring his children's obvious displeasure.

Lilah and Alec nodded glumly.

"OK, well, Zell said to come on over whenever you were ready!" He opened the door, a blast of hot air hitting him in the face as he did. On the heels of the early spring came the unrelenting heat and humidity of summer, something he'd never gotten used to and would not mind leaving behind if he got the chance to return to Ohio, something he'd been discussing with his sister lately. She thought it would be a good idea, considering the circumstances, and he didn't entirely disagree.

"Have fun, guys!" he said, waving them in the direction of Zell's house.

Obediently they trotted out the door. As Lilah passed him, he looped the bag over her capable shoulders, ignoring the way they slumped forward. This had been awful for the kids, too. Their summer vacation had probably not felt like a vacation at all. He tried not to think too much about their feelings. Because what could he do about it? What could he change? Debra was gone, and he was holding things together without her. He was doing the best he could. It had become his mantra.

He closed the door behind them and paused to take in the quiet house, inhaling the silence like a drug. He stood utterly still, just breathing. Usually when Zell took the kids, he increased his pace, scurried around doing laundry and dishes and paying bills and squeezing in work wherever he could. He worked when he should be eating, sleeping, showering. Taking this time for himself felt decadent, wasteful, as luxurious as that spa Debra had convinced him to go to with her years ago. It felt . . . selfish. But he wouldn't think about that now. He would enjoy this.

He watched from the kitchen door as Zell ushered Lilah and Alec into her car. He stayed just out of sight as the car's engine whirred into motion and the lights came on. He stood frozen in place until the car—and his children—were gone, feeling guilt wash over him as he thought of Alec's words upon hearing that it would be Zell—and not Lance—who would be taking them to the pool today. "You never have fun with us anymore, Dad."

He'd told his son to quit whining, and yet, the kid had a point. Lance never had fun anymore. Period. He cast a longing glance at the TV and at the fridge with the six-pack of beer inside, bought for just this occasion. Then with a sigh of surrender, he headed upstairs to change into his swim trunks.

But he was taking the beer with him.

BRYTE

She held Christopher's hand as she led him over to the pool, barely listening to his chatter about the ducks on the lake and the clouds in the sky. Instead, she tried to watch Jencey without appearing to. Jencey's girls were playing with another girl, all three running from the girl's brother whenever he came near them. Jencey, seemingly oblivious to their shrieks, was reading a *People* magazine on a chaise lounge.

She helped Christopher into the pool and glanced longingly in her old friend's direction, looking away too late when Jencey unexpectedly looked up from her magazine. Busted, she raised her hand in greeting as if she'd meant to catch Jencey's eye the whole time. "I thought that was you!" she said, her voice too loud and excited. As kids, she'd always been the awkward one, the tagalong just trying to match her steps to Jencey's. It was funny how lightning fast she could fall back into her old, awkward ways. She wished some of her friends were around—friends who only knew her now—but the overcast day had kept them away.

Jencey returned her wave and went back to reading her magazine as Bryte, disappointed, focused on her son and took her designated seat on the hot concrete, the heat radiating through her swimsuit. She talked to Christopher, cheered his continued attempts to submerge his face underwater, and did her best not to look back over at Jencey, who, finished with her magazine, had closed her eyes and appeared to be sleeping.

Bored, Bryte's mind wandered to the e-mail she'd received that morning from her former boss, the one marked "Urgent," asking her to come in for a meeting regarding her return to work. Minutes later, according to the time stamp, she'd received another e-mail from a coworker begging her to come back.

The place isn't the same without you! We miss you! We NEED you!

While it was nice to be wanted, she wasn't sure she wanted to go back there. She wasn't sure she could get excited about selling technical training to Fortune 500 companies again. And yet, returning to work would stop the second-child discussion in its tracks, at least for a while.

"Ouch!" Jencey said as her backside made contact with the hot concrete, jarring Bryte from her internal debate.

Bryte gave her a welcoming smile, glad for the distraction. "Hi," she said.

"I'd tell you that I used to have to do this when mine were little, but I mostly had help with this part of motherhood," Jencey said, gesturing to the shallow end and to Christopher donned in water wings.

"You were lucky," Bryte said, even though she didn't really feel that way. Tiring as it was, she wanted to experience every moment with her only child. Because he would be their only child, if only she could figure out how to make Everett understand that. Using a return to work as an excuse to put the debate off was sounding even more appealing.

"Mom, when can Lilah and I have a sleepover?" Jencey's oldest ran over to ask, breathless from running. Her name was Pilar. The youngest was Zara. As girls, Jencey and Bryte had dreamed up baby names.

Neither Pilar nor Zara had, so far as Bryte could recall, ever been on Jencey's list. But then again, Christopher hadn't been on Bryte's.

"We can talk about it later," Jencey said, her voice kind and patient in front of Bryte.

"But, Mom, Lilah wants to." Pilar was relentless, which was expected, seeing as who her mother was. But Pilar didn't look like Jencey. Bryte guessed she looked like the father, whose name, Bryte knew, was Archer, Arch for short. This name so suited the man who would marry Jencey that Bryte had laughed when she read it on the wedding announcement tacked to her parents' refrigerator. Bryte had been certain the marriage meant Jencey would never return to Sycamore Glen. At the time, she'd been relieved at the thought. Yet here she was, sitting beside Jencey on the edge of the same pool where they'd played Marco Polo as children, Bryte feeling around blindly for Jencey as she listened for "Polo" in reply to her "Marco."

"I'm sure she does, and we will," Jencey said, her voice firm, with an edge that hadn't been there before. "But we're not going to discuss it anymore today."

Pilar turned and, grumbling, marched back over to her friend. The two girls took their spots in line to jump off the diving board, waiting behind the little boy who made Bryte nervous. She'd taken to keeping an eye on him whenever she and Christopher were there. He wasn't a strong swimmer, and there was never a parent with him. He had an older sister who usually looked out for him, but the sister seemed to be caught in Pilar and Zara's orbit. Bryte remembered the feeling, how strong that pull could be.

With Pilar gone, Jencey turned back to her. "Sorry about that," she said.

"No problem," Bryte said. Christopher had grown tired of the pool and was hanging on her legs. She moved them up and down in the water, giving him a ride. It was the closest thing to exercise she got these days. If she went back to work, she could use her lunch hour to go to the gym like she used to.

She and Jencey lapsed into silence again, both of them watching Christopher ride up and down in the water, his little face filled with a smile. "He's really cute," Jencey mused aloud. The comment felt weighted with unsaid words. This was not just Bryte's son; this was Everett's son, too.

Would they ever talk about what had happened after Jencey left? Part of Bryte wanted to just say it already, get it all out in the open. But part of her didn't want to broach the subject of Everett and her, because that would mean she'd have to talk about Jencey and Everett, which was not something she liked remembering, even years later.

"He's a good baby," was all Bryte said in response.

Jencey patted her arm and started to stand. "I hate to tell you this, but he's hardly a baby anymore."

Bryte looked up. "You sound just like Everett," she said, the name slipping from her lips without meaning for it to. There was no avoiding him. In the end, they'd have to acknowledge his existence. It was there between them, as obvious as the child hanging on her legs.

"He's right," Jencey said, and shrugged. She turned her attention to Zara on the diving board and clapped her hands loudly. "Come on, Zara, let's see a flip!" she called.

Zara, from the diving board, tried to get her mother to be quiet. "Mo-om," she intoned before making a polite, unobtrusive jump into the deep end. The little boy came after her, his eyes on his sister. But she wasn't looking. She was helping Zara out of the water with effusive praise.

"That kid makes me nervous," Bryte said to Jencey. She pulled Christopher from the water and stood him beside her before standing up herself.

"Why?" Jencey asked.

Bryte took Christopher's hand and pulled him closer to her side, as if by keeping him safe, she could vicariously keep the little boy safe, too. "Watch him," she said, and pointed.

The two women watched as the boy leaped from the diving board, sank under the water, and disappeared from sight for several seconds. Bryte held her breath, as did Jencey. She felt Jencey's hand reach for her forearm. Her fingernails, painted the color pink a child might choose, dug into her skin as she strained forward. Together, they willed the boy to the surface. When he finally did rise, he was sputtering and coughing up water, his hands flailing. In unison, their eyes went to the male lifeguard, who was talking to the gorgeous blonde female lifeguard and not watching the scene in the deep end at all.

"Should we do something?" Jencey asked.

"No, look," Bryte said, directing her attention to the struggling child, who had, once again, made it to the side. But his sister wasn't there to help him out of the water this time.

"My heart is going ninety miles an hour!" Jencey said, grabbing for her chest. "I need a drink after that!" She pretended to check her nonexistent watch. "Is it five yet?"

The two laughed as Bryte led Christopher over to where her bag of tricks was. She had a juice box and animal crackers ready for him. She opened the box and took a handful for herself, then offered it to Jencey.

"Oh, what the hell," Jencey said, and reached into the box, taking a handful. Bryte wondered if the taste reminded her of her childhood.

"You should come for dinner tonight," Bryte said, her mouth still full of crackers. It was an impulse, but she didn't regret saying it once it was out. She wanted to bring Jencey into her life, the one she had now. She wanted her to see how it had all turned out. And perhaps with a few drinks in her, Jencey would spill the details of what had brought her back. Bryte listened as her old friend accepted the invitation, made plans even as she tried not to think of what Everett would say.

ZELL

The sound of Zell's name being called interrupted her attempt to eavesdrop on Jencey and Bryte's conversation. She never learned. Guilty, she looked over to see Lance walking toward her. She was glad to see him even if she had been the one to encourage him to take a break from the children. Lord knew he needed it. Sometimes when she got up in the middle of the night to get some water after being awakened by one of her hot flashes, she saw his light on, knew he was burning the midnight oil as the kids slept. Without his wife, the man was running pillar to post.

"I can't believe you came up here!" she called out to him, her guilt complex mostly forgotten.

He gave her a bashful smile. She saw the other mothers' heads turning as they noticed a new man in their midst, a very nice-looking man. She was older than all of them, but she wasn't blind.

"Well, I felt bad," he said. "I mean if I have time to goof off, I guess I should use that time to spend with the kids."

"I know they'll be glad to see you." She returned his smile and called out to the kids, "Lilah! Alec! Look who's here!"

Alec had spent the last hour following the head lifeguard around, peppering him with questions about the chemicals they put in the pool and begging to let him help take measurements of the samples they pulled from the water. Lilah had become thick as thieves with Jencey Cabot's girls in the weeks since the pool's opening, the three of them moving in a tight cluster. They'd picked up a stray today, that little girl who usually hovered on the edges looking anxious.

Both kids broke away from what they were doing and scampered over to their father with big, grateful grins on their faces. "Daddy!" they said in unison, forgetting they were too cool to call him that. He hugged them both, and they told him what they were up to as Zell looked on proudly.

"They're having a good time," Zell said. It felt good to be part of something, but Lilah gave her a look that told her she'd gone too far. Sometimes when Lilah looked at her, she thought that the child knew the truth even though she couldn't possibly. Zell saw the scar on Lilah's pencil-thin leg, forever white against her tanned skin, and remembered the day the girl had gotten it. That had been the beginning.

Lilah turned to Jencey's girls to introduce them to her father. "These are my friends Pilar and Zara," she said, waving her hands at them. The two girls giggled and waved, but the third girl—the one who'd been tagging along just today—stood silent and overlooked. Zell's heart went out to her.

"Nice to meet you," Lance said, his tone formal as he shifted his weight and looked around the pool, perhaps wondering why he'd come, where he fit.

"Will you throw me, Dad?" Alec asked, his voice husky and reserved in front of the girls.

"Sure, buddy," Lance said, looking relieved to have something to do. He glanced over at Zell. "Thanks," he said to her, and then he let Alec lead him away. She tried to catch the other little girl's eye, to give her a smile of encouragement. But she turned away too quickly, intent on following the other girls, her eyes focused on staying in step with them, her legs hurrying to keep up.

JENCEY

She hurried back to her chair, fuming internally over her stupid mistake. She straightened her towel and threw herself down. What was she thinking, saying yes to Bryte's invitation? She'd been caught up in nostalgia, maybe, her resolve weakened by the heat. She had no business attempting a social engagement of any sort, much less a social engagement with her old best friend and her first love, now married to each other and living in the same neighborhood they'd all grown up in.

She was in no shape to see Everett again, much less Everett flanked by his wife and son. She had enough on her plate without adding that stressor. Her therapist back in New Canaan would have had a fit. Of course, therapists were a luxury from the past. Ironic that now that she had real, actual problems, she could no longer afford one. Of course her parents would help pay for a therapist if she really needed one, but to ask for that was to admit she needed help both financially and mentally. She was loath to admit either.

From the opposite side of the pool, she watched as Bryte fed Christopher sections of apple, smiling like a woman who had the world by the tail. Through slitted eyes (she'd forgotten her sunglasses), Jencey studied her former friend, marveling anew at just how lovely she'd become. Gone was the awkward uncertainty that used to characterize Bryte. In its place was a glow that radiated from within, as if that inner beauty people used to talk about when referring to Bryte had finally, over time, worked its way out.

When they were friends, she used to tell Bryte she was pretty, reassure her that, even though her chest was flat and she had thick glasses, she still had a lot of good attributes. But she was mostly just trying to make Bryte feel better, and they both knew it. Bryte, Jencey had believed, would always be the sidekick. But something had changed. Bryte had gone from looking like Velma in *Scooby-Doo* to looking like Audrey Hepburn. Jencey's reassuring little lies had come true: Bryte had come into her own.

Old friends or not, Jencey didn't want to see more of Bryte and her idyllic existence than she had to. Not when her own life had turned to shit. She could be happy for her friend without having to witness the happiness. She had to come up with an excuse to get out of the evening, and fast. The little boy was crying and probably getting tired, ready for his nap. She would get Bryte's phone number before she left, then take the chickenshit way out and text her regrets. It wasn't a very grown-up way to handle things, but it would get the job done.

She stood up and hurried back over to catch Bryte before she disappeared and left Jencey with no other option but to show up at the address Bryte had enthusiastically rattled off. "It used to be the piano teacher's house. Remember? You could always hear music when you walked by?"

Jencey nodded. She remembered the house well: a white two-story with black shutters and a front porch much like the other houses in the neighborhood—not big but not small, just right for the middle-class neighborhood they'd all called home.

"Seven!" Bryte had said. "See you then!" Then she'd scurried away, leaving Jencey to feel the regret whoosh through her veins.

At seven she was usually preparing for her nightly walk. At seven she was still promising herself she wouldn't end up in the hideaway as darkness fell, playing remember when. Last night she'd heard twigs snap as if someone was walking around, someone who'd also come to those woods. She'd sat quietly until the sounds disappeared, then bolted out of the woods, running nearly all the way home, the bad memories nipping at her heels.

Now she moved almost as quickly to get to Bryte before she left, her eyes locked on her and not much else. Which is how she ran smack into the man she'd noticed earlier. He was handsome, in a dad sort of way, a way Arch had never succumbed to. She'd once been proud of this, the way Arch had remained distinctly "Arch," without giving himself over to the domesticated look that seemed to seize most of the men she knew. And yet, in hindsight, maybe that hadn't been for the best. Maybe a surrendered man was a trustworthy one.

"I'm so sorry!" she apologized as she steadied herself, using his forearms to stop the force of their impact from knocking them both to the ground.

He stepped back, gazing down at her with a look that was half amusement, half confusion. "It's OK," he said, looking embarrassed even though he'd done nothing except wander into her path.

"I'm so sorry," she said again.

He laughed. "So you said."

She glanced over at Bryte, who was obliviously gathering her things. She wasn't gone yet. That was good. "I was rushing to speak to my friend." She pointed in Bryte's direction. "I wasn't watching where I was going."

"No worries," he said. The little girl who'd been playing with her daughters for the past several weeks sauntered over to them.

"Dad," she said, addressing the man, "I thought you were going to play with us." She looked up at the two adults. A giddy look crossed her face. "Are you two talking about the sleepover?"

"What sleepover?" they both asked at the same time, with the same degree of alarm in their voices. Then they both laughed.

"We want to have a sleepover. All three of us." The girl said it in a huff as if they, the adults, were just so slow.

"Well, uh, now might not be the best time," the man said, shifting uncomfortably as he spoke. He looked over at Jencey with a pained expression. "I'm, um, a newly single dad and not really ready to host an, um, event for the kids."

Jencey waved her hand, dismissing his apology. "Oh, gosh, sure. I don't blame you. I get it." She refrained from explaining just how much she got it.

She looked over. Bryte was on her way out. She was going to miss her. She needed to get away from him, yet her southern manners prevailed. Her friends in Connecticut used to tease her about her accent, her sense of decorum, her general southernness. Try as she might, she couldn't shake it.

She spoke quickly. "We're just in town visiting my parents for a bit this summer, so I can't really, um, host guests, either." She patted his daughter's wet head. "You guys can see each other here at the pool, OK?"

The girl sighed deeply. "OK," she said. Deflated, she slumped away with heavy, dramatic footsteps.

"Well, nice to meet you," Jencey said, offering parting words.

He turned to her with that same amused/confused look on his face. "But we didn't really meet, did we?"

She looked up at him and blinked, then glanced over at Bryte again. Thankfully, she had stopped to talk to someone. "Oh, I guess not." Obliged, she thrust her hand out. "I'm Jencey."

He shook her hand briefly, then squinted at her. She noticed that his eyes were exactly the same color as his hair. She liked the uniformity of it, how utterly congruent he was.

"Jencey?" he questioned. "That's different."

She rolled her eyes. The name was a relic of her childhood. In school she'd been one of several Jennifers. She was Jennifer C, or, as her second-grade teacher coined it, "Jen C." There had also been "Jen L." As second grade went on, the teacher ran the abbreviations together so fast that they came out as one word. So "Jen C" became Jencey, and "Jen L" became Jennelle. As far as Jencey knew, Jennelle also went by that name to this day.

"It's an old nickname," she explained hastily to him now. "My real name is Jennifer, but no one calls me that."

"I like it," he said, nodding as if he'd considered it and found it acceptable. "My name's Lance, short for Lancelot." He grinned. "My mom had a thing for Camelot."

She laughed. "Seriously?"

He raised his eyebrows, held her gaze for a second, looking totally serious. But he couldn't hold the look for long, as his smile broke through. "No, my name's just Lance. But I had to come up with a story to keep up with yours."

She laughed along with him, then noticed Bryte swinging her bag over her shoulder and sliding on her flip-flops as she wrapped up her conversation. She quickly clapped him on the shoulder. "Well, Lancelot, it was nice to meet you, but I've got to catch my friend over there." She hitched her thumb in Bryte's direction. "Good luck finding Camelot."

She walked away, shaking her head. *Good luck finding Camelot?* She was clearly out of practice at this whole opposite-sex thing. She'd once been so *good* at it. But that was a long time ago, before the hearts had started arriving, before Arch had claimed her as his own.

She got to Bryte in the nick of time, reaching for her in order to stop her from walking away. Bryte turned around with a startled look. But her face immediately relaxed when she saw it was just Jencey. "Oh, Jencey! Hey!" she said, her face filling with a grin that lived up to her name. "Everything OK?" she asked. But then her smile faded and her eyes strayed to the pool as a whistle erupted and someone screamed and, all around them, people started running.

LANCE

He was standing there staring into the water, thinking about the beautiful woman's comment about finding Camelot, feeling like the furthest cry from a brave and gallant knight, when he saw the little boy, a dark shape gone still beneath the water. It took him a moment to realize the child wasn't playing; he wasn't seeing how long he could hold his breath or pulling a prank on his friends. Lance dove in without thinking, a reflex that extended, it turned out, beyond his own children. As he pushed deeper under the water toward the boy, he had two thoughts: *What do I do now? And where the hell is the lifeguard?*

He reached the child in seconds, but it felt like it took half an hour to get his hands on him. Eyes wide in spite of the way the chlorine was burning them, he scooped the boy up, just like he did when his own children fell asleep watching TV and he had to carry them up to bed. But this child wasn't sleeping.

Unready for the heft of the boy's weight—the words *dead weight* flashed through his mind, but he pushed them away—he struggled for a second, his lungs beginning to burn as he dragged both himself and the child to the surface. At the surface, there was air, there was solid ground, there was surely someone who knew CPR. He cursed himself for never learning it. From under the water, he could hear the clamor as people responded to what was happening—a whistle blew, a child screeched, a woman yelled. He could make out someone yelling, "Call 911!"

He broke through the surface just as the lifeguard materialized at his side saying, "I got him. I got him," in a confident voice that made Lance want to say, "Well, you didn't have him when it mattered." But the lifeguard knew CPR; the lifeguard was trained in things like this. He'd probably waited his whole lifeguarding career for this, the moment he got to play hero.

Lance loosened his grip on the boy, and the child was taken from his arms. A trio of lifeguards gathered on the hot concrete as they laid out the too-still child and began working on him. Lance swam to the side and, exhausted, balanced his elbows on the edge to watch what was happening as he caught his breath. His eyes burned and he blinked rapidly. He sucked big, grateful gulps of air into his lungs.

The entire pool had gone quiet. All around him the people stood still and watched the little boy, the silence simultaneously eerie and reverent. Someone had turned off the never-ending radio they kept cranked over the speakers at an obnoxious volume. He looked around for the child's mother, but no one stepped forward. A little girl was crying hysterically; he assumed she was the boy's sister. He saw Zell slip an arm around her, and the girl struggled against the restraint, trying in vain to get to the boy's side. The lifeguards kept working on the boy, who was blue and unconscious. Lance prayed for the first time in a very long time. "Please, please, please," he said, his voice barely a whisper.

Suddenly he remembered his own son and scanned around to account for his children. He found Alec frozen in his spot in line for the diving board. Their eyes met, and Alec gave him a smile so fleeting he wasn't sure he saw it, then gave him a thumbs-up, an affirmation that his father had done something right when it counted most. But would it count if the boy didn't survive? Lance pulled himself from the water just as the distant wail of sirens approached. He caught the eye of the beautiful woman, and they exchanged grim looks.

After the EMTs arrived, things moved fast. From a distance, it was hard to make out exactly what they were doing. Lance just saw arms flying and faces frowning. In short order they'd secured the boy's neck, put him on a stretcher, and headed to the ambulance. The boy's older sister, a little girl Lance had seen playing with Lilah just a few minutes before the whole episode began, ran after him, screaming his name. "Cutter!" And then, "I have to go with him!" Lilah and Jencey's daughters did their best to comfort her, but she was inconsolable, shaking them off and attempting to catch up to the ambulance and climb inside.

The EMTs, intent on helping the child and seemingly unconcerned about his hysterical sister, bustled past as if she wasn't there. One, filled with a grace the other two did not possess, turned back. "We're going to take your brother now," he said. "We're going to help him." He squeezed the little girl's thin shoulder and raced after his coworkers. Moments later the ambulance shrieked away with lights flashing and siren blaring. The nearby adults, suddenly linked by the situation, formed a messy circle around the girl, offering words of comfort and trying to decide what to do. The children gathered there, too, wide-eyed and silent.

Zell, ever helpful, rubbed the little girl's back and assured her that she could go to the hospital just as soon as they got the boy settled in. She said "settled in" as if he were going to a bed-and-breakfast. But her voice was soothing and even and seemed to calm them all down.

"Someone needs to call his mother." The woman standing beside Jencey spoke up, her voice shaky. She had scooped up her little boy and was more clinging to him than holding him.

Zell spoke to the girl. "Do you know your mom's number, honey?" Zell leaned over to Lilah. "What's her name again?" she stage-whispered.

"Cailey." Lilah's attempt at a stage whisper came out sounding more like a hiss.

The little girl ceased crying long enough to give her a "duh" look and nodded. Zell handed her a phone, and she punched in the numbers. Before it could start ringing, Zell took the phone from her hand.

"But I want to talk to her," the girl cried out, trying unsuccessfully to get the phone from Zell.

Zell turned to the girl. "Cailey," she said, gentle but firm in the face of the girl's hysterics, "you can talk to her once I've explained the situation." She took a few steps away from them and turned her back to speak to the boy's mother, a woman who, at that moment, had no idea that something terrible had just happened to her son. Lance could hear Zell's voice, slow and deliberate, relaying the news in a way that was almost businesslike.

Cailey went back to sobbing, repeating the same words over and over again. "She's going to be so mad at me. She told me to watch him." Lance and Lilah looked at each other as, helplessly, Lilah attempted to stroke the girl's bare back, flanked by two straps of her bathing suit, the little nodules of her spine poking out from beneath her skin. Lance got a towel and wrapped it around Cailey, who turned to see who had done so. She looked up at him.

"Are you the guy who saved him?" she asked. Her eyes bored into him, unsettled him.

He nodded and attempted to give her a little smile, but it fell flat. He wanted to offer her something, promise her that her brother would be OK, but he couldn't say that, not with any certainty. He didn't make a habit of lying to kids, at least not any more than he had to. He'd had to lie to his own children a fair amount lately, more than he ever thought he'd have to in his entire parenting career. It was for their own good, he told himself. It was so they'd believe there was still some good in the world. Of course that was a lie. Just look at what had happened here, today, in a place that should be reserved for happiness.

"Will you take me to him now?" Cailey asked.

He searched for the right words to respond. Trucking over to the hospital with his kids and this girl all in wet bathing suits in search of a little boy who may or may not be dying didn't sound like the most prudent thing to do at that moment. And yet, how could he say no?

Suddenly Jencey was at his side. She looked knowingly at Lance, then crouched down and looked at Cailey. She spoke in that same measured, even tone Zell had been using. It must be a mom reflex. Standing so close to Jencey, he could smell her skin. It smelled like Coppertone and sunshine. He inhaled deeply, imagining the scent of her going inside him, inflating his battered lungs. He scolded himself for thinking such a thing at a time like this.

"Cailey, honey, why don't you let one of us take you home and wait for your mom to call and let us know what she'd like us to do? I'm not sure that going to be with Cutter right now is the best thing for any of us." She gestured to the girl's bathing suit. "Wouldn't you like to get some dry clothes?"

Cailey shook her head emphatically. "I want to be with Cutter!" The three of them—Jencey, the woman holding the little boy, and Lance—all looked at one another helplessly. Just then Zell bustled back over and handed the phone to Cailey.

"Your mama wants to speak to you," she said.

"Is she mad?" Cailey asked, her voice gone hoarse.

"She's upset, honey. But not at you." Zell patted her shoulder. She took a few steps away and motioned for the others to follow her. Lance obeyed, as did the rest of them. "That mother is a basket case," Zell said quietly. "I mean imagine getting news like this in the middle of your workday. I don't think she even entirely understood what I was telling her. She just burst into tears and didn't make a whole lot of sense after that. I told her I'd be happy to take Cailey home with me until we can figure out what to do." She looked into the pairs of eyes looking back at her for confirmation.

They all nodded dumbly, lacking a better idea. There was no protocol for such things.

Zell nodded twice. "OK. That's what we'll do."

Lance had no idea how these strangers had suddenly become a "we." Zell was his next-door neighbor who had somehow made herself indispensable to him since summer began. The other woman was someone he'd met five seconds before he saw the boy in the pool, and he still didn't know the other woman's name at all. He glanced over at Cailey, hunched over in a white plastic chair, her body all but curled into a ball around that phone, and thought of the weight of her brother in his arms. Something terrifying had happened in their midst, and they were the witnesses, now united by the trauma.

"So, right," he spoke up. "Zell will take Cailey home with her. I'm right next door, so maybe Alec and Lilah can check in on her, or I can answer any questions she may have or . . . whatever. And we'll just wait for news from the mother and go from there?"

"That sounds like as good a plan as any." Zell's voice was less hearty than usual. She went over to get Cailey. Lance heard her say, her voice comforting, "Your mom needs to drive to the hospital now, honey. She needs to get off the phone so she can drive safely, OK?"

He looked around at the pool, the water now still and empty. The lifeguards were in panic mode, calling their bosses and filling out forms, unaware that anyone else was there. The music was still off, and the place had cleared out. Their own children spoke in hushed tones, huddled off to the side to process what had happened without the aid of an adult perspective. They probably thought the boy was dead. Lance wasn't sure he wasn't.

He looked back at Jencey and her friend.

"This is Lance," Jencey said to her friend. "The hero." She gave him a smile, one that was genuine but fleeting. He missed it as soon as it was gone.

CAILEY

When the snooty girl talked to me, I thought she thought I was some-one else. When she smiled at me, I looked over my shoulder to see who she was looking at. I know my face looked shocked when I realized she was talking to me. We'd been coming up to the pool for almost a whole month, played a few feet away from each other in the water many times, and stood next to each other in line for the diving board more than once. But she'd never acted like she knew I was alive. So I'd stuck with Cutter, keeping an eye on him like I was supposed to, and pretended I didn't notice that the girls my own age didn't care two flips about talking to me.

What was different about that day? I don't know. I was in the right place at the right time or the wrong place at the wrong time. It was one way, then it was another. The two things switched like how one minute the sun is there, the next minute it's the moon and you're not quite sure how it happened. Why did she decide to pay attention to me, and why did I have to respond? If I'd ignored her, everything might've been different. But I didn't. She asked me my name. I told her. She told me hers (I already knew; I'd heard her sister shout it about a hundred times by then), and we started playing Cross Pool. Everything that came after that was irreversible. It just was.

Once when Mom was between both jobs and boyfriends, she sent us to stay with her aunt Ruby, who lived on a farm out in the country. We stayed there for a long time, though Mom says it wasn't that long. I'm not sure that's true, but it doesn't really matter. What matters is that while we were there, I saw two things I'll never forget: a calf get born and then, a few days later, that calf dying. I still remember how we found it, cold and stiff in a corner of the stall. Aunt Ruby didn't know what happened to the calf. She said that sometimes things just aren't strong enough to make it in this world.

Standing there with those strangers at the pool all looking at me, I thought of that calf, and about Cutter splashing around all desperate-like every time he got in the water. He wasn't strong enough, either. But I was supposed to be strong for him. I thought of all the times I'd been cruel to him, ignored him, said awful things to him. I hoped he knew I didn't mean any of it. I felt the tears sliding down my face, and I didn't bother to wipe them away. I didn't care if those strangers saw me cry.

The adults held a little meeting and decided I should go to the old lady's house, the one who always brought Alec and Lilah up to the pool. She always had good snacks, so I figured it wouldn't be awful to go with her, even if she was a stranger and my mom told me never to go with strangers. My mom also told me to keep an eye on Cutter at all times, and I didn't do that, so maybe I deserved whatever happened to me at a stranger's house.

But when we got there, nothing terrible happened. The old lady—who told me to call her Zell—made me a glass of Coke in a bright turquoise metal cup that turned as cold as the ice she put in it. My throat was so tight I couldn't swallow the Coke, so I just held the cup in my hand until it got too cold to stand, then I put it on the coffee table and watched the condensation drip down the sides while the old lady—Zell—went to find me a coaster.

Her house was nice. Cozy. The kind of house you'd see on a TV show. Zell also seemed like she could be on a TV show, playing the plump neighbor who's nice but kind of obnoxious, the one you just have to love because she means well. She stared at me while I took a polite sip of that Coke, and that's what I told myself: *She means well.* She'd brought me there, hadn't she? She'd taken me in when she didn't have to. The whole lot of them could've left me there, crying and wailing like I was, all of them hoping I'd get myself together and get myself home eventually.

But they didn't leave me. They huddled like a football team and made a decision. Maybe they drew straws and Zell got the short one. But however they made it, she was the one elected. She told me I was going home with her as if it were the best news she'd ever heard. And when we left, the other people walked out with us, each of them promising to check in on me later, like they actually cared. Alec and Lilah's dad said, "Feel better," and looked really sad, and I wished I had a dad like him. I knew they didn't have a mom, but sometimes I thought a dad would be better anyway. I mean, if you had to pick just one.

As I drifted off to sleep on Zell's couch underneath the afghan she put over me when I couldn't stop shivering, I thought about the sign at the pool's entrance that said: **WE'RE ALL FAMILY HERE.** Maybe, I decided, it wasn't a lie.

EVERETT

Jencey Cabot was sitting at his kitchen table, looking for all the world like she belonged there. Like she'd just been by last week to drop off some blueberries she'd picked and was back to eat the muffins Bryte made from them, or whatever women did with one another when he was at work. He tried not to stare at her, taking in the changes that had occurred since the last time he'd seen her, which wasn't nearly as long ago as Bryte thought. He couldn't let on about that. So far Jencey was doing a good job of pretending it had never happened. Was it possible she'd forgotten?

His gaze flickered back over her. Damn but she was still beautiful. Whether her hair was still the same color blonde as it had been in high school or she'd had some help keeping it that color didn't matter. Except for the faintest lines around her eyes and a bit more wisdom in them, she looked just like the girl he'd loved first. He forced himself to look away and smile at Bryte, who was all revved up about what had happened at the pool that day. She'd talked of nearly nothing else.

"So then what happened?" he asked, feigning the same level of interest, when all he wanted to do was grill Jencey about what she was doing back in town and ask her if she was mad at him. She had a right to be.

"Well, they took him in the ambulance. But the saddest part"— Bryte and Jencey exchanged mournful glances—"the saddest part was his older sister. They didn't take her with them, and it just broke her heart. So she's falling apart and we're all just standing there wondering what to do." Bryte looked at Jencey again, and he could see the faintest bit of that old hero worship in her eyes as she did. "Jencey was really great with her."

Jencey shrugged. "She's close in age to my daughters. I just talked to her the way I do with them when there's a crisis."

Have you had a lot of crises in your life? He refrained from speaking the words aloud. He liked to think her life in Connecticut had been good, better than the one she'd left behind. The one that had once included him.

"Well, you got her calmed down." Bryte stood and began clearing the plates from dinner, shooing Jencey back into her place when she attempted to stand as well. "I was useless."

Everett didn't like the tone this conversation was taking. His wife was regressing in front of his eyes. Where was the confident, capable woman she'd become in her twenties, sans Jencey? He wasn't sure that Jencey's reappearance in their lives right on the heels of the infertility issues was the best thing. He'd been close to talking her into subjecting themselves to all of it again, shoring her up for battle. He couldn't afford for Jencey to reduce her to that uncertain girl she'd been back when they were in high school. That girl could never have gone through all that his wife—grown-up, confident Bryte—had.

"I'm sure you weren't useless, honey," he spoke up.

He saw Jencey's eyes cut over to him and away in a flash. So she didn't like him calling Bryte "honey." Interesting. Or maybe he was just reading too much into the situation. Projecting. Isn't that what Bryte called it when he said things he wished were true as if they already were? Did he want Jencey to be bothered? To be jealous?

Yes, he did. God help him, he did want Jencey to eat her heart out over how it had all turned out. Never mind the way things had gone down that last time. Never mind that things might've been different.

"Everett?" Bryte asked. "Would you mind getting Christopher out of his seat?" Without waiting for his reply, Bryte handed him a wet washcloth. And why not? This is what they did every night. This is who they were. This was the choice they'd all made.

He used the washcloth to attempt to remove the remnants of dinner from his son's face as Christopher squirmed and whined his disapproval. Jencey watched the domestic scene silently, and Everett wondered what she was thinking. Satisfied with his cleaning job—the rest would come off in the bath—Everett released the booster-seat tray and helped him down. Christopher immediately went to Jencey, sidling up to her with a charming grin as he thrust a toy car in her face to impress her. *Like father, like son,* he thought, and suppressed a grin of his own.

"You're quite the little charmer," Jencey said, and pulled Christopher onto her lap.

Bryte turned around and looked at the three of them there at the table—the boy in Jencey's lap, Everett sitting beside them. He could only wonder what Jencey's thoughts were, but he could take one look at his wife to know what hers were. He caught her eye and winked. *I love you. You're my wife. This is our son. I wouldn't want it any different.* Bryte smiled and turned back to the dishes.

"So where's the little girl now?" he asked, circling back to the most innocuous topic of conversation he could find. It was awful of him, but he was actually glad for the scene at the pool today. It had given them all something to talk about, allowed them to detour away from the land mines that lay in any other conversational territory.

"Well, she's with Zell. Remember Mrs. Boyette? JJ's mom?" Bryte started loading the dishwasher, speaking without turning around.

Everett laughed, thinking of big, lumbering JJ Boyette, the quintessential jock. Everett hadn't thought about him in years. "Yeah," he said, thinking of the time JJ had chased him and his friends through the woods by the lake. People said those woods were haunted, and as a child he'd been terrified of going into them. Later, he'd come to love those woods.

He forced himself not to look over at Jencey, not to think of their hideaway. At some point he wanted to talk to her alone, to make sure she wasn't ever going to mention anything to Bryte, who still had no idea what had happened in New York. He couldn't afford for anything to knock them off course, not when he'd laid so much groundwork for attempting a second child. Bryte would use any excuse to postpone another round of fertility treatments.

He understood—last time was hell—but he also knew that in the end the treatments had worked. He glanced over at Christopher, whose eyes were growing heavy as he sat on Jencey's lap. He didn't want his boy to be an only child. He'd been an only child. His world had been lonely until Jencey and Bryte had come into his life when he moved to Sycamore Glen at ten years old. He'd thought of them like sisters, until he didn't.

"Have you heard anything?" Jencey piped up. "From Zell?"

Bryte shook her head and shut the dishwasher door with a thud, the glasses inside clinking loudly against one another as she did. "Tell you what, I'll go call her. I've got a neighborhood directory around here somewhere." She strode out of the room, leaving Jencey and Everett alone.

"I'm sorry." Jencey waited a moment, then spoke quietly, knowing they had precious few moments alone. "If this is awkward."

He shrugged as if it were no big deal, not letting on how desperate he'd been to cover his bases, to beg her not to mention anything that could damage his marriage. And yet, with Jencey sitting there, he didn't want to bring up that awkward and embarrassing night. From the back bedroom they used as an office, he heard Bryte using her telephone voice, slightly louder and more formal than her normal speaking voice.

"It's just weird," he brought himself to say. "Seeing you again." He gestured to Christopher. "Here."

"I'll never bring up . . . the past," she said. She looked over at him and their eyes held. "I wouldn't do that," she added.

He looked away, focusing his gaze on Christopher's face, but he could still feel her eyes on him. "Thanks," he mumbled as relief flooded his body. Bryte returned to the room, talking a mile a minute.

"So, Cailey is still with Zell, and it looks like she's going to be there for a while. Terrible situation. Cutter has—hang on, let me make sure I say this right—acute respiratory distress syndrome. He's in intensive care, and the mom basically can't miss work because she's the sole bread-winner for the family. They're monitoring Cutter for possible brain damage because he was under the water for who knows how long. I'd like to string those lifeguards up for not paying attention!" Bryte said, her voice growing more animated. "I told you, didn't I, honey?" She didn't wait for an assent from him before continuing. "I told you how those lifeguards are not doing their jobs. I hope they fire every one of them. I mean, what would've happened if Lance didn't see him and jump in?"

"I shudder to think," Jencey agreed, nodding vigorously. She took another gulp of wine. Everett noticed she was knocking the wine back. And Bryte, ever the hostess, kept her glass filled. He didn't exactly blame Jencey. If he didn't have to get up early for work, he'd definitely get hammered.

Christopher yawned and reached for him. "Come on, buddy," he said, lifting him into the air as he stood and settled him on his hip. "Let's get you into the tub."

"Oh, let me get him some clean pj's," Bryte piped up, scuttling back out of the room.

"It looks good on you," Jencey said to him before he could follow his wife.

He turned back to her. "What does?" he asked.

She held her hands out to indicate the room, the house, the wife, the child. "All of it, Ev."

He nodded his understanding, then quickly walked away.

BRYTE

She'd had to walk away from the two of them. She'd seen it. Of course she had. The way he couldn't look at Jencey for very long. The way he snuck glances at her when he thought no one noticed. She'd spent her formative years studying Everett Lewis with the devotion of a scholar. She knew his mannerisms by heart; his face spoke as loudly as his voice. He still thought Jencey was beautiful. Bryte couldn't blame him. She did, too. And the truth was, she somehow wanted to see them together, wanted to subject herself to the pain of it, as if that would make them even.

But she hadn't anticipated the intensity of her own pain. The idea of punishing herself had been appealing in concept, but the reality of it was too much to be contained in their small kitchen amid the scraps of the dinner she'd cooked, the scent of barbecue chicken mingling with Dawn dishwashing liquid. She'd run from the room, landing on the first excuse that came to mind. She ran straight to the drawer that, yes, contained the neighborhood directory to look up Zell's number. But it also contained stray business cards. She'd added that business card to the rest years ago, hidden it in plain sight. As she left Jencey and Everett alone in the kitchen to say whatever it was they needed to say without her around, it was that card—and not the neighborhood directory—she had in mind.

She tugged open the drawer and removed the directory first, just in case Everett followed her back there. But he wouldn't. He would take the opportunity she'd given him. She rummaged through the haphazard pile, riffling through cards from the electrician and the plumber and the babysitter and, inexplicably, a baby-diaper service when she'd never used anything but disposables. She kept sorting through the cards, hearing the murmur of voices in the next room. She refused to think about what they might be saying. They had their secrets and she had hers.

Her hand fell on the card she was there to find, and the pace of her heart picked up as she eyed the familiar lettering, the swirl and curve of the name printed on it: Trent Miller. She could picture his face as he handed it to her. "Promise me you'll call if you're ever in the market for a different position," he'd said. "Someone like you I could place a thousand times over, for about a thousand times more money than you're making now." He'd given her that cocky, confident look. She'd gone to take the card from his hand, and he'd pulled it away, teasing her. "Promise me," he'd intoned, holding the card out of reach.

She'd promised, never thinking that would be the case. She was happy in the job she had at the time and wasn't in the market to be recruited elsewhere. She cared about her clients, and they cared about her. She could solve the technical issues while relating to the human ones, making her invaluable in a field where people usually had one skill or the other but not both. In fact, it was at the specific request of a former client that her name had come back up again, causing her employer to come knocking. She thought of the e-mails waiting in her in-box from her old boss and coworker. And yet, maybe Trent knew of other, better opportunities. Could he offer options she hadn't thought of that would give her more leverage now? Would it be the worst thing for her to call him?

She ran her fingers across the card and waited for her heart to slow. Then she pocketed it and picked up the neighborhood directory, flipping expertly to the listing for Boyette, John and Zell. Their children were still listed under their names though none of them lived with them anymore. Bryte found that a little sad. She dialed the number, thinking as she did of Zell's second son, Ty. She'd kissed him once, in the woods behind the lake, near the little circle of trees that Jencey and Everett used to disappear into. She'd kissed Ty because she was bored, because he was there, and because she was determined to get over Everett.

She listened to the sound of Zell's phone ringing in the house two streets over from hers, thinking that no kiss had ever been powerful enough to break the spell Everett had over her, no desire had ever been as strong as the one she had to make him hers. She traced the outline of the card in her pocket. She'd made him hers; now she just had to keep him. But Jencey wasn't the threat anymore. She'd become that all by herself.

CAILEY

Three days went by. I told my mom I would just stay with Zell since she offered, and it was better than being at home alone all the time since Mom was always working or going to the hospital to be with Cutter. It wasn't so bad being with Zell, except for how she kept talking to people on the phone about Cutter. She went into another room and lowered her voice, but I could make out enough to know that 1) this was just about the most exciting thing that had happened to her in a long time, and 2) Cutter was not doing so well. But you know what she would say to me? She would say he's doing just fine and that I should be able to see him soon. I hate when adults lie to kids.

I wanted to see Cutter, even if he was out cold and hooked up to a lot of tubes and machines. I wanted to see my mom. I wanted to get it over with, the look she was going to give me, that one of utter disappointment that made me wish she'd just yell at me already. I wanted her to say out loud that I'd ruined everything and that I might've cost her her job and the house we rented and who knew what else. I'd talked to her on the phone twice, but both times it was really fast, and she wasn't going to get into it with Zell hovering nearby anyway. My day of reckoning would come later, and the thought of it made my stomach hurt.

Zell tried to occupy my time so I wouldn't think about Cutter and how awful everything was. She had me help her in the kitchen and tried to teach me how to play cards and took me to the library to check out books on her library card. I told her I might lose the books, and she said well, then, she'd just pay for them if that happened, but she didn't think it would. I was glad she got me the books. It gave me a reason to go to my room (which was really her son's room) and be by myself. But if I stayed in there too long, she knocked on the door and asked me if I was OK and wouldn't I like something to drink or eat. She was always trying to feed me.

I guess if I had to stay somewhere, it wasn't the worst place I could've ended up even if she did put me in a room that smelled like a boy. Zell was nice, if a bit peculiar (I like that word), and her husband, John, was funny. We ate dinner together, the three of us at the table talking about the news and the weather and the things I always imagined families talked about around the table. And for just a moment, I would imagine that it would stay that way forever, that I could change into someone else completely—someone who grew up in a house like that one and not the eyesore of the neighborhood. But then I would feel terrible for thinking about myself, especially considering the fact that Cutter got hurt because I was only thinking about myself. In those moments I would whisper, "I'm sorry" and imagine that wherever Cutter was, he could hear me.

Late at night when Zell and John thought I'd gone to sleep, I would tiptoe to the window in their son's room and stare up at the stars in the sky, wishing on every one of them just for good measure. And every wish I had was for Cutter to be OK. I thought only of him and not me, forcing my brain not to think about the coming school year or the friends I didn't have or whether I'd ever fit anywhere. I promised whoever made those stars that if Cutter got better, I'd never care about anyone but him for the rest of my life. And, mostly, I believed it was possible.

ZELL

She'd hauled a stool out to the garden to get some weeding done and was awkwardly crouched on it, ripping weeds out down to the roots—an activity she found quite therapeutic—when she heard footsteps approaching. Before this summer, the footsteps would've been heavier, those of John plodding out, wondering what was for dinner or asking where was such-and-such, even though he'd lived in that house the last thirty years.

But it wasn't John. These footsteps were too light to be his, little fairy footsteps. She turned to greet Cailey, whose presence was fast becoming a fixture. John had warned her just last night not to get too attached. She'd turned from him, busying herself with stirring the beans until he gave up and walked away. It was good to have someone to take care of, someone to cook for.

Last night she'd made a big meal, the kind her mama used to make—country-style steak, mashed potatoes and gravy, fresh corn, green beans, and sliced tomatoes. She'd even made biscuits, something she hadn't done in a coon's age. Cailey loved her cooking and ate like there was no tomorrow. Zell worried that the child hadn't been fed properly and made it her mission to get some nourishment in her.

For dessert she'd made real banana pudding, only to learn that Cailey didn't like bananas. But that was OK because she had some ice cream in the freezer, and John was only too happy to eat the banana pudding himself, though Lord knew he didn't need it. She glanced down at her own belly, brimming over the top of her waistband, then looked up and gave Cailey a smile. She adjusted her wide-brimmed straw hat so she could see the child better.

"Have a good sleep?" she asked her.

Cailey nodded, chewing her lip and casting her eyes about like she was casing the joint.

"Give me just a minute to finish up here and I'll make you some breakfast." Zell turned back to the weeds, wincing as her knee protested the movement. The stool wasn't really helping. She missed being able to kneel, missed getting her nose and hands fully immersed in the earth.

"I could help you with that . . . if you want," Cailey offered. She moved closer, coming into Zell's line of sight.

"Do you know about gardening?" Zell asked, unable to keep the surprise from her voice.

Cailey shrugged. "I helped my teacher at my old school. We were making a wildlife habitat. It was a class project, but . . . I moved away before we finished." Cailey thought about it for a second. "That was two schools ago." She shrugged as if it meant nothing, but Zell could see the lie in her pensive little face. She heard John's warning again about getting attached, his words echoing from the night before. He knew her all too well.

"But you liked it?"

Cailey nodded. "I liked making a place for, you know, the animals and stuff. We planted special plants they could eat and made places for them to hide." She shrugged again. "It was pretty cool."

Zell's voice was tight when she spoke, and she cleared her throat. "I bet you wish you'd seen it all finished."

Cailey nodded, her eyes focused on the landscaping. She blinked a few times. "Yeah. My mom said we could go back one day, but . . . she never has time."

"Is the school nearby?" Zell asked.

Cailey thought about it. "I think it's like an hour away. Maybe."

"Ah," said Zell. She thought about her own life with young children, how overwhelming things had seemed then, and she'd been a stay-at-home mom with no outside responsibilities. There were so many things she'd intended to do with them, for them, but the time got away and then it was over. "I'm sure your mom would love to take you sometime."

"Yeah," Cailey agreed. "I know she would if she could." She glanced over at Zell. "She's a good mom."

"She sure is, honey." Zell had noticed Cailey's penchant for defending her mom even though no charges had been levied against her. The woman, Lisa, was clearly in over her head, cursed with more responsibility than she had resources to handle, exacerbated, Zell guessed from things that Cailey had said, by a tendency to pick cruel, freeloading men. Zell had seen it before. Her own sister, for example, was now living in Arkansas with husband number four. She wasn't judging Cailey's mom—at least she hoped it didn't come across that she was. She was just trying to help. Somewhere deep inside her a warning bell went off, but she ignored it.

"Can I go see her?" Cailey asked, seeming to sense a weak moment, an opportune time to strike. Kids, Zell recalled, were exceedingly good at that. "I want to go see her and Cutter."

Zell had spoken with Lisa just yesterday when she'd stopped by to see Cailey. Cutter was still touch and go. He was hanging in there, but not improving as they'd hoped. Lisa and Zell had agreed that it was best for Cailey not to see Cutter until he was awake. That was exactly how they'd put it, stringing the words *until* and *awake* together in an act of good faith—both of them wanting to believe that this kind of positive talk could make all the difference. Zell had said a little prayer for the boy after Lisa left, even though she wasn't in a position to be asking for favors from the Almighty.

"Soon, honey," Zell promised. "I'm waiting for your mother to let me know the doctors have cleared Cutter for visitors." When all else fails, blame it on the doctors. This was also something she remembered from raising her own children. The doctor said you have to eat that. The doctor said you have to go to bed now. The doctor said you have to have sunscreen or you can't go swimming. The doctor was always a good scapegoat. Zell held her breath and hoped her ploy would work on Cailey like it did with her own kids.

"I wish those doctors would hurry up," Cailey grumbled, sinking down beside Zell on the lawn.

"What if . . ." Zell spoke aloud, her mouth uttering the words even before the idea had fully taken shape. Cailey looked up, her face expectant, eager. Like most children, she knew that questions that started off with "What if" were usually good questions. "What if," Zell continued, "you and I turned my yard into a wildlife habitat? It could be our little project while you're here." She watched Cailey's reaction, hoped this wasn't a colossal mistake. Something inside her said, *You never learn.* But something else said, *Maybe this time will be different.*

Cailey hesitated for just a moment, as if she were having an internal dialogue of her own. But then the eager, expectant look returned, and a grin broke out across her little face. Cailey's genuine smiles were rare, and Zell let herself take this one in, because this one was just for her. "Yes?" she prompted, wanting to hear the word on Cailey's lips.

Cailey nodded vigorously and the grin widened. "Yes!" she said. She sprang up and started sprinting away, then turned back to beckon Zell to follow her. "I know the website we have to go to!" she hollered from across the yard. "Come on! I'll show you!"

Zell smiled and started the slow process of getting herself up off the stool, her knee already protesting with even the slightest movement. In a flash, Cailey was back at her side. "Here," she said, extending her small hand, "I'll help you up." Zell did the only thing there was to do: she took Cailey's hand and allowed the child to help her stand.

BRYTE

She sank down onto the cold tile of the laundry-room floor and willed herself to get a grip. She'd found the business card in the pocket of her shorts, rescued seconds before being thrown into the washing machine and destroyed by the hot water she was about to send pouring into the tub. Her heart pounding, she remembered and pinched it out of its hiding place, nestled there between the layers of denim, put there as a protective weapon on a night she'd felt vulnerable. She thought not of Jencey's face, but of Everett's as he looked at Jencey. She worried that Jencey's return had put everything she'd created for herself at risk.

As a child, she'd wanted exactly what she'd grown up with. She wanted to replicate the life she'd known. She was the only one of her friends who felt that way, her teen years spent listening to various accounts of how the future was going to be different for them. Jencey wanted a big house. Everett wanted Jencey. Other friends wanted more religion or less, more freedom or less, more money (but never less), different politics, different traditions, different lives from the ones they'd been brought up in. She would listen politely, nod when appropriate, and make encouraging comments. But inside she was thinking, *Is it wrong to want more of the same?*

She loved her parents, her home, her neighborhood, even her school. She loved swimming with the same kids each summer at the pool, the big Fourth of July celebration that lasted all day and into the night, the way the sun's rays glinted off the lake and the breeze rippled the water. She loved church on Sundays and takeout pizza on Fridays, the Christmas-card photos of friends and family members affixed to the refrigerator door for months after the holidays were over, and afternoons reading in the backyard hammock. She loved belonging to this place and these people. She knew she was lucky—many kids didn't have what she had. What more was there to want?

Crouched on her laundry-room floor, running her fingers across the raised black letters, she waffled between remembering and forgetting, between who she was, then and now. She'd gotten exactly what she wanted, but it had come at a price she'd never expected. She stood, feeling restless and anxious, her heart beating much too hard for a stay-at-home mom doing laundry on an ordinary summer Tuesday.

She palmed the card and walked it back to its original spot in the drawer. But before she could hide it away again, she paused, taking one last look. She took in the name, then the phone number, then the e-mail. Could it still be the same? Would it hurt to try?

She took a deep breath and reached for her cell phone, charging on the desk where she left it each night. She gave herself a pep talk as she entered the numbers on the card into her phone's keypad. This was about a job, and that was all. She was doing her due diligence in the face of the repeated requests from her former employer; she was just being smart. Her heart hammered as the line rang and rang and rang. It went to voice mail, and the minute she heard his voice, she hit "End"—a reflex. This was wrong and dangerous and stupid. She stood there panting as if she'd run a marathon, her insides churning. She paced back and forth a few times in front of the desk, calming herself, still holding her phone.

This morning before he'd left for work, Everett had said he was going to make an appointment at the clinic, that they couldn't keep putting it off. He'd brushed aside her objections, put his hands on her shoulders, and with a serious look told her that he'd be with her every step of the way. He'd never understand that this was the last thing she wanted. She would do anything to keep from hearing the same verdict, the same options she'd heard before. And going back to work could stop that from happening.

She looked down at the phone, debating placing a second call and this time not hanging up. *If you do this,* she coached herself, *everything could change.* But everything was going to change anyway. She pulled up her recent calls and hit the number again. She cleared her throat as the phone rang, readying herself to leave a message. There was that voice, strangely familiar even though it had been years since she'd heard it last. She smiled at the sound of it, then began to speak after the beep.

"Hi," she said. "This is Bryte Lewis. We met several years ago at the ATXS show, at the cocktail party. I'm not sure you'll remember, but you mentioned I should call if I was ever looking for a job, and I am. So, if you can, I'd love to talk to you about it. I know tomorrow is the Fourth, so you're probably not even working this week, but if you can give me a call, my number is—" The beep sounded, and she was cut off.

A voice inside her said, *This isn't just about a job.* But she ignored the voice, pushing it into that place deep within her where the truth resided. She watched as the phone's screen returned to a photo of the three of them at Easter, all dressed up. She'd put Christopher and Everett in adorable matching pastel bow ties. She exhaled loudly and considered calling back to leave her number. No, the number would show up in his list of incoming calls. If he wanted to respond, he'd figure it out.

JULY 2014

JENCEY

The impact of a little body landing on the mattress jolted her awake in her old bedroom, never changed since her departure, a pastel wonderland with its boy-band posters and various other accoutrements of the teenage female. Her girls were fascinated with the time capsule that was her old bedroom, holding long-since dried-out bottles of nail polish up to her with a kind of wonder. "Mom," Pilar had asked, astonished, "*you* wore glitter nail polish?"

She supposed it was astonishing to a child who'd only seen her mother with French manicures, which was what all the women had back in her old neighborhood. She'd taken the bottle of nail polish from Pilar's hand and studied it for a moment, seeing in her mind's eye sitting with Bryte on her bed, doing one another's nails. Bryte was always so careful, so serious about the polish being just so. She'd been fastidious then, and—from what Jencey could tell—was still that way. She was just as serious and careful in her devotion to her home, her cooking, her son, and Everett. Jencey tried not to think about those few moments alone she'd had with Everett after dinner. There were things she'd wanted to say to him, but didn't dare, the unsaid words still rolling around like marbles in her mind.

"Get up, Mom!" Zara hollered, shaking the mattress as violently as her small body could manage, her shrill voice too loud and piercing on the cusp of a sound sleep. Jencey had been dreaming she was in the woods by the lake, but there was someone else there, too, someone she didn't know, but who knew her—the presence disturbing, threatening, and all too real. She tried to shake off the dream even as she pulled back the sheets so Zara could snuggle under with her. She hugged her daughter tighter and kissed her head several times, the action warding off any lingering bad mojo from her dreams. Zara giggled and wrenched away. "Mom, we have to get ready for the parade!" she scolded.

Jencey moaned aloud and pulled the covers over her head. "Can't your grandmother take you?" she said from under the sheets. She'd known today was the Fourth and had vaguely thought of the neighborhood to-do over the big day, but hadn't actually expected to take part in any of it. Pilar and Zara had spent the day yesterday helping her mother make the traditional dishes to put out at the neighborhood potluck. Things just wouldn't be the same in Sycamore Glen if her mother's potato salad wasn't among the dishes. Jencey wasn't in the mood to participate in a large celebration that most likely would involve people she hadn't seen in over a decade, fielding questions about her husband and why she was there, which she'd so far, for the most part, been able to avoid. But the girls were invested now, which meant she was as well.

Zara's head appeared underneath the covers, her grin so wide her dimples showed. She scooched down to get into Jencey's line of sight. She was her mirror child, her baby, her sweetest girl. "No, Mom, you have to come. You promised."

It was true; she'd agreed at dinner last night, acquiescing to the girls' pleas without much of a fight. That would teach her to drink wine at dinner. She tossed the covers back with a world-weary sigh, her eyes falling on a poster of Marky Mark before he'd become the more respectable Mark Wahlberg. "You're right. I said I would go, so let's go watch this amazing, elaborate display of patriotism!" she said, her voice containing so much false enthusiasm she expected Zara to see right through it.

But she didn't. "Pilar!" Zara hollered as she hopped up from the bed. "I told you she'd come!" She scampered from the room, her little feet thundering down the hall in search of her sister. If her parents weren't awake, they would be now. *Serves them right,* she thought. She was tempted to pull the covers back over her head and fall headlong back into dreamland, but she wasn't sure her dreamland was a safe place to go.

She took her spot on the sidewalk with the other neighbors, waiting for the parade to start. Her mother had prepared a thermos of coffee for her, and a friendly man she didn't recognize handed her a donut to go with it. She accepted the fried ring of dough and sugar just because it was the Fourth of July and the donut had red, white, and blue sprinkles. It felt unpatriotic to turn it down. She watched the parade, such as it was, begin its long trek from the entrance of the neighborhood to the clubhouse. As tradition dictated, the local fire department had sent an engine to lead the way, and she waved back at a fireman who hung off the side, pointing at her as he passed, waving enthusiastically when he was sure he had her attention.

"I think he likes you." Bryte sidled up, pushing Christopher in his stroller. After all their days at the pool together, Jencey had come to recognize that stroller as well as she recognized other people's vehicles.

Jencey grinned at her and said hello even though her mouth was still full of donut. She broke off a bite of the donut and handed it to Christopher without asking Bryte first. Christopher looked up at her with utter gratitude on his face, stuffing the donut in his mouth before his mother could think better of it and take it away.

Bryte laughed. "Donuts are his love language."

"Smart boy," Jencey said. She looked around for Everett and was glad when she saw that he wasn't with her.

Reading her mind, Bryte explained. "We came to see Daddy ride his bike, didn't we, Christopher?" She raised her eyebrows and gestured to the pack of paraders still waiting for their turn. A big red tractor decorated with an abundance of streamers putted by. The man driving it spit a big brown stream of tobacco juice onto the pavement. *Only in the South,* she thought.

Beside her, Bryte shuddered at the sight of the spit, then continued talking. "Everett got roped into riding his bike with some of the other neighborhood guys." She looked down at Christopher, his mouth stuffed with donut. "Christopher helped decorate it last night," she added.

"I'm sure it's lovely."

Bryte laughed. "It's um, colorful," she said with a smile. She looked around. "Your girls in the parade?"

"Oh yes. My parents decorated their golf cart. They'll be along any minute."

They stood in companionable silence for a bit as girls on horses and a man in a huge old convertible made their way past. People cheered and clapped and screamed, more for the sheer excuse to do so than because the entries were anything spectacular. Children ran up and down the parade route, shrieking their excitement and waving their arms so the people in the parade would throw them candy. She tried to imagine this sort of spectacle in her old neighborhood, but she might as well have been trying to envision a parade of elephants or spaceships traversing down the main drag of her former residence. For one thing, aliens and pachyderms would never make it past the gatehouse. For another, her old neighbors only did things with elegance, distinction, class—a hodgepodge, anything-goes parade like the one she was watching would have caused horror and dismay among the people she'd once called friends.

She felt a little foot nudge her in the back of the leg and looked down to see Christopher kicking absentmindedly as he took in the sights, his brow knit together, his face serious. She tried not to think too much about whether he looked like Everett. He was all decked out in red, white, and blue, as were most of the other kids. Her own girls had cobbled together white T-shirts and denim shorts at the last minute, and her mother had come to the rescue with red-and-white polka-dot ribbons for their ponytails, completing their patriotic ensembles. In her old neighborhood, she'd have planned weeks in advance, ordered special coordinated—heaven forbid they matched!—outfits for them to wear. This year she hadn't given it a second thought.

A man on a unicycle rolled by them, throwing candy out of a fanny pack as he went. Bryte caught a piece of gum, unwrapped it, and handed it to Christopher, who looked like he'd hit the jackpot as he greedily stuffed it into his mouth. "Do you remember doing this as kids?" Bryte asked when she turned back toward the action. Everett still hadn't been by.

"Oh, sure," Jencey said, as if it was old hat, unwilling to admit all the memories the event was stirring in her. So many memories she faced each day, all coming at her like a mental assault.

Her parents came by in the golf cart with Pilar and Zara waving shyly from the backseat as they passed. Jencey attempted to wolf-whistle and saw Pilar duck her head in embarrassment, her face taking on a rosy blush. Zara hollered, "Mom! Hey, Mom!" and waved more furiously. Jencey laughed and waved back just as furiously. Zara's ribbon had come untied on one pigtail, but the other was hanging in there, giving her a lopsided look.

She spotted the man—the one who'd saved the little boy—heading toward them, a meek and uncertain smile on his face. The unlikely hero who'd teased her about being named after a legendary one. She gave him a little wave. He looked momentarily surprised, then waved back and headed their way with a little more confidence in his step. He stopped when he got to them. "Hello," he greeted them. "I was hoping I'd see you guys here."

"Wouldn't miss it!" Bryte said.

He waited until he caught Jencey's eye. "Hi," he said, and it felt like a special greeting just for her.

She blushed in spite of herself. "How are you?" she asked. She hadn't seen him since the incident and hoped he was doing OK after what had happened. She hadn't been able to get it too far from her mind, and she hadn't been the one to pull the child out of that pool. She'd heard Cutter was not out of the woods.

He shrugged. "Hanging in there." He gestured at the paraders going by. "Just celebrating our nation's birth."

She grinned in response. "Well, you've come to the right place." She knew all their minds had to be on what they'd witnessed, in spite of the forced celebration. It was the only reason she wanted to go to the pool today, to be around the people who'd been there that day. "Do you come every year?" she asked, just to keep the conversation going.

"Yeah, my wife—Debra—she loved all this stuff. So the kids think it's a requirement to come." He rolled his eyes, and she could sympathize with his reticence to be somewhere people were having a good time. It took a lot out of you: celebrating when you wanted to do anything but.

"I'm sorry for your loss," she said.

He looked at her and squinted his eyes in confusion. "Loss?"

"Your wife? She's um . . . deceased?" She winced at her words. First she brought up the little boy, then his wife's death. Way to keep things positive. She was definitely rusty at conversing with the opposite sex.

Thankfully he didn't look upset. Instead, he surprised her by laughing. "Debra? Dead?" He shook his head. "I might've wished her dead sometimes, but no, she's very much alive. We're just living apart while she 'figures out what she wants out of life.'" He made air quotes with his fingers as he said the last part, his voice dripping with sarcasm. He gave her a meaningful look. "Turns out she's not so sure she ever wanted any of this life, after all." He gave her a "what are you gonna do?" shrug just as Bryte broke into whoops and applause, startling them both.

Jencey turned in time to see Everett ride by on a mountain bike bedecked in streamers and paper flags. He was wearing an Uncle Sam top hat, which he tipped in Bryte and Christopher's direction.

"See, Daddy?" Bryte yelled and pointed, as if Christopher could miss him. From his stroller, his somber expression changed, and he also began waving and hollering. When he smiled, dimples creased his cheeks and his eyes danced. He clapped his hands together, marveling at the sight of his dad.

Jencey clapped as well. When her eyes locked with Everett's, she smiled at him. He didn't tip his hat to her, and she didn't expect him to. He belonged to someone else now. He rode past her, but she didn't watch him go.

CAILEY

I didn't want to go back to the pool ever again, but Zell said I had to. She said the Fourth of July was going to be fun and told me all about the stuff they do, which I thought sounded lame. But I wasn't going to tell her that, seeing as how she was giving me a place to stay. She gave me a pep talk about conquering my fears, and how I couldn't avoid water for the rest of my life. She said that the longer I waited, the harder it was going to be, and the more I was going to let the fear own me. She said that part of growing up is facing your fears and doing the things you didn't want to do. Then she got a funny look on her face, like maybe her knee was bothering her. It bothered her a lot, but whenever I told her she should go to the doctor, she just shook her head.

"Are you OK?" I asked her.

"Oh, sure," she said, and made her face look right again. "Now go get your bathing suit on."

Before I went upstairs, I said, "Zell?"

And she said, "Hmm?" but she sounded like she was thinking about something else.

And I said, "You don't make growing up sound like all that much fun."

Then she laughed and said, "Well, honey, sometimes it's not." Then she shooed me upstairs.

As I got dressed, I thought about things we'd done on other July Fourths. We'd never really made a big deal out of it. Usually my mother had to work. Sometimes at night, she and whoever her boyfriend was at the time would take us to see fireworks, sitting on the hood of the warm car. Her boyfriends always said the same thing to her, as if they were the first ones to ever think of it. "Later we'll make fireworks of our own." And she always laughed like it was the first time she'd ever heard it.

Once we went to a family picnic back when my mother was still speaking to her family. We ate hot dogs and hamburgers that my mom's dad cooked on the grill, and my mom's stepmom, a woman she insisted was evil but seemed nice enough to me. She made apple pie for dessert. We ate big, warm slices with rivers of vanilla ice cream melting into the crust. The pie made me feel good inside: warm and full and happy. Then my mom said her stepmom probably made those pies from poisoned apples, and I spent the rest of the night thinking of Snow White eating the poisoned apple and sleeping for years. I was afraid to go to sleep that night. Instead, I lay in my bed and looked up at the ceiling, replaying the fireworks we'd seen, trying to recall the patterns of color they'd traced across the night sky. Cutter had been scared of the fireworks, hiding his eyes.

I tried not to think of Cutter, how he was missing the Fourth of July this year and how much he would've wanted to be there. No matter what Zell said, I didn't want to go back to that pool, to see the spot under the water where Mr. Lance had found him, to watch other kids have fun and worry Cutter would never get a chance to have fun like that again, to watch the fireworks over the lake and know he wasn't scared of them at all, because he couldn't see them. And to know that it was all my fault.

LANCE

Lance hated the pool on the Fourth of July. People came out of the woodwork, jostling for space in the water, taking up all the available chairs, and generally causing mayhem in a place that was normally quiet and restful. Debra had dragged the family there year after year after they'd moved into the neighborhood. She'd marveled over how quaint it all was, delighting in the old-fashioned traditions—the pie-eating competition, the greased-watermelon contest, the coin and egg tosses, the prayer before the potluck dinner, everyone's heads bowed in unison. "This is all just so southern," she'd gushed happily.

He'd gone along with it, but he hadn't been happy about it, and he'd let her know it. When she left, she'd called him "passive aggressive." She'd silently stored up his transgressions throughout their marriage, then spewed them at him all at once, a human hydrant.

So it was ironic that this year of all years, he actually wanted to be there. Without Debra there to drag him, he went of his own accord, hustling the kids up there as soon as the parade was over in an effort to secure a good spot. He'd even saved a chair for Jencey, having promised to do so when they'd parted ways after the parade. Shy as a schoolboy, he'd asked her if she was planning to come up to the pool for the festivities. She'd shrugged nonchalantly and said, "Not much else to do."

"Come on," he'd said, and elbowed her. "It'll be fun." And when he did it, he thought of Debra doing and saying the very same thing on previous July Fourths. In that moment, a shock traveled through him, the shock of Debra being right. It wasn't the first time it had happened since she'd left. There were many times since she'd gone that he'd been struck by the evidence that all those things she'd said just might've been true. If he knew where she was, he would say he was sorry.

But Debra had gone into hiding, and he'd given up trying to find her. Her sister had assured him that she was safe, and that was all he needed to know. Debra wanted to be gone, and she would stay that way until she didn't want to be gone anymore. He understood this more with each passing day, and hated her less the more he understood. He even respected her just the tiniest bit for having the courage to go.

He sprayed the children with sunscreen as they wiggled and complained, then released them to play. He tried his best not to look over at the deep end of the pool where he'd found the still form of the boy under the water. From the looks of things, the pool management company had stepped up their lifeguard presence and done some serious training on vigilance since the near drowning. The lifeguards sat alert and attentive in their high chairs, surveying the crowds with whistles around their necks and flotation devices at the ready in their laps. Their postures were that of attack dogs barely restrained on leashes. *Good,* he thought. He tried to relax, trusting his services would not be needed again.

Every hour on the hour, a new contest took place, with James Doyle—a neighborhood fixture—officiating. Known for his devotion to his elderly mother and mentally delayed brother, he was particularly invested in the Fourth of July celebration. He used personal money to buy the fireworks for the neighborhood show and made sure that there were plenty of eggs for the egg toss, and snack cakes for the pie-eating contest. He kept everything on schedule and even purchased trophies for the winners of the various contests. Everyone seemed to appreciate his efforts to keep the tradition going, because the truth was, no one else would if he didn't.

Lance caught James's eye and gave him a friendly wave, as he always did. They were neighbors, but Lance had never made an effort to do much more than wave at him from a distance, across their respective yards. It wasn't like they had anything in common. Sure, he felt sorry for the guy, who'd certainly gotten a raw deal in life. And he respected him because he seemed to make the best of things in spite of it. But he left it there, which was admittedly not the most neighborly way to be.

A volleyball game of middle-aged men formed in one of the pools, and he turned his attention to it, idly taking in the action more as a way to keep his attention off the empty chair beside him. He tried not to care about Jencey showing up, but more than once, he'd turned someone away who wanted it "if you're not using it." He felt the slightest bit selfish, taking up a perfectly good chair that others could use in the hopes that Jencey would show. But then he would think of seeing her that morning, and how he hadn't been that glad to see someone in a long, long time.

"I'm sorry," he said again and again. "I'm saving this one for someone."

The first game ended, and the men all climbed out of the pool to swig beer and trade barbs, their guffaws echoing even over the noise and hubbub of the crowd, calling to him, or at least to part of him. He supposed he could join them, if he was so inclined. He had, after all, fallen into the category of middle-aged man, a fact that still surprised him.

He heard a female voice say, "Is this seat taken?" and turned his head in the direction of the voice, but it wasn't Jencey. He frowned, explained yet again that he was saving the chair, then pulled the cooler from underneath the umbrella where he'd stowed it and added it to the towels and beach bag that were already marking the chaise as "taken," in hopes it would make it more obvious. If she didn't show soon, he'd have to surrender the chaise. And maybe that would be for the best. He was, after all, technically a married man. And judging from the rock she wore on her left ring finger, she was a married woman. He suspected they each had stories to tell, about missteps and miscommunication, about regret and resignation. He wanted to hear her story, and reasoned there could be no harm in that. They could be friends.

He scanned the perimeter of the pool until he accounted for each of his children. Alec was by himself, as usual. And Lilah was sitting beside Cailey eating grapes with her. Lilah had become fiercely loyal to the poor girl, and Lance hoped that spoke of his daughter's character. They were sitting next to Zell, who waved at him so demonstratively her visor nearly came off her head. He gave her a polite wave in return and turned back to watch the game, but the men, while back in the water, were still horsing around, swigging more beer, and leering at the women—girls, really—who'd congregated nearby.

On the end closest to where he sat, a heavyset, balding old man he'd seen before shuffled to the opposite end of the pool and, in spite of the crowds, made a motion for the lap lane to be cleared. Lance leaned forward, anticipating the response of the volleyball players. They weren't going to like the old man making them move their game over. Lance was drawn into the drama, such as it was. The rest of the men moved over good-naturedly, but one stood his ground, his barrel chest puffed up, a beer gripped tightly in his hand. He was wearing, ridiculously, a red, white, and blue bandana in his hair, a youthful look he wasn't able to pull off.

One of the guys tried to pull him out of the lane, saying something to him that Lance couldn't hear. The man shrugged his friend off and stayed put, his chin jutting out as he waited for the old man to swim the length of the pool and reach him. When the man got closer, bandana man began yelling at him, his face red and his language definitely not appropriate for a family gathering. One of his buddies attempted to stop him again, and his attempt was met with a forceful shove. "I just want to know why this asshole has to come up here today of all days." He gestured with his arm at the crowd. "I mean, look at this place, man. He shouldn't ask to take up a lane on the fucking Fourth of July."

With bandana man distracted by the exchange, the old man saw his opportunity and veered around him in order to make it to the wall. Lance couldn't imagine why it mattered so much that he make it all the way across the length of the pool. He suspected it was tangled up in his pride, which was understandable. But the old man was too large to just slip by, and bandana man, alerted by the churning water, turned back and jumped into his path, colliding with him. What happened next brought Lance to his feet, and stilled the entire pool as all attention turned toward the drama in the shallow end.

The old man stood up and shoved the man, spitting water and hollering at the same time. Within seconds, James Doyle had turned from tossing coins into the water and was there, too, along with the rest of the volleyball players, jumping between the two before their punches could connect and make the situation worse. Lance, too, had automatically moved closer to the action, his blood pumping and his synapses firing as he watched the fight being contained. The two parties, now separated, pled their respective cases to anyone who would listen.

He could hear the old man grumbling to James about his right to swim in the lane reserved for that purpose no matter what day it was. James, whose glasses had fallen off in the melee, squinted at him and nodded his understanding as he fumbled to place the glasses back on his nose. James put his arm around the old man and began guiding him away. Lance worried about the old man, whose wheezing could be heard from a distance. Bandana man was being led out of the pool, amid loud protests. Some idiot handed him another beer, and he sucked it down like a big, thirsty baby.

"You didn't tell me the Fourth of July was so exciting." Lance heard the voice behind him and wondered how he could've ever mistaken it.

He turned to find Jencey there, wide-eyed as she processed the scene. "I mean, I knew there were contests, but actual fights? That's something to see!" She gave him a little smile, and he laughed.

"Guess this isn't standard where you're from?" he asked. He hoped the question would prompt her to tell him more about where she'd come from.

"I told you," she said, shutting down his hopes, "I'm from here. Born and raised in this very neighborhood." She shifted a heavy-looking beach bag on her shoulder. "So did you manage to save me a seat?" She looked around the pool, taking in the wall-to-wall people.

"As a matter of fact, I did," he said, and pointed toward the chairs. She gave a pleasantly surprised look. "Lead the way," she said.

CAILEY

Lilah led me over to the tables they set up for the pie-eating contest. "I almost won this last year," she said, then pointed at her flat stomach. "I can eat a lot more than you might think."

I thought of Cutter shoveling in food at our kitchen table, the way my mom always teased him about having a hollow leg. Now a machine was feeding him through his veins. I wanted to tell Lilah that she should be glad that Cutter wasn't there or she wouldn't have a chance. But my throat closed up and I couldn't say it.

"I bet you'll win today," I said instead. We were all friends, ever since the accident. That part was nice. Lilah gave me a thumbs-up as if she were reading my thoughts, then I realized she was referring to the contest and not Cutter. She turned to Pilar on her other side, who'd arrived minutes earlier and was still out of sorts that they'd been so late.

"My mom got some stupid call from her stupid lawyer. I mean, it's the freaking Fourth of July. Why is he even working?" Pilar asked, and shook her head in answer to her own question. Lilah and I nodded our understanding, even though we had no idea what Pilar was talking about. But we did feel bad that she'd missed out on both the coin toss and the egg toss. Well, Lilah felt bad. I was glad I'd had a partner for the egg toss, though Lilah and I hadn't even come close to winning that.

I heard my name being called and looked over to see Zell with her camera. Why she wanted to take a picture of me, who wasn't even a relative, was beyond me. But Zell did things I didn't understand a lot. She was a nice old lady, and I shuddered to think what would've happened to me if she hadn't given me a place to stay since the accident. I'd be spending a lot of time all alone, that's what.

As we'd driven to the pool that morning, Zell had told me that today was Independence Day and that meant we should think about being free, free from anything that makes us feel bad. Then she was quiet for the rest of the ride, and I guessed we were both thinking of the things we wanted to be free of.

Pilar and Lilah and I squished up together with our arms around each other and big smiles on our faces so Zell could snap the picture with her phone. "Will you send that to my mom?" Pilar hollered at her. Zell waved like she would, but I doubted that 1) she even heard her, and 2) she knew how to send a photo to Pilar's mom. I still couldn't imagine why she wanted a photo of me, someone who probably wouldn't even live here this time next year. Next year I would be almost a teenager. I tried to picture a teenage me, but I couldn't.

The man in charge of the contests came to stand in front of me. "You ready?" he asked, and gave me a smile.

I made myself smile back and nodded.

He raised his eyebrows. "You sure? You don't look ready. You look like you're a million miles away."

"I was just thinking," I said.

"About your brother?" he asked. I wasn't shocked that he knew. Most people in the neighborhood had heard about Cutter, the news spreading like spilled milk across a table. And the man in charge of the contests lived right across the street from Zell, to boot. I saw him sometimes when he mowed his grass, stopping to mop sweat off his forehead with a towel he kept tucked in the waistband of his shorts. Sometimes his younger brother got out of the house and he had to chase him to get him back.

"Sort of," I answered. "He would probably win this contest, if he was here." I had to force the words out around the lump in my throat.

"I'm sorry, Cailey," he said, looking into my eyes in a way most people around here avoided doing. "That your brother's not here." He gave a sad smile. "So whaddayasay we make sure you win this contest for him?" He made his voice sound weird, trying to be funny.

I smiled back and shook my head. "I never win anything."

He cocked his head. "Well, I don't know about that. You look like a winner to me." He winked and turned to address the horde of kids who'd assembled around the table, laughing and pushing and eyeing the snack cakes piled on the table. Behind us, all the parents gathered to watch and take pictures and cheer their kids on. I knew better than to look for my mom. She was sitting in a hospital room, and though I wished she could be here, I understood she was where she needed to be.

The lump in my throat grew, and I swallowed a few times, trying to make it go away. I caught the man's eye, and he nodded. He believed I could win this contest, and that counted more than he knew. I looked down at the lone snack cake sitting on my plate and swallowed a few more times, willing the lump to go down enough for me to swallow around it. There was no reason I couldn't win this. I would do it for Cutter. Maybe if I won he'd open his eyes. Maybe I could still somehow make everything OK.

When the whistle blew, I dove into that cake, inhaling it without even really chewing. I could feel the barely chewed cake collecting in my esophagus (thank you, fourth-grade health class) as I inhaled snack cake after snack cake. The spongy, thick mass seemed to swell and it hurt, but I welcomed the pain. Deserved it. I thought of Cutter's damaged lungs. I kept eating and swallowing, adding to the mass until it felt like I would choke to death.

The world fell away, and it was just me, the plate in front of me, and the cakes as they came and went. I didn't think of Pilar and Lilah, also trying to win the contest. I didn't think of Zell, snapping pictures of a kid who wasn't hers. I didn't think of my mother, who wouldn't be there to see if I won. I just thought of Cutter, of him getting better, and that somehow I was making that possible in this moment, eating snack cakes on the Fourth of July at the same pool where he nearly died.

I heard a whistle blow and felt someone tug my arm into the air. The man looked down at me, my arm aloft as I struggled to swallow what was in my mouth. "Water," I managed to gasp, and he handed me a water bottle as if he'd known I was going to ask.

"You won," he said. "I told you that you would." I didn't answer him. I was too busy gulping the water, thinking as I did how weird it was that something that nearly killed my brother could also be the thing that was saving me.

ZELL

Zell watched as James handed Cailey her trophy for winning the pie-eating contest. (She didn't know why they called it a pie-eating contest, as the kids weren't really eating pies—they were eating Little Debbie Snack Cakes. But that's what it had been called for as long as she could remember. And who was she to call attention to it?) She'd been surprised by Cailey's fierceness, the way she tore into those little cakes one after the other, her body hunkered over the plate, her intensity visible.

James gave Cailey a hug that went on a second too long, if you asked Zell—not so much that anyone would notice it, but enough that Zell felt her guard go up. She'd known James since his family had moved in. He'd been attending college then, coming and going like young men do, not really connected to his family or the neighborhood. But in his senior year of college, his father had suddenly dropped dead. James had quit school and come home to assume his role as man of the house: earning a living, mowing the grass, and chasing after his mentally delayed brother, Jesse, when he got loose. Living across the street from the Doyles, Zell could attest to the orderly way

James kept up the house, to his comings and goings from whatever job he held, and the way he cared for both his mother (who had dementia and was little more than a shell of a woman anymore) and Jesse. She was sure it wasn't an easy life for him, and she did feel sorry for him at times. But . . .

One time she caught him outside her daughter Melanie's window trying to look in. At first she thought her eyes were playing tricks on her, and she stood and watched for just a moment, wondering what was happening. It took her mind a second to catch up, to register that she was witnessing a Peeping Tom in action. She hollered out his name, "James!" and he turned toward her voice with a look of horror and guilt on his face. "What are you doing?"

She marched over to him. He began backing away, and before she could get to him, he broke out in a run. She hollered at his retreating figure, disappearing in the gathering dark. "I better not catch you around here again!" She'd stood there for a moment, listening to her heart pounding as she caught her breath enough to go back inside. She watched as a light went on in the Doyles' house, signifying James's successful escape.

The next day, after double-checking the locks on Melanie's window, she went outside to see if he'd left footprints, debating whether she should call the police and report him. It was in looking for the footprints that she saw a soccer ball, and remembered that Jesse had been in the front yard kicking a soccer ball as far as it could go just before she found James by the window. One of her sons had remarked that it was too bad Jesse was mentally delayed because he sure could kick the hell out of a soccer ball. She'd picked up the soccer ball and carried it to the Doyles' front porch. She left it there for Jesse, but she never apologized to James for accusing him. She still wasn't sure what she'd seen. Now, watching him hug Cailey, those same concerns returned.

Cailey skipped over to her, holding her trophy aloft. "I won, Zell!" she crowed, and Zell clapped her hands together, managing, she hoped, to look happy and not concerned.

"That is just amazing, Cailey! I mean I've seen you chow down, but never quite like that."

Cailey grinned, her first real smile of the day. "I can't wait to show it to Cutter." She inspected her trophy. Then quieter, she added, "I'm going to tell him I won it for him."

"I think that's a great idea." Cailey handed over the trophy, and Zell tucked it into her beach bag for safekeeping.

Cailey dug into the cooler for a water and took a long pull from it. "I'm so thirsty. I can still feel that cake stuck in my throat." She took another drink.

"I saw you met Mr. Doyle," Zell said.

"You mean the guy doing the contest?" Cailey asked. "The one who lives across the street?"

"Yes, I've known him a long time." Zell weighed her words carefully.

Cailey thought about it. "His mom's in a wheelchair. I've seen him push her around. What's wrong with his brother?"

"Well, now, I don't rightly know. That family has just had its share of hardships."

Cailey looked thoughtful again. "Kind of like mine," she said.

It was not the direction Zell had wanted this to go. She didn't want Cailey identifying with James, sympathizing with him. "I guess you could say that," she said. "But he's a lot older than you. He's an adult, and he's got adult problems," she added.

Cailey gave her a "duh" look. "I know," she said.

"Well, I just saw him talking to you, and I wanted to make sure you knew that he is not really someone I'd want you to . . ." She had run out of words.

Cailey raised her eyebrows. "Yes?"

Zell waved her hand in the air. "I'm just being silly. Worrying like old ladies do."

Pilar called to Cailey, and she hopped up from the chair. "I'm gonna go swim," she said, already forgetting Zell's warning.

"Sure thing," Zell said, relieved that the conversation was over. But before Cailey could walk away, she called out to her. "Just don't ever go in his house, OK?"

Cailey gave her a quizzical look. "Like I ever would," she said, then shook her head and scampered away.

EVERETT

The fireworks terrified Christopher. He shrieked so loudly that Bryte scooped him up and ran out of the pool area, stumbling over chairs and mumbling "Excuse me" multiple times as she hastily made her exit. Everett watched his wife and child leave. The darkened pool area was packed, making it hard for Bryte to move with ease, much less while clutching a screaming child. Every few minutes, the lights of the fireworks illuminated a path while simultaneously setting Christopher off again, his shrieks ringing out over the tinny patriotic music playing through the speakers.

Everett, embarrassed by the spectacle, wondered what he should do. Did he wait for her to settle their son down and return? Did he go after her and create another disturbance? He surveyed the various items he would have to collect in order to leave. There was no way he could accomplish that in the dark. They'd spent the whole afternoon at the pool and had participated in the potluck dinner there that evening. All around him were dishes and clothing and towels and several bags strewn about the area where they'd set up camp. He turned his attention back to the fireworks, reasoning that he'd just wait until the show ended, gather up their things, and leave. It had to be close to over, though down by the lake, he could see James and his buddies still lighting fuses and scurrying around.

Everett wondered idly just how much money the man had invested in fireworks, only to see it all go up in smoke. Literally. He smiled at his own joke. He felt someone's eyes on him and turned to see Jencey looking at him. She smiled back, and he wondered guiltily whether she thought the smile was for or about her. Jencey turned her attention back toward the fireworks, but he didn't. In the dark, he could make out her blonde hair, and the two blonde heads on either side of her, leaning into her.

He wouldn't have pictured Jencey as the consummate mother, and yet it suited her. He thought with a pang of Bryte's resistance to having more children, of her recent announcement that she might just look for a job instead. He never thought it had to be one or the other and didn't understand why she was making it sound like it had to be. But whenever he tried to bring it up for discussion, she closed up like a book slamming shut.

Jencey was sitting with Lance, the "hero." Everyone had been making such a fuss over him all day, slapping him on the back and thanking him. *Come on,* Everett thought more than once, *the guy just did what any man would do who saw a child drowning.* It seemed as if Jencey had fallen under his hero spell as well. Everett would be lying if he said it didn't bother him, seeing her at the pool where they used to watch fireworks, their fingers laced together and her leaning against him the way her daughters were leaning against her now. "Get a room, you two," Bryte would tease. And later, after everyone had gone home, they would get a room of sorts, only it wasn't a room at all.

He hadn't gone to their spot in years, felt guilty visiting that place now that he and Bryte were married. It would hurt her too much to know he did that. And yet, sometimes he could feel it calling to him, the tree branches waving in the breeze, beckoning him to come . . . and remember. He shook his head and forced himself to look back at the fireworks, concentrating on the light arcing across the sky, feeling the explosions in his heart. Lee Greenwood sang "Proud to Be an American," and on the other side of him, he could hear John Boyette's mother singing along off-key but loudly. In his pocket, he felt his phone buzz. He looked at it. A text from Bryte: Took him home. Will you just bring everything when it's over? I'm putting him to bed.

He texted back: Will do. Sorry you missed the rest of the show. Fireworks of our own later? and pocketed his phone. He would never admit what had put him in the mood.

After they'd started dating, Bryte had confessed to him that each time she saw him and Jencey together during high school her heart had broken a little more. He'd been so slow on the draw, unaware of Bryte's unrequited love for him until Jencey was out of the picture and Bryte finally, after too much to drink one night, blurted it all out. Until that moment, he'd always thought of Bryte as his best friend, his confidante. And, actually, seven years of marriage later, she still was. "Today I marry my best friend," their wedding invitations had said. And it was true.

The screech of chairs being slid back into place startled him out of his thoughts. He looked around as the floodlights around the pool came back on and people began the leaving process. He stood, stiff and sore, and stretched before gathering their things. It would take several trips to the car to get it all loaded. Someone poked him in the side, and he turned to find Jencey there, looking concerned. "Is Christopher OK?"

"Yeah. He just got scared." He shrugged. "Funny because last year he loved them."

She nodded. "That's the age. One year they love Santa, the next they scream bloody murder if you get within ten feet of him." She rolled her eyes playfully. "Kids."

He pointed at Jencey's girls. "They're beautiful."

She glanced over at her daughters and smiled proudly. "Thanks."

"I guess it's not really how I pictured you, when I pictured you as an adult," he said.

She squinted at him while nudging her daughters in the direction of Lance's kids. "What do you mean?"

Now he'd put his foot in his mouth. "I mean, you just always talked about this supersuccessful life, and I guess I thought you meant this high-powered career. You know, *Sex and the City* kind of stuff."

She laughed and shook her head. "I probably thought that, too, but . . . then I met my husband, and well, he wanted the life we built and I . . . didn't stop to question it." She paused. "I didn't question a lot of things." The last bit seemed more to herself than him.

"And where is he now?" he asked, giving voice to something he and Bryte had discussed after Jencey left the night she came for dinner. Jencey still wore a wedding ring, so they didn't think she was divorced, and yet she was there alone, and didn't seem to be going anywhere. Bryte had told him she'd even asked about the schools.

Maybe it was due to the beers he'd seen her sip throughout the fireworks display. Maybe it was because, he hoped, she trusted Everett. Maybe it was the fact that none of the neighborhood busybodies were around. Whatever the reason, Jencey didn't hesitate to answer his question. "Jail," she said, the word almost flippant, but he detected a catch in her voice. "Federal prison, to be exact." She raised her eyebrows. "For the next ten years at least."

His eyes widened at the news. "What'd he do?" He thought of the big, bad things—murder, rape, bank robbery.

"Wire fraud, mail fraud, money laundering, and bribing city officials." She ticked off her husband's offenses as if it were no big deal, but her eyes gave her away. "Turns out he was not the prince I thought he was."

He pointed at her ring. "But you're still married?"

She twisted the ring around self-consciously, lowering her eyes. "Not officially divorced. Not yet. And, until I am, I've sort of kept it on for the girls. And, I guess, for me. Old habits and all that." She glanced back up at him. "Had to get used to the idea."

"And are you? Used to it?"

She shook her head. "Not really. Still not sure what I'm going to do next. I have to reinvent my life, make a new life for the girls. I came back here because I . . ." She looked around at the pool, and he wondered if she too had memories. She took a deep breath and turned back to him. "I would've told you I came back here because I had nowhere else to go. But I don't necessarily think that anymore."

"What do you think now?" he coaxed.

"I think I needed to come home."

He nodded, swallowed, thinking of why and how she'd left, how he'd failed to protect her. He could still see one of those damn hearts, this one under *his* windshield wiper, fluttering in the breeze. The crowd had thinned out. Jencey's girls were chasing Lance's kids around the pool, and no one was stopping them. He could see Lance waiting for her, off to the side, shuffling his feet as he tried to be polite. Everett still had to gather their things, make the multiple trips to the car, go home to his wife and son. "I'm glad you did," he said.

She reached out, grabbed his hand, and squeezed it lightly before letting go. "Me, too," she said. She gave him a little wave and was gone. To his credit, he did not watch her go.

JENCEY

She watched Everett leave. He gave her a weak smile as he passed by, then trudged out of the pool and toward the parking lot. Lance cleared his throat, and she turned to face him. "Is there a story there?" he asked, pointing at Everett's retreating back.

She raised her eyebrows. "You could say that." She worked to make her voice playful and light. This was flirting, as best she could recall.

He shook his head. "Something tells me you're a woman of many stories."

She nodded and gave him a sage look. "You could say that, too."

He glanced down at her wedding ring but said nothing. She had to take it off, and soon. She'd told herself that the moment the final papers came from her attorney, that would be her signal that it was time. It was really and truly over.

"I better get them to bed," she said, indicating the girls, who'd left the pool area and were swinging in the adjoining playground with Lance's kids. She heard their giggles ringing out in the night air. Other than the lifeguards and a few teenagers, they were the only people left.

Lance ran his hands through his hair, and when he did, she took in the muscles flexing in his arms, the obvious strength there. She found herself wanting to feel those arms around her, and wondered if that was just a normal reaction for someone who hadn't had physical contact with a man in months, or if she was actually attracted to this one.

"Yeah," he agreed, "I should do the same with mine." He reached for the bag that was sitting on the chair near them and hoisted it onto his shoulders. "Thanks for hanging out today. It was fun."

She nodded. It *had* been fun. They'd talked and laughed and teased each other. He couldn't believe she'd never seen *Monty Python and the Holy Grail* and tried to express the many, apparently hilarious one-liners from the movie. But hearing him attempt a British accent was what really made her laugh. They'd socialized with the neighbors, met some new folks, eaten potluck with her parents. He'd talked for a long while with her dad. Her mother, to her credit, had not asked any questions, though Jencey suspected she was dying to. Their kids had played together most of the day, sinking into the chairs beside them as the fireworks began. They'd made a little unit, him with his kids and her with hers, yet all together, looking up at the night sky, their chins tilted at the same angle. She'd watched the colors explode and expand across the blackness, unable to keep herself from recalling the last time she'd seen fireworks.

Last Fourth of July she'd been with Arch and had no idea of what was coming. They'd gone out of town without the girls, leaving them behind with a college-age sitter she used from time to time. She and Arch and their friends had eaten gourmet small plates and drunk champagne on a yacht anchored in the Charles River as fireworks exploded over Boston. They'd gone to hear the Boston Pops and taken a historical tour of the city where much of America began.

It had been a quintessential Fourth celebration, and Arch had delighted in showing her all that money could buy. She had, as he'd so kindly pointed out to her from behind bars, reveled in it all. Gushing to her girlfriends about the experience after it was over had been almost as much fun as doing it. She and her friends had each tried to outdo one another with how they'd spent the holiday in a never-ending game of one-upmanship that, in hindsight, kept her breathless and anxious a lot of the time. But she'd been too immersed in the game to even know she was playing it.

It was only sitting there, relaxed and at ease, flanked by her girls, wearing an old T-shirt with grape Popsicle dripped down the front, that she could see her former life for what it was. Exhausting. Soul sucking. As empty as her former home now was. She hadn't really missed any of the women she once called friends, hadn't heard from even one of them after Arch was exposed and arrested. They avoided her as though she'd caught a plague. She supposed she had—the plague of poverty. And yet, sitting there by the pool with normal people observing a normal Fourth of July, she didn't feel poor at all. She felt fairly rich.

"So," Lance said as they walked together to their cars, the kids lagging behind, complaining that they had to leave. "Think you might want to come over sometime and watch *The Holy Grail*?" Continuing to kid around about being named Lancelot, he'd joked that the knights in that movie were more like the kind of knights he would be. Jencey let him joke, but she sensed that his self-deprecating humor was an attempt to deflect all the compliments and kudos he'd been receiving from neighbors who'd heard about him saving Cutter. She'd felt proud to be beside him, but not proud like she used to be beside Arch. She was proud of who Lance was, not what he had.

Now he raised his eyebrows at her. She tried to process just what he was asking with his invitation. Sure, they'd flirted and spent the day together. Now he wanted to see her again. But was this a date? Or was he just being neighborly?

"I mean, you really shouldn't go much longer without seeing it." He kept his voice nonchalant, which didn't exactly help her figure things out. He pressed the latch on his trunk and stowed the bulging bag of pool paraphernalia, then slammed the liftgate shut and turned back to her.

She nodded. "I'm not sure how I've survived this long without it."

"Well, then, we need to get it scheduled as soon as possible," he said. She knew he hadn't dated since his wife's departure. She'd come upon that information courtesy of Zell, who seemed to be matchmaking. Jencey had laughed Zell's insinuation off, assuring Zell that the last thing Jencey needed was a relationship. What she needed was a plan for getting on with life. But in the meantime, she told herself for the hundredth time, he was good company, another grown-up to pass the time with.

"OK, so when would be good for you?" she asked.

"Well, today's Wednesday—it *is* Wednesday, right? I never know what day it is since summer started. So . . . maybe Friday? Bring the girls and we'll put them in front of a movie in our playroom while we watch our movie? Order some pizzas?" He was doing a good job of looking spur-of-the-moment about it, but she had a suspicion he'd worked out the details of this invitation before extending it.

She pretended to think about her plans, though of course she had none, unless she counted her nightly jaunts to the hideaway in the woods, a habit she should probably break. "Sounds great," she said. "What time?"

"Six thirty?"

"We'll be there," she said. "And thanks. For saving me a seat today."

He smiled. "No problem." He held out his arms for a hug and raised his eyebrows in question.

It was only a hug. What harm was there in it? She walked into the same strong arms that had pulled that boy from the bottom of the pool, letting them encircle her for a brief moment, pulling her into an embrace she hadn't known she needed until she stepped inside it.

BRYTE

Christopher's meltdown over the fireworks was a blessing in disguise, in spite of the embarrassment. There'd been a message waiting for Bryte on her cell when she got home. If Everett had been with her, he might've asked her who'd called or, worse yet, played the message himself, not out of suspicion but just curiosity. A strange out-of-town number might raise questions. And she wasn't ready to answer them.

She listened to his voice mail twice, which was a purely professional response to her own. Yes, of course he remembered her. Yes, he would still like to talk to her. Yes, he had some thoughts about her options. She could call whenever she wanted, and he hoped she had a nice Fourth of July.

Had she had a nice Fourth? She thought back over the day, culminating in her flight from the pool with a screaming boy in her arms as people watched her instead of the fireworks. The day, she concluded, hadn't been bad or good. It had been a day like any other, another bead in a very long string. Working would add a variety to her days, challenge her, broaden her outlook past her own front yard. She'd been good at what she did. She'd had friends to chat with, respect from coworkers.

She just had to ignore the pang she felt when she thought about being away from her son all day.

She opted to put Christopher to bed without a bath, dodging feelings of guilt as she did. He'd been in water that day; he was clean enough. The meltdown had exhausted him, and he needed to get to bed lest anything else set him off. She moved slowly and gently, keeping the lights and her voice low as she soothed and eased him. He was high-strung at times, unfamiliar to her, unfamiliar to Everett as well. But still she had learned how to approach him, how to be his mother. She was good at it. Mostly.

She managed to get him into bed without a story—he was so tired he didn't even ask for it. She smoothed the covers over him and hummed the same lullaby she'd sung to him since that first night in the hospital when she'd been left alone with him. The lullaby worked then, and now. He closed those eyes of his and blissfully drifted off to sleep as she sang, surrendering the fight for another day. Bryte was relieved every time this happened.

She went into the kitchen and poured herself a glass of wine. She took the baby monitor with her and went to sit on their back deck. At this time of year, the trees were full of leaves and blocked her view of the neighbors behind them. In the winter, she could see right into their kitchen. She sipped her wine and listened thoughtfully to the night noises around her—cicadas and frogs and other summer creatures all singing to one another, making their own kind of music, a nature symphony.

She finished one glass, then poured another, noticing as she did that the fireworks should've been long over by now. She wondered what was keeping Everett. Her heart quickened at the thought of Jencey being at the pool. Jencey was back and Everett wanted another child and she was thinking about going back to work and had called Trent Miller about it—she'd actually done it—and he'd returned her call, on a holiday no less. And now she was sitting outside, drinking alone on the Fourth of July, wondering where her husband was. Her stomach rumbled, but she didn't know whether it was from nerves or from Jencey's mom's potato salad that she was sure now had sat out in the heat a bit too long. She thought of the food she'd piled on her plate—barbecue and watermelon and potato salad—and regretted it.

She'd passed her parents' house on the way home from the pool; a light was burning in her old bedroom window despite the late hour. She'd wondered what crafting project her mother was into. After she and Everett had bought their own house in the neighborhood, her mother had decided to turn her old bedroom into a craft room and called her over to get anything out of it she might want to keep. She'd been hugely pregnant then but had dutifully waddled over, sinking awkwardly onto the floor, wondering as she did if she would ever get back up again. The baby had been due in mere weeks, and the activity had been a good diversion from the rabid thoughts chomping away inside her brain as his birth neared.

Alone in her old closet, she'd pulled out the boxes of birthday cards and letters exchanged between her and Jencey, paged through the yearbooks on the shelf, rereading what her husband had written to her on the page she reserved just for him. She'd laughed at how banal his note to her was, reflecting over just how smitten *she'd* been and how utterly oblivious *he'd* been. She'd put the yearbooks back and pulled out a single spiral-bound notebook resting on the shelf beside the yearbooks, there in plain sight, just waiting to be discovered. She'd looked at the cover and hoped to God her mother had never seen it. There, written in bold, black Sharpie were the words EVERETT MICHAEL LEWIS and nothing else. "So hokey," she'd said aloud, then turned the cover.

It was a notebook she'd started, and kept with an embarrassing devotion, all about Everett. She had written down any information she gleaned about him—his favorite teams and hobbies, the names of his childhood pets, and his favorite flavor of ice cream. She'd written down the sizes he wore and what clothing he liked to wear, and on what days. She'd written down his daily schedule and what his dreams and aspirations were. None of those dreams or aspirations included her.

She'd been both surprised and horrified to find this document, this proof of just how much she'd pined after him, and for how long it had gone on. It was clear she would've done anything to have Everett, and to keep him once she had him. Embarrassed, she'd quickly shoved the notebook into a trash bag and fled the room. Downstairs, she'd found her mother in the kitchen, frowning over a basket of tangled yarn.

"Did you find anything you wanted to keep?" her mother had asked, her attention still on the yarn.

She'd shaken her head and smiled, the taste of vomit still lingering in her mouth. "It's just old stuff," she'd said.

"So you just want me to toss it all?" her mom had asked, looking up from the basket with surprise registering on her face.

"You know what they say," Bryte had quipped and rubbed her belly. "Out with the old, in with the new."

She hadn't believed herself then, and she didn't believe it now. Especially not this summer.

She was about to stand up and get her phone to call Everett when she saw headlights swing into their driveway. She exhaled breath she hadn't realized she was holding, and felt her stomach settle. She took another sip of wine and waited for Everett to find her instead of calling out to him. She waited in the dark as he entered the house and searched for her, feeling like a child playing hide-and-seek. He finally did, rushing onto the deck, panicked. "What are you doing?" he asked, a note of accusation in his voice. "You scared me."

She wanted to tell him that he'd scared her, too, that she'd imagined Jencey sending her girls home with her mother so that she and Everett could go find their old hiding place in the woods by the lake. But she couldn't say those words out loud even if she could picture it fully in her head, Jencey's late-night whispered confessions when they were girls coming to mind unbidden. She knew it all: how Everett and Jencey had dragged a blow-up mattress out to the woods. How they would lay there and stare up at the stars at night, talking and dreaming.

Bryte didn't think that mattress could possibly still be there after all these years. She resolved to venture into those woods again. Just to see.

"I just felt like sitting outside," she said.

He looked around. "It's a nice night. Cooling off some now that the sun's gone down." He gestured to the wine. "Should I pour a glass and join you?"

She smiled at him, feeling relief flood her body. Surely he wouldn't do that if anything had happened with Jencey. She willed herself not to ask and ruin the moment. "Sure," she said. "That would be nice." He disappeared inside again, and she looked up at the stars as she waited for him.

He returned quickly and sat across from her at their little table. They were quiet for a moment as they both sipped their wine. She could feel the second glass beginning to blur the edges of her mind, doing exactly what she'd hoped it would.

"Sorry you missed the end of the fireworks," he said.

She thought again of the voice-mail message. "It was OK. It was way past his bedtime. He crashed as soon as we got home."

"I wonder how much James spent on those fireworks," Everett said. He was making small talk, and she was grateful for it. "They went on forever."

She nodded. "They must have. I was surprised by how long it took you to get home." She had no right to challenge him, considering, but she also wanted to know. Her words hung in the air between them, and she saw him shift in his seat, then take a sip of wine. Her heart pounded and she, too, took a sip of wine. Only hers was more like a gulp.

"Well, I talked to some folks as I was gathering up our stuff and loading the car. You know, being a good neighbor. Channeling my wife." He gave a little laugh and nudged her.

"Did you talk to Jencey?" she asked. She tried to keep her tone light, saying the name as if she was naming any other resident of Sycamore Glen. But she could tell her voice betrayed her by the barely perceptible wince on his part. This was ridiculous. They were married. They had a child. They had a good relationship, were good friends at their core.

Her inexplicable unease about Jencey was either women's intuition or complete paranoia. Or residual from their past, creeping in, never fully vanquished no matter how much they all moved on.

He put his glass down. "Do we need to talk about her?" he asked, turning to face her.

She shook her head, a reflex. That was the wrong answer—they probably did need to talk about her, but she wasn't ready to, and probably never would be. They'd spent their courtship and married life successfully avoiding the topic of Jencey.

"Are you sure?" he pressed. "Because I did talk to her. If that bothers you, then we need to talk about why."

She forced her mouth to smile. "Did she say she's in love with you and can't live without you?" She hoped she sounded like she was teasing. "Because if that's the case, then, yeah, maybe we need to talk about Jencey."

His laughter in response was as forced as her cavalier tone. "No." He reached over and laid his hand on top of hers, the weight and size of it so familiar. "She did tell me why she came back, though."

Bryte felt her heart pick up speed. She hadn't felt comfortable enough to ask Jencey something that personal, yet Jencey had told Everett. She didn't know if she was threatened by that degree of honesty between them, or jealous that Jencey had chosen Everett to confide in instead of her.

"Oh?" she tried her voice. "And?" She moved her hand from underneath his and reached for her wineglass. Her wine was almost gone. She couldn't remember the last time she'd had three glasses of wine in one evening, but this might be the night to do it.

He raised his eyebrows. "It's pretty bad. Her husband's in jail. They're getting divorced. She was basically left with nothing and had no choice but to come back here and live with her parents."

"But she wears her wedding ring," Bryte argued, as if it would change anything. Jencey wasn't just here for a summer visit, Bryte had come to realize. She was staying.

"She said she needs to take it off but . . . well, you can understand how final that has to feel."

With the thumb of her left hand, she felt for her own wedding ring, remembering both the night Everett had put the engagement ring on her finger at their favorite restaurant in town and the day he'd put on the band to match it, completing the set. It had been such a happy day, made even happier by the knowledge that Jencey wouldn't be there. Jencey's mother had relayed the news as if it was a disappointment, when it was anything but. Though she'd felt obligated to invite her former best friend, her presence on their wedding day was the last thing Bryte had wanted. Bryte had believed then that they would probably never see Jencey again, and that had been OK with her.

"Yeah." Her voice cracked and she cleared her throat. "Yeah," she tried again. "I'm sure it is." She stood up and grabbed her wineglass, her head spinning a little. "I think I'll go get another glass. You want some?" She started to walk away without waiting for him to respond, but he stood up and stopped her, blocking her entry to the house.

"Don't let it freak you out, Bryte. Jencey being here changes nothing." He looked down at her and gave her a reassuring smile. He put his hands in her hair, leaned in, and kissed her. She tried to go with it, to focus on him there, with her. Everything was OK. There was no reason to panic. Nothing changes, as he said. She kissed him back, trying to think about how much her adolescent self had craved this very thing. She had everything she ever wanted; they had everything they wanted. She longed to melt into him, to lose herself in him just as she had always done. Except. Except Jencey was back.

She let him take the wineglass from her hand and put it on the table, leading her inside. He led her right past her phone where she'd left it. She followed her husband upstairs to the room and bed they shared, knowing as she did that the next day she would return the call. She would blame Jencey for it, because it was easier than blaming herself.

ZELL

It was Cailey's fault Zell was outside in this heat. The brim of her sun hat fell into her eyes once again, and she impatiently pushed it out of the way, feeling a smear of mud left behind on her forehead where her gloved hands had touched. With her gardening clothes and floppy wide-brimmed straw hat, she knew she looked every bit like Shirley MacLaine's character in *Steel Magnolias*. But it was for a good cause. She straightened up and felt her knee respond. Cailey kept suggesting she see a doctor, not understanding Zell's hesitance to do so. It wasn't something she could explain.

Cailey crouched down beside her with an intent expression, studying their efforts, trying her best to learn all there was to know about gardening in the short amount of time they had together. The kid was a sponge. Zell tried not to think of that eyesore house she lived in with the desert of a front and back yard. There were no trees, and no shade, shrubs, or plants. It would be cruel and unusual to send the child back to that hellhole, and yet she had to sooner or later. She didn't like to think about that, didn't want to face what would surely end. "That kid has an expiration date stamped right on her forehead," John kept warning her. "Don't get all wrapped up in her and forget that."

Though he was right, it didn't make it any easier to think about saying goodbye. Cailey had given her someone to dote on, someone to nurture just as surely as she nurtured the plants and flowers in her yard. Cailey wasn't taking her own children's place, but she was a nice balm for Zell's hurting heart. And, Zell liked to think, it worked both ways. What would Cailey have done this summer if Zell hadn't offered her a place to stay? Spent a lot of time at home alone watching the boob tube and not learned nearly as much about the great outdoors, that's what.

"Zell, are you listening to me?" Cailey asked loudly, and Zell turned her gaze to meet those blue-gray eyes that commanded her attention. "I was asking you what you meant when you said that a garden is like a neighborhood?"

She smiled and went into teacher mode. She'd taught Sunday school for years, substituted at her kids' schools. She had it in her. "OK so we're all pretty much living in our own houses, right? Doing our own thing?"

Cailey nodded.

"But sometimes we need the people around us." She almost said, "Like you needed me," but decided it was best not to say that. "Like sometimes Mr. Lance needs me to watch Lilah and Alec so he can get some work done, and I help him out." Cailey nodded again. "Well, plants can help one another out, and a good gardener knows which plants make the best neighbors—and which ones don't."

"Like neighbors who deal drugs or steal cars?" Cailey asked. Sometimes Zell had to work hard not to let the shock show on her face when the child revealed the parts of the world she'd been exposed to.

Zell tried to steer the conversation back to a more positive light. "Well, like some plants take more than their share of water or sun, or they grow too fast and hurt the roots of other plants. Some give off toxins that can kill other plants."

"They're the bad guys," Cailey said.

"Yes, some plants are bad guys. But some are good guys—they add nutrients to the soil or attract insects that are good, or repel insects that are bad. So when I'm planting my garden, I look for plants that work together well—that are good for one another, that help one another out."

Cailey pointed at the garden. "So that's why you put beans near corn."

"Right. The beans add nutrients to the soil so the corn can grow better. And the corn provides a stalk for the beans to climb."

She looked around the garden. "And the marigolds are near the beans because they keep beetles away," she added, recalling information Zell had shared days ago.

Zell held up her hand for a high five, something she'd learned from her kids. "You got it."

"Plus," Cailey continued, "marigolds are just pretty, I think."

Zell nodded. "I do, too."

Cailey wandered away, and Zell tugged at a few more weeds she'd spotted during their impromptu gardening lesson. Satisfied for the day, she pulled off her mud-caked gloves and called over to Cailey, who was over on the deck studying a piece of paper they'd printed off the computer. The paper detailed the steps needed to have your yard declared a wildlife habitat. "OK, where's that hummingbird feeder we bought? We could hang it right over here."

"I think we need to build a pond!" Cailey hollered back, looking up from her paper. "Says here that ponds are good for frogs and also provide water for animals and insects. D'ya think Mr. John would dig us a hole?"

Zell frowned at the girl, feeling another trickle of sweat snake its way down her chest and into her bra, which was already soaking wet. She didn't say what she was thinking, which was that standing water also attracts mosquitoes.

"I think we need to complete step one before we move to step four," Zell responded. "You're getting ahead of yourself again. What's our motto?" She huffed her way across the yard to get closer to Cailey.

Cailey rolled her eyes, already approximating a teenager just a little too closely. "One step at a time," she moaned.

Zell smiled. "Well, now, taskmaster, do I have your permission to go inside and fix us some lemonade?"

Cailey grinned and nodded. "That sounds good."

"OK, you wanna come in, too? Get out of this heat?" The July sun was particularly brutal, a blinding white orb relentlessly shining above their heads. Truth was, summer wasn't the best time to undertake such a project—spring or fall would've been much better. Zell had tried to convince Cailey that they didn't have to make the wildlife habitat in a rush, but she could tell the girl knew she didn't have long before she went home and didn't want her efforts to be lost again.

In her frequent check-in calls and stop-in visits, Cailey's mother had offered for her to come back home, but Zell had always replied, "Well, she's no trouble at all. You just let her stay, and it'll be one less thing for you to worry about."

John thought the whole habitat idea was plumb crazy, and he'd told her so in private, but she just told him to mind his own business. "I don't tell you that chasing a little white ball all over God's creation is crazy," she'd scolded. He'd given her that look that told her there was more he wanted to say, but thirty-five years of marriage had taught him it was best not to. He'd kissed her instead and strolled out of the house, his golf shoes clacking across the hardwoods. She'd told him a hundred times not to put those damn things on in the house.

Zell mixed the sugar and water to heat on the stove, then got out the juicer to juice some lemons. Cailey had never seen lemonade made this way—she'd had only the powdered kind—and now she begged her to make it. The girl had put on some weight since she'd gotten to her house. Zell supposed that was a good thing even if that simple syrup was wreaking havoc on her own waistline. But she couldn't resist at least a small glass if she went to the effort of making the stuff. She'd been cooking up a storm for Cailey in the weeks she'd been there, reveling in the girl's delight at what she prepared. It was nice to cook for someone who appreciated it.

She fished her cell phone out of her purse just to check and make sure none of the kids had called or John hadn't had a heart attack on the golf course (a real fear she'd had ever since that very thing happened to Lars Petersen several years back). She saw that she had indeed missed a call, but it was from Lisa. She peeked outside to make sure Cailey wasn't coming inside, Zell's heart thrumming in her chest as it did any time Lisa called. Zell always feared bad news about Cutter. How in the world would she break that kind of news to this child she'd grown so fond of?

Cailey had ventured into the front yard and, from the looks of things, was trying to find a good spot for the pond that John would probably never consent to (though Cailey had charmed him no matter how much he said otherwise). Her heart in her throat, Zell clicked on the number and listened as it began ringing. Lisa answered on the third ring, her voice husky and gravelly, typical of smokers, though Cailey said her mother had quit. She guessed that she'd probably gone back to it due to the stress.

"Lisa?" she asked. "It's Zell Boyette." She almost explained who she was but stopped herself.

"Oh, Zell! I tried calling you earlier!" Lisa chirruped, her voice rising higher than Zell had heard it before. She got the feeling there was good news.

"I saw that. Cailey and I were outside working on that wildlife habitat she was telling you about. Boy, when that girl gets a bee in her bonnet—"

"Cutter's awake!" Lisa interrupted. "He's awake! He's got a long road ahead of him, but they expect him to make a full recovery."

"Well, that's just . . . just wonderful," Zell replied.

"Can you bring Cailey up here? Today?" Lisa asked. Zell didn't know her heart could lift and fall at the same time. This was the best possible news, and yet, Cailey would be leaving. Even as she was gushing to Lisa about how happy she was that Cutter was going to be OK, she was thinking about finishing that habitat. She'd just make sure she could have Cailey over to visit as much as it took until school started back. She would make sure the girl got to see the sign declaring it an official habitat planted proudly in the yard.

"I can definitely do that. She'll be thrilled."

"Cutter's been asking for her. He doesn't remember anything from that day, so please just warn her we'd like to avoid talking about it. Don't want him getting upset."

"She just wants to see him. She's been so worried." Zell took a deep breath. "I think she feels guilty, at fault somehow."

"Well, I'll talk to her. Reassure her," Lisa said.

"That would be nice," Zell said. She got the room number they'd been moved to since Cutter was out of intensive care and promised to head to the hospital just as soon as possible. She ended the call. Before she went anywhere, she was going to take a shower.

"Cailey!" she called. She bustled outside, rounding the corner of her house to the front yard, where she'd last seen Cailey. But Cailey wasn't there. She scanned the yard, but it was empty. She moved to the backyard calling out for Cailey. But the backyard was empty, too, the squirrel feeder they'd planned to mount later still sitting on the patio.

She ran back to the front yard, yelling Cailey's name loudly. Her mind ran to the little girl who'd disappeared months ago, the one they'd never found. She'd lived not too far from Sycamore Glen. Zell raised her voice and yelled the child's name even louder still.

CAILEY

I was sitting on Mr. Doyle's back deck eating a fudge pop—my favorite—when I heard Zell hollering for me. "I think someone's looking for you," he said and gestured in the direction of her voice, loud and panicked sounding. I hopped up and went running toward Zell's house, the pop still in my hand.

"Hey! Hey!" I yelled when I rounded the corner and spotted her pacing back and forth in her front yard. "I'm over here!" I waved my arms over my head, the Popsicle dripping a little as I did, droplets like brown rain sprinkling down.

Zell was in the front yard, and as soon as she saw me, she stopped moving and stared at me like I was a ghost coming toward her. I crossed the street in a hurry and met her in the middle of her yard. I looked over to see if Mr. Doyle had followed me, but he hadn't. I guessed he went inside to check on his mother. She was taking a nap, but later he was going to take her for a walk in her wheelchair. He said he was waiting till it wasn't hot as Hades to go. He said I was welcome to walk with them, but I said I'd have to ask Zell. He made a face and said it wasn't likely she would say yes. I asked why, and he said, "Long story."

Zell gave me a quick hug when I got to her, then she looked at me like my mother did when she was disappointed. I tried to figure out what I could've forgotten to do for Zell, but I couldn't think of anything. The nice thing about Zell's house was I didn't have to do a thing. She mostly did it all, which was a nice change.

"Where were you?" Zell asked. "And where'd you get that fudge pop?" She was acting like I stole it.

"From Mr. Doyle," I said, and pointed toward his house like Zell didn't already know where he lived. Then I remembered. At the pool she'd seen me talking to him after he gave me my trophy and asked me not to ever go to his house. She'd said I didn't have to understand, that I just needed to listen to her. When he offered me the Popsicle, I forgot all about that. All I could think of was eating that fudge pop, how cold and good it would taste on a hot day.

"I didn't ask him for it," I said really quickly. "He offered." I wanted Zell to see I had good manners even if I wasn't the best listener in the world. The last thing I wanted was for her to get mad at me and send me home.

"Cailey, please stay away from him. I'm telling you, it's for your own good," Zell pleaded with me, casting a glance at Mr. Doyle's house as she spoke.

"He just gave me a Popsicle. He said I looked hot out here. He was being nice." I tried to assure her, but she wasn't buying it. Grown-ups sure do like to worry. Even when they don't have anything to worry about, they invent stuff. It was kind of like my mom, telling me not to talk to strangers. My mom had been so wrong—just look at how nice people had been. I mean, before Cutter's accident I didn't even know Zell, and now I practically lived with her.

Zell waved her hand in the air. "Oh, well, it doesn't matter. You're OK and I've got exciting news." She put her arm around my shoulders and began walking me back toward her house. She kind of stunk after working on the habitat all morning, but I didn't dare say so.

When she said she had news for me, I honestly thought she was going to tell me that Mr. John had said he'd dig us a pond. I was starting to feel at home with Zell and John, starting to think we might actually finish this project of ours. I wasn't even thinking about Cutter. The truth was, lately, I hadn't thought about my mom and brother much at all. First, my selfishness had landed my brother in the hospital, then I went off and lived the good life while he was there and forgot about him. I was the worst sister in the world.

"Yeah?" I asked. "What is it?" I was already thinking of the special fish I'd ask Zell to buy for the pond. I'd seen them on a show on TV before. They were big and fat and orange, like overgrown goldfish. I would name them—

"Your brother's awake," Zell said. "We've got to get ready and get up to the hospital." She beamed at me, and I felt the Popsicle start to drip down my hand. "He's going to be so happy to see you!" She gave me a little hug, and I made my face smile back at her because I should've been happy.

I mean, I was happy. Relieved, too. But in the same moment, at the exact same time, I was sad, too. Because I would be going home. Possibly as soon as that night. No more dinners with Mr. John and Zell. No more Zell asking, "So what do we feel like for supper?" No more wildlife habitat. No more going over to hang out with Lilah next door. No more waking up on the sofa with an afghan covering me because Zell thought I looked cold. I'd have to take my Fourth of July trophy off her mantel.

"That's great," I said, hoping I sounded the way a normal kid would when she heard that her brother who might have died wasn't going to die after all. "I can't wait to see him." When tears welled in my eyes, I made it seem like it was because I was so relieved. And I was. But I was also thinking about what it would be like to go back to being the one who took care of people instead of being the one who got cared for.

Zell and I took showers superfast and got dressed. I met her downstairs in the kitchen, and she handed me a big, shiny apple. "You haven't had lunch, and I don't think that Popsicle is going to hold you." She gave me a wink that told me I was forgiven. "We'll go get lunch after the hospital to celebrate. How's that sound?"

It sounded nice. It sounded like a fitting end to what had been the best summer I could remember.

On the way to the hospital, we passed a billboard of that little girl who'd disappeared. It had a big picture of her, smiling and looking at us all as we drove past, heading to our everyday lives while she remained lost. I could tell it was her school picture. (School pictures always look the same no matter what school you go to. I'd been to enough to know.) The billboard asked the question, "Have you seen me?" with a phone number and the promise of a big reward for anyone who helped find her. It gave me the heebie-jeebies, and I had to look away really quickly, even though her face stayed in my mind.

I saw Zell notice it, too, but neither of us said anything about it, even though I knew both of us were thinking about earlier when Zell couldn't find me. Zell had it wrong, though. Mr. Doyle was a nice man who was just a little lonely. He had to take care of other people a lot so he didn't have the greatest life. I understood how that felt.

After we passed the billboard, we stopped and got candy and balloons for Cutter, and I got him a puzzle he could work on now that he was awake. It was a picture of Superman flying through the air, his fist raised. If I'd been brave enough, I would have told Cutter that he was Superman, surviving drowning the way he did. But sometimes it was hard for me to say mushy stuff to other people, especially if other people were watching.

I got butterflies in my stomach when we parked in the lot at the hospital, and they spread their wings and started flying around when we got into the elevator to go up to the eighth floor, where Cutter was. I was worried about seeing him and my mom. I was afraid of what she would say to me, the way she would look at me, her smile frozen on her face for Zell's sake, but her eyes cold and hard. I was nervous about Cutter looking at me with those dark eyes of his, eyes that told the real story about what had happened at the pool that day, how I'd failed him. The elevator door opened, and Zell reached out and gave my hand a quick squeeze. In just a few weeks, family had become strangers, and strangers had become family.

I took a deep breath and followed Zell down the hall, my feet heavy as I walked past the framed artwork done by sick children. I kept my chin up, trying not to think about those suffering children taking crayon to paper, and made myself smile at the nurses as they walked by. When at last we reached room number 810, the butterflies were whipping around my stomach so hard I felt like I might need to lean against the wall. But Zell pushed open the door (without even knocking), and I had no choice but to follow her inside my brother's hospital room.

I think it was because Zell didn't knock first that we caught Mom and the man together, leaning against each other the way only two people who are very comfortable would do, his arm casually tossed across her shoulders. If they'd had some warning, I bet my mother would've put some distance between them and not looked so cozy. She hadn't let Joe come around us for the first several months they dated. (I wish she'd never let him come around at all.) But I guessed this was a different situation.

I recognized the Ambulance Guy right away. He was the one who stopped and talked to me while the other two got Cutter loaded into the back. He was nice and everything but, jeez, how did he end up with his arm around my mother? In the split second between when the door opened and when they realized we weren't just another nurse entering the room, I got the picture.

They weren't hiding anything from Cutter, who was sitting up in bed picking at a tray of food on a table stretched across his bed. They were laughing at something Cutter said, and he was laughing, too, and for just a moment, I wondered if maybe it would be better for all of us—them, too, not just me—if I stayed with Zell and let them be a family. They looked comfortable and familiar, like they belonged together. And when their heads swiveled around to take in Zell and me standing in the doorway motionless, it was clear just who the outsider was.

I felt Zell's hand come to rest on my shoulder, and then she said with that bright, happy voice she used sometimes, "We came to see the miracle boy!" She pointed to the stuff I was carrying. "And we brought presents!"

My mother got up and rushed over to me, wrapping her arms around me and hugging me so big I could hardly breathe. Ambulance Guy came over and took the things from my hand, exclaiming, "Cool! Look, Cutter!" a little too loudly.

From inside my mother's arms, I could see Cutter. He gave me that Cutter grin I'd seen a thousand and one times before, and in that moment, with my mother hugging me and Ambulance Guy in the room and Zell saying all her Zell things, it hit me: Cutter was OK. He was OK. He was OK.

Which meant, I guessed, so was I.

LANCE

In the year before Debra left, she'd gotten into new foods, her devotion to all things healthy pursued with the kind of zeal usually attributed to cult followers. She'd eaten carrots dipped in hummus, and smoothies made with strange ingredients, and apples dipped in almond butter instead of peanut butter. "What's wrong with peanuts?" Lance had asked, but she hadn't answered, already buzzing to the next thing.

She'd never stayed still, as if the healthy foods were giving her excess energy she had to keep moving to burn off. She'd eschewed anything made with flour or sugar, waxing eloquent on how fruits had all the natural sugar she'd ever need. She'd made and devoured huge salads, nibbled on nuts and seeds, avoided beef in favor of chicken or seafood. She'd rarely spoken to him unless it was to sermonize over the health benefits of the foods she was eating and, therefore, foisting on the entire family. There had never been anything good to eat in the house. He'd grumbled and complained, even as the weight fell off her and she'd started to resemble the girl he'd married again. Trouble was, she'd acted nothing like that girl.

She'd taken up running. She ran all the time, even when it rained. "Shouldn't you join a gym or something?" he'd asked, concerned, as she'd taken off into the rain one cold day when he was sure she'd catch her death. "You could run on a treadmill. Wouldn't that be . . . safer?"

Debra hadn't answered. She'd just run away.

She even ran in her sleep, a phenomenon he'd witnessed one night as she'd lain splayed in their bed, sleep sacking her midsentence. Her mouth had still been open, her unspoken words escaping into the air. He'd watched her, wishing he had the courage to rouse her and tell her all he was thinking. *I feel like I'm losing you. I fear that we're drifting apart. And yet you seem so happy, so purposeful, for the first time since the kids were born, and I'm scared to death to mess with that.* He'd watched her sleep and thought of all the things he couldn't say to his wife. Watching her, he'd noticed twitching under the sheets, and it had taken him a moment to realize she was running even in her dreams. Her feet had moved as though she were rhythmically plodding along the asphalt. Even in her sleep, he could see in hindsight, she'd been running away.

Lance watched for Jencey and her girls to arrive in that mammoth SUV she drove. He was always a little shocked when he saw a tiny woman climb out from behind the wheel of one of those intimidating vehicles. He wasn't even sure *he* wanted to drive a car that big, that high, through traffic and down narrow suburban streets. And yet, he'd seen many a mom whip one of those things into a parking space without a second thought.

He busied himself by emptying the dishwasher, a chore he normally made the kids do (Debra hadn't required them to do enough around the house, and that only added to her stress and unhappiness in his opinion), but he needed a distraction so he'd stop pacing by the front windows, looking out for Jencey, who must've been going for fashionably late. He hoped she hadn't forgotten about their date.

He scolded himself for even thinking that word. This was not a date. And yet, he looked forward to spending time with her, had spent the better part of the day with an anticipatory grin on his face. Lilah had even noticed it. "Stop smiling, Dad," she scolded. "It makes you look weird."

He'd done his best to comply with her request, forming his lips into a straight line. But moments later, he was smiling again. Lilah shook her head and went outside to investigate whatever Zell and Cailey were up to in the Boyette backyard. They'd been outside a lot lately, busy as beavers. He supposed he should be neighborly and inquire, but he'd been preoccupied with thoughts of Jencey, coinciding with more and more memories of Debra and thoughts about it being over. He was, he knew, beginning to let his wife go. But letting her go meant he had to find her and do it officially, which was an idea that was forming more and more each day, almost independent of his conscious thought life. His subconscious was deciding for him: it was time to move on, to pronounce the time of death on his marriage and start living—for real—again.

He saw the SUV pull into his driveway and tried not to attach symbolism to its appearance at that moment. And yet, as Jencey climbed out of the big vehicle, he felt his heart lift and hoped that when she saw him waiting for her in the doorway, maybe hers did, too. He raised his hand in greeting, and she gave him that smile he'd been waiting to see, the one that made him think about a future apart from Debra, something he hadn't thought was possible.

JENCEY

Jencey was on a rooftop with Arch, sitting at a café table overlooking a splendid view of the city below on a perfect day. Arch was wearing the dark-gray Armani suit she loved with a crisp white shirt and a deep-red tie. The gray suit complemented his starting-to-silver dark hair, and he was tan from a recent trip to Miami that he swore had been no fun at all. He couldn't stand the clients, he'd said upon his return. She saw the lie but said nothing.

They sipped champagne, the bubbles tickling her nose as they always did, making her feel happy and light. He reached for her hand and took it across the table, trailed his fingers up and down the soft inner skin of her forearm, a signal that he wanted to make love later. She wasn't even sure he knew he did it, but she knew his cues. She knew everything about him.

Suddenly a group of men in black suits surrounded them, guns drawn, shouting, "Mr. Wells, you're under arrest!"

She began to shake her head no, no, no. This couldn't be happening. They were having drinks before a lovely dinner in the restaurant downstairs. She was going to have She Crab Soup because she'd heard it was excellent there, and she loved a good She Crab Soup—the delicate meat, the rich, creamy broth with a hint of sherry—if it was made right. After dinner they were going back to their hotel to climb into bed. How could these men drag him away? What right did they have?

"Arch!" she cried, attempting to lunge toward him even though one of the men restrained her. "Arch, don't let them do this!" He looked back at her, his face a mask of panic and terror. He turned from her and allowed the men to drag him away. She turned to the man holding her back and tried to look into his eyes, but the black glasses he wore prevented her from seeing them. She pulled them off, only to find that where eyes should be there were just vacant black holes. His mouth opened, and before she could scream, the man in black spoke to her. "Jencey," he said. "Wake up."

She opened her own eyes to find herself on Lance's couch, her legs thrown across his knees with an inappropriate air of familiarity, *Monty Python* frozen on the TV screen. He stared at her, his brows knitted together. "Sorry I woke you," he said. "You were having a nightmare."

She sat up quickly and pulled her legs to herself, self-conscious. She blamed the wine they'd had before the movie started while the kids scampered around the backyard playing the same night games she'd once played in this neighborhood—freeze tag, hide-and-seek, capture the flag—the games made more difficult by the darkening sky. They'd drunk several glasses on his deck before herding the kids upstairs and into their pajamas to watch their own movie in the bonus room, freeing the two of them to be alone in the den. She'd felt loose and warm and comfortable when they'd started the movie, and between the darkened room, the cozy couch, and the effects of the wine, she'd started fading only a few minutes into the movie.

Still disoriented, she looked back at this man who was not Arch, blinking for a few seconds as she tried to recall what this nightmare had been about. What had been so clear and vivid minutes ago was quickly dissolving into a murky memory of disturbing images. The images faded, leaving behind feelings of threat and foreboding. It was always this way. Many of the nightmares were similar—she had a husband, and then he was gone. Her brain kept dreaming up a new and creative way to lose him. Though the dreams were different, the sense of loss was persistent.

"I d-don't remember what it was about," she said, hugging her legs to herself and looking at her hands, wrapped around her legs. "I just remember being really scared." She felt his eyes on her, but she couldn't look back at him. If she looked at him, she would spill the secret. And she didn't feel ready to talk to this man she barely knew about the ugliest part of her life. She liked him and didn't want him to think less of her. What if he, like Arch, thought she was somehow complicit in what Arch had done? What if he kept his distance from her once he knew the truth? This was hardly first-date conversation.

"Maybe you were dreaming you were a witch, about to be burned at the stake," he quipped.

She laughed. That was the scene they'd watched just before she'd faded into sleep. She was grateful to him for lightening the mood. She liked him enough not to screw it up by draping her woes on top of their evening. "That was probably it," she said.

And yet, he'd had no qualms in telling her that his wife had decided she needed time away from their marriage, walking out and leaving him and the children. *What happened to cause her to do that?* she wondered. She got the feeling he was leaving it up to Jencey to decide if he was at fault, to determine for herself if he deserved to be left. She studied his profile as he looked back at the image frozen on the television screen. He certainly didn't look like someone who deserved to be walked out on. Does anyone?

She pointed at the TV, the image of a man on a horse banging coconuts together. "What'd I miss?" she asked. She forced herself to smile.

"I could easily rewind it back to where you fell asleep so you won't miss anything," he teased. He scooted closer to her and gave her what she guessed was his attempt at a leer, but with his baby face, he couldn't quite pull it off. "Or . . ." He pulled her to him.

She let herself be embraced, let herself feel comforted by his arms encircling her. Counting the hug after the fireworks and the hug when she arrived, this was the third hug of their relationship. Was that what it was? A relationship? A friendship? Friends hugged one another all the time. She felt his eyes on her and turned her face to look back at him. The only light in the room came from the TV. Upstairs, from a distance and behind a closed door, she could hear tinny cartoon music. She wondered if they were still awake.

Reading her mind, he said, "I think they all passed out."

She swallowed. "Oh." She licked her lips one second before his lips landed on hers. The kiss lasted less than a second, no more than what she'd give one of her girls before bed. A peck.

He fixed her with his gaze, his mouth so close she could feel his breath on her lips. "Should I apologize?"

She supposed the right answer, the responsible answer, was "It's too soon." But she liked the smell of his skin, the gentleness in his eyes, the way the light from the television made everything in the room look blue.

"You really think they're asleep?" she asked. She arched one eyebrow up—a talent Bryte had always envied—and wondered if he saw it in the dark.

He grinned his response. "Want me to go check?"

She nodded, and he sprang up like a released coil, trotting away and up the stairs. She had seconds to come to her senses, to talk herself out of whatever came next. To determine just how far she would go. She was just passing through. Last week she'd talked to an old friend from college who had her own all-female law practice in Virginia and could hire her to do admin stuff. She would most likely start over there and leave this neighborhood behind just like she'd left it before. And this night—this man—would be just a fun blip, a funny little confession for the girlfriends she'd have in the future about the night she behaved badly. They would titter over her admission, raise their glasses in a toast to strong women.

When those girlfriends asked, "How'd you ever get through it?" she'd tell them about finding hidden money and eating McDonald's and living with her parents and seeking consolation in the arms of someone else who'd also been left. She'd smile bravely and inspire them. The scene played out in her mind like one from *Sex and the City*, and she remembered Everett's words. Maybe it could still come true.

She heard Lance's footsteps returning. "They're all out. Crashed," he said. She could hear the smile in his voice without even looking at him. He bent down and kissed her again, this time as tentative as before. He straightened up and extended his hand, an invitation. She knew just where he would lead her if she took his hand. She looked up at him and blinked once, then reached up with her own hand, lacing her fingers through his as he pulled her to him for the fourth time.

Now Jencey awoke in Lance's house for the second time, but this time it was light outside and no nightmare had awakened her. She stretched, lifting her arms above her head as she listened to the birds chirp outside the window. She looked beside her and found the space empty, the sheets tangled and the imprint of a body the only evidence he'd ever been there.

She stared at the empty spot, grateful she'd not had to wake up to him. She wasn't ready for morning conversation, for an analysis of what had happened, or even admitting it had happened at all. She'd given in to an impulse and he'd done the same. That was all. This was what grown-ups did. They moved on and found comfort wherever they could along the way.

She looked around on the floor for where her clothes had fallen, collecting them and putting them on quickly, eager to be dressed in case the girls came looking for her. At some point in the night, they'd discussed how they'd explain it to the kids, voices urgent and hushed as they concocted a story even as they unzipped zippers and undid buttons. They'd fallen asleep watching the movie, and Lance had offered her the guest room. He would go back to his bed, and that was how their waking children would find them, separate and chaste, as far as they knew.

She tried to block the images that came to mind as she dressed, her recall of last night instant and fresh in spite of how little sleep she'd gotten. She remembered how different his body, his smell, his touch was from Arch's. Arch had been tall and wiry; Lance was almost exactly her height and broad-chested. Arch was dark; Lance was light. Arch always smelled of this expensive cologne that he applied a bit too liberally (though she never said so). Lance smelled like Dial soap.

Dressed, she turned her attention to making up the bed. As she straightened and smoothed the twisted sheets, her thoughts turned to the unavoidable comparisons she'd made, even as it was happening. Arch was aggressive and in charge in the bedroom—just like in life— but Lance had been tentative and solicitous. Arch had rarely spoken during sex, but Lance had been verbal, his voice a low, compelling murmur in her ear, telling her what he was doing and asking if she liked it. He was like the eye doctor: "Better this? Or this?"

Satisfied that the bed was adequately made, she left the room, and her thoughts, behind. She found Lance and the four kids in the kitchen. Lance was scrambling eggs and frying bacon, a pitcher of orange juice on the counter and a pot of coffee—blessedly—at the ready. He looked over at her the moment she entered the room.

"There's your mom!" he said to the girls, who leaped up to greet her with hugs and kisses as if she'd been gone forever. Their eyes met over the top of the girls' heads, and he winked.

"We finally got to have a sleepover, Mommy," Zara said, beaming. "Isn't that cool?" She thought suddenly of her parents at home, probably worried, or at the very least, disapproving of her staying out all night at Lance's. She hadn't answered to her parents in fifteen years and wondered how it was that she was back to making excuses as to her whereabouts. She wondered if they would buy the same lie the girls had.

Disentangling herself from the girls' octopus arms, she poured coffee, added cream and sugar, and sat down with the kids to wait for the food. At the stove, Lilah stood stirring a pot of grits with a pensive look that told Jencey she wasn't quite sure about all this. She attempted to catch the girl's eye and give her a smile, but Lilah wouldn't look her way. *I'm not looking to take your mom's place,* she wanted to assure her. Because she wasn't. She was just looking to fill the time between her old life and her new one, letting this strange summer back in Sycamore Glen be the transition she needed, a bench on the side of the road before she continued her journey.

Lance, oblivious, just kept smiling and cooking, looking like the cat who ate the canary, a secret smile playing constantly at his lips. She thought of those same lips on hers, how they'd traveled the length of her body and back again. Though it might've been the stupidest thing she could've done, at that moment, as long as she didn't look at Lilah, it didn't feel stupid at all. It felt like progress. She'd passed through a place she had to go through in order to get where she was going. It was nothing more than that.

BRYTE

Before she could get to her intended destination, Bryte had to make a stop off at Myrtle Honeycutt's to pick up Rigby. He was part of her ploy. As far as Everett was concerned, she was just going to walk the dog, like any other day. She just failed to mention that she was going to veer off the usual path and check out the hideaway while she was out. Ever since the idea had taken root on the night of the Fourth, she'd felt compelled to go, to know. Though to know what, she wasn't quite sure.

When Everett and Jencey were dating, Bryte hadn't let on that she was in love with him, at least not to anyone else. The closest she'd ever come to admitting her feelings to Jencey was when they were seventeen years old. Bryte had uttered three words, exhaled like a sigh: "I want that." She'd meant she wanted Everett's love, but she guessed that Jencey took it that she wanted love at all. She'd spoken so low she wasn't even sure Jencey had heard her.

There'd been a pause, then Jencey had given her a little smile in response and patted her shoulder. "You will," she'd said, her quavering voice belying her words. Everyone knew that what Jencey and Everett had was rare. Jencey knew. But still she left it behind.

It was Jencey's leaving that enabled Bryte to get that desperate wish. Still, she couldn't stop the doubts that plagued her mind, made her crazy. Did he ever look at Bryte the way he used to look at Jencey? When Bryte and Everett had started trying and couldn't conceive, it was clear that she'd never give him the child they'd dreamed of together. When he was Jencey's, she'd thought only about getting him; she'd never considered being a failure once she got him. Her desire—their desire—to get pregnant became her personal quest, pursued the same way she'd once pursued Everett.

She thought she'd be happy when she got pregnant, that she'd get the same feeling of elation she'd experienced when she got into Chapel Hill, was elected treasurer at school, or scored her dream job. She thought she'd high-five the doctor, the nurse, and anyone else she could find, then float home on a cloud of joy to celebrate with her husband. But by the time she sat across the desk from the doctor to confirm the news, she'd been so broken, gone so far afield of what having a baby should be, that all she could do was nod mutely and ask about risks to the pregnancy.

Later, when she'd told Everett the news, he'd hugged her tight, but she'd barely registered his arms around her. Her mind was elsewhere, lost in a tangle of emotions and fears. Thankfully, Everett wrote it all off to hormones, joking about her anxiety with her parents and his. But sometimes she saw her mother-in-law watching her with concern, worried, Bryte was sure, that all the negativity was somehow harming her unborn grandchild.

Now she pushed that child, who seemed no worse for the wear—her mother had promised her that babies were resilient, and as always, she'd been right—in his stroller up to Myrtle Honeycutt's back door. Myrtle had been old when Bryte had lived here as a kid, so she was positively ancient now. Her dog Rigby was a medium-size mutt of indeterminate origin who had more energy than Myrtle could handle, but the dog was a good companion for her, living all alone. And Christopher loved his daily dose of dog. It was like having one, only not.

She rapped lightly on the door and heard Myrtle's shuffling steps in response. Her wavering voice called out, "I'm a-comin'," just like it always did. And when she opened the door, she already had Rigby on the leash, just like she always did. There had been a bad spell a few weeks ago when Myrtle seemed confused when Bryte came to the door. Then she couldn't find the leash. Bryte had feared the end was near, but then she'd snapped right out of it. Bryte hated to think what they would do when Myrtle passed. She guessed they'd probably inherit a dog, for starters.

"You doing OK today, Miss Myrtle?" she asked, just as she always did. Myrtle's answer was the one thing that varied in their routine.

"Well, I 'spect I am," was the answer she got today. "Except this heat is just ungodly."

"We can thank the good Lord for inventing air-conditioning, huh?" Bryte asked as she cinched the leash to keep Rigby from straying too far.

"I'll say," Myrtle Honeycutt agreed. She looked past Bryte at Christopher in his stroller. "You mind you don't get that boy overheated now," she cautioned.

"Oh, I won't, Miss, Myrtle. We've got lots of water, and we'll stay under the trees, in the shade," she assured her. The woods were full of shade, after all. "We'll see you back in a little bit." She gave the old woman a wave and pulled the door shut, then tugged Rigby down the stairs, fixing him at her side with the short leash as she began pushing the stroller.

They made a tidy knot as they moved forward. Christopher hummed a tune from one of his TV shows, and she fell back to debating the job issue, her thoughts on an endless loop of pros and cons. Christopher was getting older, and another baby was impossible without intervention. If she got a job, that would make it even more so—and give her a reason to indefinitely postpone going back to the fertility clinic with Everett, like he was pushing for. It wasn't really about the job. It never was. The job was just the lesser of the two evils. If she reentered the workforce, she would have a reason to tell Everett it wasn't a good time to go through infertility treatments. She knew that would placate him, for a while at least. Some day she might have to tell him the truth about why she never wanted to go back to the clinic, but her intent was to avoid that as long as possible.

The way she saw it, she had no choice but to follow up with Trent Miller. He could connect her with the best opportunities in her field and potentially link her to a better situation than her former job. With the gap she'd taken to have Christopher, she needed an edge. His references and contacts would be invaluable, his interest a little push for her past boss to step up any new offer he was thinking about. She grew more certain about this decision as she walked to find the hideaway, to confirm with her own eyes that it was still there, preferring to think about her job prospects than whether Everett could be meeting Jencey in their former meeting place. She tightened Rigby's leash.

Up ahead she saw Zell Boyette and Cailey in Zell's front yard, both of them staring down at something, unmoving. As she got closer, the little girl looked up and waved, then ran toward them calling Christopher's name. Cailey always asked to help Bryte with Christopher at the pool.

"Wanna come see what we're doing?" Cailey asked, breathless and grinning. Bryte wondered what the latest was on Cutter. She'd heard through the neighborhood grapevine that he'd woken up and was on the mend. She wondered why, then, Cailey was still with Zell. From his stroller, Christopher held up his arms for Cailey, eager to escape his confines and knowing a sucker when he saw one.

"Sure," she said, releasing him. Cailey pulled him out of the stroller and carried him over to Zell, balancing his heft even though he was half her size.

"Hello!" Zell called to Bryte. "Don't mind me. I look a sight." The older woman wasn't exaggerating. She was streaked with dirt, and her hair stood up in clumps around her head. She laughed at Bryte's expression. "Is it that bad?"

Bryte came over to peer down into what was, so far, a small circle of dirt in Zell's front yard. "We're making a koi pond," Zell explained.

"It's for our wildlife habitat," Cailey added. She turned to Christopher and pointed at the hole, changing her voice to a baby voice when she spoke to him. "We're going to put water in that hole and make a pond," she said. "And then we're gonna add fishies."

"Fishies?" Christopher asked. His little eyebrows scrunched together, and he looked so much like his father.

Bryte turned to Zell. "This is quite a project," she said.

"Cailey and I are trying to get it finished before she goes back home," Zell said.

"Can I take Christopher to the backyard so he can see the feeders?" Cailey's question was posed to both of them, and they answered in unison, "Sure." They looked at each other and laughed. Intent on keeping hold of Christopher, Cailey lurched toward the backyard with her arms locked around him. Bryte heard him say, "Wanna get down," but she couldn't hear Cailey's response. She wished the girl luck; he was not easily dissuaded once he got something into his mind. In that way he was like his father, too.

"I heard Cutter's doing better, thank the Lord. So when is Cailey headed home? I'm sure you'll miss having her," Bryte said.

Zell nodded. "Cutter's coming home from the hospital in the next day or two, but he's going to be back and forth doing all kinds of rehab stuff. Lisa, God bless her, doesn't know which end's up. She's exhausted and—get this—seems to have taken up with the ambulance driver from the pool that day, if you can believe that, so she's got a new relationship, to boot." Zell waved her arm in the air. "I don't know. It just doesn't seem to be the best environment to send Cailey back to right now. So I offered to just keep her a bit longer while they get settled. Lisa's come by a few times to see her, and she's taking her out to dinner soon. I know she misses Cailey, but she agreed to let her stay. I think on one level Lisa was relieved."

Bryte couldn't imagine letting her child spend such a long time away from her, but then again, Bryte wasn't a single mom with two kids, living in the eyesore house of the neighborhood and juggling two jobs, trying to make ends meet. "That was nice of you," Bryte offered, for lack of something better to say.

Zell laughed. "Nice of me?" She shook her head. "I get just as much out of that child being here as she does." Zell thought about it. "Maybe more."

"She's a sweet kid."

Zell nodded. "That she is." She picked up the shovel and scooped out another bit of dirt, carefully depositing it on top of the small mound they'd created. "So what brings you this way today?"

"Just out taking a walk." She held up Rigby's leash, though the dog had flopped down beside her. "I walk Myrtle Honeycutt's dog every day. My mom used to do it, but then she got plantar fasciitis and couldn't do it anymore. So I said I would." She shrugged. "It makes me get out."

"Well, it sounds like I'm not the only do-gooder around here." Zell gave her a wink and scooped out more dirt. Bryte felt like she should grab a shovel and help.

"Gonna have any more, ya think?" Zell asked. Her face was turned toward the hole, and for that Bryte was grateful. It was amazing how people could toss that question off so casually. People had been doing it with some regularity since Christopher turned two, as if it were up to them to determine when it was time for Bryte and Everett to add to their family.

"Well, we had a bit of trouble even having him, so I'm not sure there'll be any more." She gave her standard response and looked around, wishing Cailey would bring Christopher back so she could go. The silence between the women lengthened, and Bryte searched for words to fill it.

"Do you ever think about coming back to book club?" She thought she saw Zell's shoulders tense at the question, but it could've just been from the shoveling. "I just joined a few months ago, and they told me you used to be part of it. I know they'd love to have you back."

Zell leaned on the shovel and studied her for a moment. "I'll give it some thought." She winked. "Since you asked."

"OK," Bryte answered. "I can send you the list of titles for the fall. We've only decided on books till the end of the year. Your e-mail's in the directory, right?"

Zell nodded. "That it is." On the ground the dog made a whimpering noise and rested his head on his paws, looking mournful.

"I guess I'd better get going," Bryte said.

"Cailey!" Zell called. "Bring Christopher back here! His mama's ready to go!"

Bryte wondered if she was actually ready, then realized it didn't matter whether she was or not. She was on her way.

She tried steering Christopher's stroller over the roots and branches and piles of dead leaves in the woods, but the overgrown path was just too precarious. One miscalculation of a root and she could accidentally topple the stroller. And negotiating both the dog and the child wasn't the easiest thing. She stood still for a moment, determining just how to get back here. She'd come far enough to be able to make out the clearing where the hideaway had been. She was too close not to lay eyes on it, to see if it matched what lived in her memory. Though this was a fool's errand, she didn't want to abandon it.

She unlatched Christopher and pulled him up into her arms, much as Cailey had done earlier. She held him close as they moved deeper into the woods and clung tightly to Rigby's leash. Without the stroller to manage, she made it to the clearing quickly, Christopher heavy in her arms. He did not ask to get down, didn't protest being carried. He was quite calm and docile, taking in the cooler, dark surroundings with a kind of acceptance, as if this were an everyday activity for the two of them. He did not ask questions as he normally would have, did not point to the squirrels and birds they passed. He just looked around with those knit, curious brows. She kissed his cheek, and he rewarded her with a grin. His breath, so close to her face, smelled of the cookie Zell had given to him before they'd left her house.

Bryte looked around, trying to remember what the place used to look like, ascertaining whether it had changed. The trees were a bit taller, the vegetation perhaps denser, but otherwise she knew exactly where she was. She heard a branch snap, and a rustling noise, and she took a step back in the direction they'd come from. These woods had creeped her out as kid, and they didn't seem less foreboding now that she was an adult.

She thought of the news reports of Hannah Sumner, gone missing from a neighborhood nearby, one very much like this one. They'd discussed her at the pool just recently, swapping bits of information they'd gleaned from various news reports and rumors, their voices low and out of earshot of the kids. She thought of the madness that would ensue if Christopher ever went missing. Losing him would be the end of her—this she knew more certainly than anything. She pulled him tighter still, and he squirmed in protest. He pointed at the copse of trees ahead. They'd reached Everett and Jencey's hideaway.

"Go in there?" he asked. She set him down but kept hold of his hand, scanning the area as she did, just to make sure. There was talk of coyotes in these woods as well.

She looked down at him, willed herself to relax. "You want to?"

He nodded vigorously, his brows unknotting, his face open. They moved closer to the hideaway. She took exaggerated tiptoe steps forward like Elmer Fudd hunting "wabbits," and Christopher laughed. They were on an adventure, nothing more, nothing less. But how would she explain to Everett if he mentioned it that night at the dinner table? She would have to say they were somewhere else; that was all. She could lie to Everett.

"I just want to be friends" was the first lie she ever told him, just after that make-out session in ninth grade. Jencey had been away with her family, and Bryte had made a good stand-in, a practice dummy. This was before Everett and Jencey had officially coupled off, but everyone knew it was coming. Bryte's lie had been a preemptive strike, an attempt to save face before he chose Jencey. What happened between them that one night, she told herself—and him—meant nothing. She stuck to that particular story for a long, long time, right up until the night she admitted her real feelings for him, the night everything changed between them and he became hers for real.

But there'd always been that nagging doubt that it wasn't real.

Pushing the branches back, she held her breath and stepped inside the hideaway, hoping that she didn't find that same blow-up mattress, and evidence that her husband and Jencey had resumed their meetings somehow. She exhaled as she stepped inside, finding nothing at all save a little clearing, the trees encircling them and blocking all visibility except the small patch of sky just over their heads. She looked up at it, the neat round bit of blue the only thing she could see that wasn't green.

She pointed at the natural skylight so Christopher would look up, too, thinking as she did of how Jencey and Everett would lie on that blow-up mattress and wish on whatever stars they could find in that circle, their arms folded behind their heads, their eyes intent on what lay in front of them. The scene was almost like her own memory, even though she'd never witnessed it, only heard about it from Jencey. Bryte knew full well what Jencey's wishes were, even if she wasn't privy to Everett's back then. She wondered if those old wishes depressed Jencey now. She could only guess at what her husband's wishes had been, and if the life they'd built together looked anything like whatever he'd thought of when he watched the stars twinkle in that small circle of sky.

EVERETT

With Bryte out of the house, Everett was able to search online for that doctor's number without her seeing. He'd been looking it up earlier when she'd come to tell him she was leaving, startling him as much as if he'd been caught looking at porn. He'd quickly flipped back to another screen before she saw, waiting for her to leave before he tried again. He got up and watched from the front window until she was safely out of sight, her back moving steadily away from him as she pushed Christopher in the stroller to go get Rigby.

He wondered what she would say if she knew he was going through with his idea to talk to the doctor, to get things moving along. He knew she was scared. He knew that the fertility issues leading up to the pregnancy had been hard on her—harder than anyone could understand. Something had changed in Bryte, beginning when they didn't immediately conceive, and spiraling progressively downward the longer pregnancy eluded them. By the time she got pregnant, it almost seemed too late, that the damage—psychological? physical?—had already happened. He'd urged her to go to support groups, to talk to someone, but she'd steadfastly refused. Ultimately, it was Christopher who brought her back. But she wasn't interested in ever doing it again.

And yet, he saw his son growing up like he did—an only child, always alone—and he didn't want that for him. He'd worked on Bryte for several months but was getting nowhere. The only thing he knew that might jump-start things was to make a grand gesture. And making an appointment to talk to the doctor himself was the best idea he could think of. When she learned he'd done that, surely she'd see how serious he was, how much he wanted this. If he could go, maybe she'd muster the courage to do the same. Granted, his part in the process had been minimal, but what man in his right mind voluntarily goes to a fertility specialist without his wife forcing him to do so? It had to make an impression. It just had to.

He spoke to the nurse, who seemed confused by what he was asking. "And this is an appointment for your wife, sir?" she asked.

"Um, actually, it's for just me," he said. "To talk to the doctor myself." He could feel his face reddening.

"It's highly irregular for the husband to come in without the wife, sir," she said, her voice clipped.

"Yes, I realize that, but I'm just trying to gauge what we're looking at this time around. And since we worked with Dr. Ferguson in the past, I thought perhaps he could, er, talk me through what we can expect. Just in case there's anything I can do to get the ball rolling, so to speak." He cringed at that particular choice of words.

"I see," the nurse said, but the note of doubt in her voice told Everett that she didn't see at all. She was humoring him at this point, leaving the rest to the doctor to sort out. She made the appointment, wished him a good day, and hung up.

He held the dead phone and tried to feel something other than foolish, something akin to hope. He strode over to the mantel and pulled down the photo his parents had snapped at Easter, the one on the front steps with him and Christopher in those goofy matching ties, Bryte in a pretty spring dress. He tried to see the three of them as any other person might. Did they look like a complete family? He didn't think so. He squinted at the photo and tried to see another child there with them, another boy or maybe a little girl, the one who would turn their triangle into a square, the one who would make their lives complete. He looked for the place where he or she might fit, if only his wife would make room.

ZELL

Two days after the visit to the hospital, she could feel herself getting sick. Those places were germ factories. She made it through the morning without letting on to Cailey, but by lunchtime, she couldn't fake it any longer. She told the child to occupy herself, and sank into the couch for a little rest. She pulled the afghan over her and rolled over to her side, so that her vantage point was the den windows, which faced the house next door. Jencey's car was there, again, and she didn't know how to feel about that. She closed her eyes and thought of Debra's leaving, and whether it was time to tell Lance what she knew about it. The thought of telling him made her feel sicker. She could anticipate the look on his face, the betrayal that would spread across his normally open features the longer she talked.

Before Debra and Lance had lived in that house, she'd never befriended the people who lived there, never really had time to. She was always dashing off to activities and commitments, running one child here and another there. John joked that they ought to put in one of those revolving doors like they have in hotels so that he and Zell and the kids could actually run in circles instead of just feeling like they were. She always felt bad for not being more neighborly, but really, who had the time?

When Debra and Lance moved in and it turned out they were Yankees, well, that just cinched it. She certainly didn't have time to fool with Yankees who didn't know how things were done. They put tacky blow-up characters in their yard at Christmas. Their Halloween decorations were just plain evil looking and, if you asked her, disturbing to children. They launched fireworks in the street on New Year's Eve and set all the neighborhood dogs to barking to the point that she couldn't sleep a wink and was tired all through New Year's Day. She could hardly make her pork and collards and black-eyed peas like she was supposed to.

Still and all, she minded her manners and smiled in passing at Debra or Lance if they were in their driveway. Sometimes she gave a little wave. She'd watched with a detached fascination as Debra had their second child, a son. She saw Debra pose in front of the gigantic (and tacky, if you asked her) stork they put in the front yard, holding up the pinch-faced baby, looking swollen and strung out. Zell felt equal parts envy and relief as she watched the scene play out. Oh, to do it all over again! Thank God I never have to do that again!

And yet, as she watched Debra maneuver the baby blankets so that Lance could get their son's face in the photo, Zell tried to recall the day she'd brought any of her babies home, the feelings and thoughts she must've had. She aimed for some vivid, standout recollection, crisp and clear in her mind. But all she could turn up was a vague sense of exhaustion and panic. She wondered if she'd retained any of the experiences of motherhood, the scope of it, if the joy would ever start to outweigh the anxiety. She felt as though she'd been sucked up into a whirlwind and periodically touched down long enough to look around, register the unfamiliar scenery, only to be sucked up and tossed about again.

She'd taken them a loaf of quick bread, still warm and smelling of chocolate and bananas, and knocked on the door, intending to leave it and dash away. Debra had answered the door, looking haggard but glad for company. "Please come in," she'd said, and the *please* sounded less polite than desperate. Zell agreed and found a seat at the nearby kitchen table.

Debra sat across from her. In her arms, a bundle of blue squirmed. "You wanna hold him?" The note of hopefulness in her voice told her she needed Zell to say yes. Debra thrust Alec into her arms before she'd even finished nodding.

She dutifully studied the baby, making appropriate comments about his size and features. "Who does he look like, do you think?"

"I think my father, but of course Lance thinks he looks just like him." Debra laughed and Zell joined in, though she didn't fully understand the joke.

They limped through small talk, covering the weather and the local schools and the headlines. But it was conversation and it filled the dead air. She'd played the part of the good neighbor that afternoon, and that had been, very nearly, that. She watched as the boy grew from baby to toddler to kid, registering the changes from afar just as she'd always done with the people who lived in that house, being a tolerable neighbor, if not an especially good one.

And then one day she'd heard screaming in their driveway. Her mother ears twitched at the sound, which was especially loud in her quiet house. She put down the book she was reading (she had book club that night and was cramming). The screaming was horrific, as if someone was being murdered. She grabbed the phone just in case she needed to call 911. She peered out the kitchen window to get a better look.

When she saw the blood, she moved toward it, carrying her phone with her as she ran out the kitchen door. She prided herself on being someone who moved toward things, even if they were frightening or gory or just plain uncomfortable. She didn't shrink back like some people. She wanted to be of help, to be that person about whom people later remarked: "I just don't know what I would've done if you hadn't been there." She ran to Debra's side and knelt there with her beside the older child, Lilah.

"What can I do?" She tried to gauge just where the blood was coming from and whether Lilah was critically injured.

It was an accident that started it all, and an accident that ended it.

The little girl's shoelace had tangled in the bicycle chain, and she'd toppled over, her sneaker still affixed to the bicycle in such a way that every time they moved her, the bicycle grated along the concrete, making a horrible scraping noise. She looked at Debra's panicked face, the way the blood was informing her reaction, and rested a hand on her shoulder.

"I think we should take her to the hospital," she said, willing her voice to sound calm and relaxed. She was almost certain the little girl had broken something, and the cut on her leg that was the source of all the blood was of concern as well. It was deep and jagged, lying open like a yawning mouth. Zell tried to brush some of the dirt from it, but Lilah went crazy trying to get away from her touch. Zell extracted the shoelaces from the chain and scooped up Lilah, carrying her as she ordered the uncertain Debra to grab Alec and follow her to her car. They settled Debra and Lilah in the backseat, with Alec tucked in, too, and set off.

Zell sat in the waiting room and entertained Alec while they waited for Lilah to be stitched up. Lance showed up and offered to take care of him, but Zell sent him into the exam room to be with his wife and child, magnanimously staying put, her arm around Alec. "You go," she said, and waved him away. "Lilah will want to see you."

Lance had looked skeptical, glancing at Alec, who was intent on finishing a drawing Zell had started out of desperation. She'd meant it to be a dog, but he'd turned it into a cat, his lips pursed in concentration as he applied the whiskers to the face. "He's fine," she said, her voice assuring. She waited for him to say that she was a lifesaver, but he didn't. Instead, he ruffled his son's hair and trotted off down the hall. He disappeared into the room they'd had Lilah and Debra in for hours.

Lilah had to have stitches in her leg, and she had a broken collarbone, which required a sling. Eventually Lance took Alec home, and Zell, uncertain what to do without the child to mind, decided to go home, too. She knocked tentatively at the door she'd seen Lance disappear into and heard a weak "Come in" in response.

She poked her head inside the room to see Lilah asleep, her arm bound to her side, her leg resting atop a pillow. Debra was slouched in a chair beside her bed, staring vacantly at a TV with the sound turned off. "I was just going to go home. Unless there's anything else I could do?" she said.

Debra shook her head. "They're about to release us." Debra covered her eyes with her hands, like Ty used to do when he was very small and thought that if he couldn't see her, she couldn't see him. She heard small sobbing sounds and waited politely for Debra to collect herself, wondering if she should just back out of the room or wait to be dismissed. She moved inside the room and let the door swing shut behind her.

Finally Debra spoke. "I'm sorry for crying." She swiped at her eyes, embarrassed.

"It's OK. You've been through a lot."

"You know what I was thinking just before this happened?" Debra asked, picking at a cuticle instead of looking at Zell. She went on with her story before Zell could admit that she had no idea what the younger woman was thinking moments before her daughter had a bike accident. Before Zell had heard the screaming, she hadn't thought of Debra at all.

Debra answered her own question, her answer coming out in a rush of words. "I was thinking that this isn't so bad. The kids are starting to get older, and Alec will go to kindergarten in the fall and I won't be so tied down. They can play outside without me helping them or watching their every move, and maybe, just maybe, I might end up like the others." She finished speaking, lifted her finger to her mouth, and began to chew at a piece of stray skin on her cuticle.

Zell's daughter had a nasty habit of doing the same thing. Her fingers were a mess. She thought about lecturing Debra the same way she lectured Melanie but decided against it. She was not this girl's mother. "The others?" she asked gently.

Debra still didn't meet her gaze. She continued to nibble at the skin on her cuticle for a moment, then spat out the piece of skin she'd been trying to chew away. "The other mothers. The ones who seem to actually enjoy this gig." Her finger began to bleed, and she put it back in her mouth, sucking the blood away. Zell was repulsed but tried not to show it.

She spoke quietly, cautiously, the way one might speak to a child. "I'm not sure any one of us is enjoying all of it fully—not the way you might think."

Debra's laugh was a scoff. "That's easy for you to say." Finally she raised her eyes. "You're already past the worst part. You're home free."

She gestured to Zell. "And look at you. You're wearing a white shirt, and there isn't a speck of ketchup or grease or a child's lip print or dirt on it. And I bet you're what—a size four?" Zell had almost corrected her—she was a size two then—but decided it was better to keep that detail to herself. Debra gestured at her own stomach, pooching onto her lap. "I've been trying to get the baby weight off since Alec was born!"

When her voice raised at the end, Lilah started to stir. She blanched and went back to speaking in an emphatic whisper. "You might be 'just trying to survive'"—she held her hands up to make air quotes—"but your survival and mine are light-years apart." Her voice got softer and her eyes flickered away again, this time toward the window.

"I watch you go running every day, and I think, 'I wish I could do that. Just run away like that.' The difference is, I'm not sure I'd come back like you do." She glanced back over toward Zell, her expression caught somewhere between shame and surrender. She shrugged her shoulders as if it were nothing and straightened her back. "Thanks for helping out today. I don't know what I would've done without you there. And I'm sorry for falling apart in front of you."

"You've been through a traumatic experience," Zell said. "You're entitled to fall apart."

A little burst of laughter escaped Debra's lips. "Tell that to my family," she said.

Zell was about to speak again, to say something—anything—to put Debra's mind at ease. She wanted to tell her that she knew exactly how she felt and that it would get better. The kids would stop needing her quite the way they needed her now. The intensity would ebb, at least. She wanted to tell her that there would come a day when she could go for a run uninhibited, when she could run away, as she put it. She wanted to tell her that this reality wasn't the only one there was, forever. That nothing stayed the same.

But just as she opened her mouth to speak, the nurse bustled in with the discharge papers, speaking loudly enough to rouse Lilah and giving Zell a pointed look that told her it was time to vacate the premises. She mumbled something about getting out of their way, but no one heard her. She slipped out, feeling vaguely guilty, as though she'd done something wrong, seen something she shouldn't have.

She stopped and picked up Chinese takeout for dinner, then at the last minute went ahead and picked up some entrées for Debra's family, too. It wasn't a homemade meal—she'd see to that tomorrow—but it was food, and it was, after all, dinnertime. She sent John next door with the neighbors' food, put some out for her own hungry brood, then made it to book club and kept up with the discussion even though she never did finish the book. She sipped wine and made small talk with the other women, all the while thinking about what Debra had said and wondering just what she could do about it. Should she invite her to book club? Offer to keep the kids for her?

It wasn't until she was doing her stretches before bed that she hit upon an idea. Years later she could still feel the little zing of inspiration that traveled up her spine at the moment she thought of it. She pictured Debra gesturing to her stomach, pointing at Zell's smaller body. Everything that happened after came from that one idea, which came from that strange encounter in the hospital room when a woman she barely knew bared her soul, admitting something Zell felt quite sure Debra had admitted aloud to no one else. Her confession left Zell feeling responsible. She had never been able to turn away from another person's pain.

CAILEY

I asked Zell what hurt and she said, "Everything." I tried to help out, bringing her aspirin and fixing her a Coke in the same blue cup she'd given me that first day. I even remembered a coaster. When Zell got sick, I knew that my days were numbered and I better do everything I had a mind to do right quick. I'd already been on borrowed time ever since Cutter woke up. Mama agreeing to let me stay with Zell those extra days had been nothing short of a miracle, and I wasn't one to ignore miracles. Zell called those extra days "bonus time." I didn't say so, but I liked it that she felt that way. My eyes got all watery when I thought of having to say goodbye. But neither one of us wanted to talk about that yet.

We worked hard to get the yard ready to be approved as a wildlife habitat, finishing up the last items on the punch list, as Zell called it. Truth is, I was sure it was all that working outside in the heat that made Zell sick. I felt bad about it, even though she told me not to give it a minute's thought. She took the aspirin and drank a little bit of the Coke; then she fell sound asleep, which was my chance.

I'd been meaning to get back over to Mr. Doyle's house ever since he'd given me that Popsicle, but I swear it wasn't to see him. I wanted to visit his mama, because he told me she'd been feeling bad. He said that she was getting weaker and weaker and he thought she might die. I drew her a picture I thought might make her happy, and I intended to take it over to her before I left. When Zell asked me about it, I told her it was for Cutter, which she said was really sweet. It was just a little lie.

I opened the door really quietly, but it still made a click when I shut it, so I stood there on the stoop for a few minutes to see if it woke Zell up. I watched her but she didn't move. I hoped she felt better when she got up. One good thing was that she didn't have to cook dinner for me that night, as Mama and the Ambulance Guy were taking me out. Just me. The thought of their four eyes staring at me while I ate made my stomach feel quivery, so I tried not to think about it. I didn't see how I was going to get a bite of food down.

I looked down at the picture in my hands as I walked. I'd drawn a rainbow and a sun and some birds. I didn't think about it till I was already across the street, but the picture was all things in the sky, which I guessed was where Mr. Doyle's mama was headed to soon. Up to the sky, with God. I didn't know if that was the right or wrong thing to draw. Does a person who's getting ready to go up to heaven want to think about it? Maybe she didn't.

I had just about convinced myself to go back to Zell's and draw another picture entirely when Mr. Doyle came out on his front porch and called my name. He yelled it kind of loud, and I was worried somehow Zell would hear and come running outside to shoo me back into her house and get that worried look she got whenever Mr. Doyle's name came up. Then I remembered how still she was on her couch, her chest rising and falling in a slow rhythm. I looked back at her house, saw no sign of her, turned back, and waved hello.

He said, "Well, Cailey, tell me what brings you this way?" He had a funny smile on his face, like he knew the answer to a riddle I didn't know.

I held up the picture. "I drew it," I said. "For your mama."

He peered at the picture, his glasses sliding down slightly when he did. His mouth was open, and I could smell the coffee he'd been drinking. I had to work hard to keep from wrinkling my nose from the smell. He looked from the picture to me and back again. "You're a very good artist, Cailey. I think my mother is going to be very pleased to receive this." He started to reach for it, but I pulled it away. "I—uh—wanted to give it to her myself." I looked at his face, to see if he was mad. I'd never been inside his house before. I didn't think anyone had in years except Mr. Doyle, his mother, and Jesse. When I'd eaten the Popsicle, he'd seemed to want to stay outside.

He got that look on his face again, that "answer to the riddle" look, and gave me a little smile. He reached out and ruffled my hair. "Well, sure, Cailey," he said. "You can come in and give my mother your picture." He kept his hand on my head, and it felt heavy and warm. He didn't seem to mind that my head was all sweaty. "You're a thoughtful girl," he said. "You don't see that too much in this world."

He beckoned me into the house, and I followed him in through the front door, which led into a front room that had a couple of couches and a big TV turned on loud to cartoons, though no one was watching it. I assumed Jesse, who was kind of like an overgrown boy, had been watching it but lost interest. Cutter did that sometimes and he never remembered to turn it off. I had to do that or else my mother lectured us about the cost of electricity and threatened to put the TV in the closet. She'd done it once before so we knew she was serious.

I followed Mr. Doyle back toward the kitchen, still holding my picture. We passed a door that was padlocked. I looked at the lock, then back at him. There must've been a funny look on my face because he rushed to explain. "There's stairs leading down to the basement on the other side of that door. My mother fell down them so I had to lock it up. I can't always be here, you know." He waved me on toward the kitchen, and I moved with him, away from the locked door. I'd heard of childproofing but not adult-proofing. I thought about saying that to him, but then wondered if he'd think it was funny. He might not.

The smell from the kitchen hit my nose before we rounded the corner—a mixture of rotting food and burned coffee. I walked in and tried to keep the shocked expression from showing up on my face, but I don't think I did a very good job because he laughed. "Guess I need to hire a housekeeper, huh?" He gestured to the mess. "Like I said, I can't always be here." Dishes with food still stuck to them were piled in the sink and overflowed down the counters. A puddle of something was in the middle of the floor. Trash was spilling out of the trash can, and other full trash bags, loosely tied off, were lined up down the wall. Once I got inside the room, the smell burned my nose, and I had to breathe out of my mouth to keep from gagging.

He pulled a chair out from the rickety table in the corner of the room, sidestepping the spill as he did so I could sit. He waved his hand over it like a waiter in a fancy restaurant and said, "Have a seat, madame," like he was trying to be French. I sat down and started to lay my picture on the table but then thought better of it, fearing I'd lay it in some sticky patch and ruin it. "Let me just see if my mother's awake," he said, and left the room. I just sat there waiting for my nose to adjust and hoping he didn't leave me long.

I listened to his footsteps fade away and looked around the room at the mess. Part of me thought maybe I should get up and wash the dishes or do something to help. I thought of Zell's perfectly clean house across the street. You could practically eat off her floors. And in that moment, I wished I could teleport myself back there, back to the place I'd just slipped away from. I thought of Zell, obliviously sleeping away. What if she woke up and I was gone? Would she even guess where I was? My stomach clenched with guilt and, deeper, something else I couldn't name.

I looked around for a clock so I could keep an eye on the time and not be gone too long. There was a clock on the wall, a round black-and-white one, the kind they had in every school I'd ever been to. But it had stopped, its hands frozen at ten and two. I looked at the microwave, but the readout said ":34," like someone had been cooking something and stopped the process before the timer ran out. I got up and moved over to the microwave to clear the readout so I could see the actual time. It was 2:22. If I hurried, I could get back before Zell woke and she'd never know the difference.

I spotted a small white bag on top of the microwave, with the letters *CVS* stamped in red on the outside. I could hear my mother's voice in my head telling me not to snoop. But I couldn't help being curious, and there was nothing else to do while I waited except look around. So I peeked inside.

My eyes took a few seconds to register what I saw inside the bag. I looked at the items, trying to make the things I saw in the bag fit with where I was. Inside the bag was a small box of tampons, a bag of Sour Patch Kids candy, and purple nail polish. I tried to think which one of the three people who lived there would have use for those items. Maybe Jesse liked sour candy. But I doubted any of the three of them had use for tampons or purple nail polish. I knew that women don't get their periods anymore after they get old, and I would think that a dying old woman wasn't going to be painting her nails. And she wouldn't be painting them purple if she did.

I heard a door close in the back of the house and the sound of feet walking back toward the kitchen. I hurried back to the table and sat down as if I'd never moved, my heart pounding like I'd just run a marathon. I was sitting there, holding my picture, trying not to look rattled, when he came back in. "I'm sorry," he said. "My mother's asleep." He held his hand out. "But I'll take that pretty picture of yours and give it to her just as soon as she wakes up. How's that?"

I nodded, suddenly mute and wishing I'd never gone into Mr. Doyle's house. The air seemed to have changed, as if it were polluted by the dirty kitchen, or something else. I didn't dare let my eyes stray to that little bag on top of the microwave, lest I give myself away. I handed over my picture, and he stared down at it for a few seconds before putting it under a magnet on the gold refrigerator.

Satisfied with where he'd placed it, he turned back. "Would you like a Popsicle?" His eyes looked eager as he spoke, and I knew saying no would disappoint him, but I couldn't stop thinking about the bag on the microwave, and how strange I felt there all of a sudden. I thought about how upset Zell had been the last time I'd gone over, the look she had in her eyes when she warned me about Mr. Doyle. I probably should've listened to her.

I stood up. "I should get back. Zell was asleep when I left, and I don't want her to worry."

Mr. Doyle nodded, his lips pursed as he looked at me. Then he smiled and put his arm around me. I could smell the sweat under his arms, the oil from his pores, the coffee on his breath.

"Let me walk you out," he said. We stopped in the doorway. "I don't suppose you'd like to help me build one of those ponds like you and Zell built? I was thinking I'd do that for my mother. Then maybe she could sit outside by it in the fall when the weather gets cooler."

I thought about how his mother would like that and how probably Zell was wrong about him.

"I'd pay you something for your trouble," he added.

I couldn't deny that I could use the money. That was one thing I'd never turn down. I figured Zell wouldn't say no if I was doing a job and actually getting paid real money for it. "I'll ask Zell," I said.

He gave me that smile again, the one that said he knew something I didn't, and whatever it was amused him greatly. "You do that," he said. I took a step back, away from him and toward Zell's house. I thought he'd let go of me then, but he didn't. Instead his grip tightened and he pulled me toward him. "Well, give me a hug goodbye," he said. His voice was disappointed, as if I was being ridiculous for even trying to leave without hugging him.

I let him hug me, my arms limp at my sides. He stopped hugging me and looked into my eyes. His were brown and green, both, which is the color they call hazel. "You have to hug me back or it doesn't count," he said.

Instead of resisting like I wanted to, I put my arms around him. I told myself I was doing the right thing, that I was just hugging a lonely man who didn't have anyone normal in his life to love him back. I gave him a little hug, like I used to give Joe when my mom made me. Then I pulled away quickly.

"I'll let you know when I'm going to work on the pond. Gotta get some river rocks to put around it first. Don't you think that'd be pretty?" he asked.

I nodded. "Sure," I said, even though I didn't have the faintest notion of what river rocks were. But I went along with it, because sometimes that was the easiest thing to do.

BRYTE

The conversation lasted less than five minutes. She knew because she looked at the timer after she pressed "End": four minutes, forty-seven seconds. They'd spent little time catching up on their current lives, no time rehashing the past (which was just fine with her), and most of the time deciding when and where to meet.

"As luck would have it," he said, "I'm going to be near you for a meeting in a few days. Does that work for you?"

This had very little to do with luck. Or did it? "Yes," she said, "I can do that." She didn't need to check her calendar to know there was nothing on it save another trip to the pool, another spin around the block with Christopher in the stroller and a dog cinched to her side.

"So you could do Thursday, August second? Say . . . five thirty? I should have my meetings wrapped up by then."

She would ask her mom to watch Christopher. Everett could pick him up from her house after work.

"Sure," she breathed. "Where?"

"I guess we could meet for a drink somewhere. A restaurant, maybe? Or we could just meet up in the lobby of the Marriott. That's where I'm staying."

She tried not to think about meeting him at a hotel, about his room upstairs that they could just walk right up to. That was the past. Things were different now. She was asking him to help her get back into the career she'd left behind. That was all. She exhaled. "The hotel lobby is fine."

"OK, doll," he said, and she could hear him smile through the phone. She remembered that smile all too well. She cringed, remembering how he called her that, how there was a time she'd found it charming.

"OK, well, see you then!" She tried to keep her voice light, happy.

"And, Bryte?" he asked just before she could end the call. "I'm, um, glad you called. It'll be good to see you again. We never really—"

"Yeah, me, too!" she said, not wanting him to finish whatever he was about to say. She blurted a goodbye before ending the call. She held the phone in her hand and blinked at the 4:47 display, thinking about how surprisingly easy it was to decide to change your life forever, and how surprisingly easy it was to keep that decision from the one you loved the most.

JENCEY

After that first night, their relationship unfolded with surprising ease. The days bled together in a summer haze. She felt as if she were living in one of those montages from a romantic movie. Here's the happy couple under the covers in bed, whispering and giggling and hiding from their kids. Here's the dad sneaking back into his own bed as the first light of dawn streaks the sky. Here are the two families eating burgers outside around the picnic table, the kids' mouths ringed with bright-red ketchup. Here's him baiting her hook as they all fish at the neighborhood lake on the tacky metal pier, the setting sun painting the sky beyond them with wide brushstrokes of pink and orange and blue.

It was weeks before she finally told him about Arch, her words coming out in a rush sometime in the wee hours of the morning. She rested her head on his chest and whispered the whole story—the flight to the college up north to escape her stalker's increasing menace, the whirlwind courtship and building a life with this man she loved far from home, the criminal behavior she'd been oblivious to, the agents who looked remarkably like the Men in Black showing up, trampling all over her flowers and her life. She breathed the tale in one long exhale, and when she was finished, neither of them spoke, each thinking, she imagined, about how far afield their lives had gone.

"Thanks," Lance finally spoke. "For telling me." He kissed the top of her head. "I'm sure that wasn't easy." She was getting used to his scent, his touch, his shape. She let herself lean into it, telling herself not to get too cozy as she did.

Sometimes after Lance snuck back to his own bed and she was left alone, she had stern talks with herself. This wasn't a permanent solution. It couldn't last between them. And yet, they behaved as if it could. The worst part was, they were dragging their children into it with them, the six of them forming this odd unit, complete with inside jokes and alliances that grew stronger with each passing summer day. Every day she told herself that soon they would talk about it. And every day it just didn't seem like a good time to bring up the future. Why put a damper on things? She would deal with it tomorrow, or next week, or . . . when he did. There was no need to mess with a good thing.

Because this was a good thing. And good things, she knew all too well, were rare. And fleeting.

She was just home from his house, arriving back at her parents' home late in the morning as usual, after they'd all had breakfast together. She'd made French toast, and her hair still smelled of bacon and syrup. She was thinking about a shower, about how long it would take him to get the work done that he needed to do, about what they'd do that evening, when she felt someone watching her. She looked over to find her mother standing on the back deck, looking in at her, a frown on her face. Jencey felt her smile die on her own face. She swallowed, gave her mother a little wave.

Instead of waving back, her mother beckoned to her, summoning her out to the deck. She nodded and walked toward her, thinking as she did just where the girls were, if they were in earshot of whatever her mother was about to say. Just to be safe, she closed the door behind her when she got out onto the deck. "Hey, Mom," she said, willing her voice to stay light and upbeat.

"Hi, Jencey." Her mother rarely referred to her by name, choosing a variety of other endearments instead: honey, dear, sweetie. Lois Cabot's mouth was a straight line, and there were more wrinkles around it than Jencey had ever noticed before. She wanted to reach over and smooth the wrinkles out like she sometimes smoothed her daughters' clothes or hair. Instead, she clasped one hand inside the other, shifting her weight from one foot to the other.

"What's up?" she asked.

"I take it this is going to be a . . . habit?" Lois asked.

She almost played dumb and asked what her mother meant. But she was not a teenager anymore. "We were up late watching a movie, and I had a few glasses of wine so I didn't want to drive. The kids fell asleep, and so I just slept in his guest room, Mom." She shrugged her shoulders for emphasis, as if she hadn't given her mother the same exact story multiple times in recent weeks.

"He's married, Jencey." Her mother using her name more than once in a conversation—this had to be some kind of record.

"It's nothing, Mom. I promise." She held her hands up like the scales of justice.

Lois continued. "And you're in the midst of a very difficult time in your life."

She refrained from saying, "Thank you, Captain Obvious." Instead, she nodded, hoping to achieve a penitent, contemplative posture. "Our kids are friends. They enjoy spending time together. He's also been through something . . . unexpected in his own life. We're good company for each other." The explanation sounded good in her own head, reasonable.

"I know all about his wife leaving him." Her mother raised an eyebrow. "You forget how active the rumor mill is in this neighborhood."

She rolled her eyes. "Oh, I remember."

"People are talking. They see your car there overnight, how much time the two of you are spending together," Lois said. "I just thought you'd want to know."

"People are always talking, Mom, in case you haven't noticed. It's whether you care what they're saying that matters."

Her mother sniffed. "If history is any indication, you'll move on. And we'll be left here to answer for you. So will he."

She knew this wasn't about Lance. It was about the past, about how her flight from this place had been a one-way ticket instead of a round-trip. Her mother always thought she'd come back, had kept her old room intact as though she'd be back in a year instead of more than a decade. Though she'd never said it outright, Jencey knew her mother had felt rejected when she'd decided to stay up north. But Jencey didn't have it in her to argue about the past. She didn't have it in her to argue about the present, come to think of it. She wanted to hold on to the happiness she'd felt when she woke up, when she made breakfast, when they said they'd see each other later. She wanted to hold on to *later*. There was always something better just ahead. Isn't that what she'd spent her life believing? Isn't that what she'd fought hard to hold on to in recent months?

"I'm sorry, Mom," she said, again angling for a look of remorse underneath her mother's intense gaze. "I'll try to be less . . . obvious." She turned on her heel and stalked away, feeling every bit the teenager she'd once been, the old arguments rising up like ghosts. All that was missing was the slamming door.

CAILEY

When Zell got to feeling better, Ty came for dinner. He tried not to show he was mad when he found out I was using his old room, but when he thought I wasn't around, I heard him ask Zell, "Why didn't you put her in Melanie's room?"

Zell said, "Shhh." Then a few seconds later, she added, "You don't live here anymore, so I'd say technically you don't have a room."

I smiled to myself and waited a few minutes before I came back in the room so they wouldn't know I heard, though I suspected Ty wouldn't care if I did. He would really hate having me in his room if he knew I'd dug all through it, looking at his old stuff from when he was a kid. He'd probably want to help me pack and walk me out himself. But I was the one who'd been around all summer keeping his mother company, and it was the first I'd seen of him. His brother and sister both lived out of town, so they had excuses not to come around. But he didn't.

The whole time he was there, he watched me like I was going to make off with the family silver or some of Zell's jewelry. It wasn't hard for me to figure out he didn't like me very much. But to be honest, it seemed like he didn't like Zell or Mr. John very much, either. He complained that Zell made chicken instead of steak, and pouted that she made roasted instead of mashed potatoes. I thought about the lame diary I'd found under his bed, covered in dust and forgotten. He'd kept a log of what he ate for dinner every night. Boring. I looked at his belly, hanging over his waistband. If you asked me, he was a little too concerned with food. And he didn't need potatoes at all. He needed one of those low-carb diets Zell was always talking about.

Mr. John and him hardly spoke, and Zell just chattered about mindless stuff: the weather, our wildlife habitat, the new way she made the broccoli. "It's roasted instead of steamed," she said. "Isn't it so much better?"

Ty just shrugged and kept shoveling food into his big open hole of a mouth. So I said I agreed it was much better roasted, which was a mistake, because then I had to listen to her explanation of how she made it, which went on way too long. Mr. John and Ty didn't seem to hear her at all.

Ty didn't stay very long, though of course I wasn't sorry to see him go. Zell made me walk him out with her, and I did, but I lagged behind. I was happy to see that Lilah, Alec, Pilar, and Zara were outside, too, and waved at them as soon as I saw them. Pilar and Zara were over at Alec and Lilah's all the time. I was a little jealous and wished my mom would date someone with kids my age, someone Cutter and I could hang out with all the time. I wondered if Ambulance Guy had kids. I doubted it.

"Can I go over and say hi?" I asked.

Zell said yes, and I started to run off, but then Zell hollered, "You forgot to tell Ty goodbye, Cailey."

I stopped and turned around, giving him my most sincere smile, which wasn't sincere at all. "Goodbye, Ty. It was nice to meet you," I said.

"You, too," he said, but his voice told me he didn't mean it any more than I did.

I skipped across the Brysons' yard toward the kids, who were swinging each other on the tire swing Mr. Lance had hung there a few weeks before. Pilar was pushing Alec, and Lilah and Zara were doing "Poof with the Attitude," a clapping game they did all the time. Mr. Lance and Miss Jencey were sitting on the picnic table, hardly paying attention to the kids. If they were, they would've told Pilar not to push Alec so high, and Alec to hang on tighter. And they would've told Lilah and Zara to find a new game to play, one that didn't get on all our last nerves because we'd heard it so much.

"Hi, Cailey," Miss Jencey called out as I walked by them, surprising me that they even saw me. She pointed out Ty's car, finally backing out of Zell's drive. "Did you guys have company for dinner tonight?" She was smiling. She was always smiling when she and Mr. Lance were together. She didn't smile much when I first met her, always wearing sunglasses and looking like she just came from a funeral.

I stopped in front of the picnic table and eyed the graham crackers, Hershey's bars, and marshmallows stacked there. If I played my cards right, I might get a s'more. "Yes, ma'am," I said, using the same voice I used with Ty. It was the voice I used with most adults I didn't know all that well. I used it with Zell at first, but now I mostly forgot and just talked to her in my regular voice. "Zell's son was here. Ty."

"Oh, Ty!" Jencey said. "I knew Ty way back when."

Then I remembered. "Oh, yeah!" I said. "You did know him." I raised my eyebrows and gave her a look. "You knew him pretty well." I looked over at Lance, who'd stopped holding Jencey's hand with me around, but they didn't fool me. "Don't get jealous, Mr. Lance," I said. "It was a long time ago." I froze, realizing what I'd done. In teasing them, I'd told on myself. But it was too late now. I could tell by the looks on their faces I was going to have to explain.

I'd found a whole box of stuff in Ty's closet that had to do with Jencey. Little cut-out hearts with her name on them, and poems he'd written about her (which were so lame I laughed when I read them), and a lot of pictures of her, some with the heads of other people cut out in them. You could tell that, at least back then, she was the only girl for him. Which kind of didn't make any sense because she seemed way too pretty for him. But who was I to know? Maybe back in high school he was a stud. He had the photo of her when she was homecoming queen, standing on a stage with a crown on her head, looking surprised and really, really happy.

I started to walk over to the kids to see if I could get a turn on the tire swing when Jencey stopped me. "What was a long time ago, Cailey?" she asked.

"Oh, well, um, when you guys were boyfriend and girlfriend," I said, wishing I'd never said anything. I didn't want to stand there and discuss an adult's old boyfriend with her, especially when I'd just gotten away from his gross self. I waved my hand in the air like it didn't matter a hill of beans, as Zell would say, and started to walk away again. But Jencey stopped me again.

"Cailey, we were never boyfriend and girlfriend. I barely knew him," she said. "Where would you get an idea like that?"

I looked at her, feeling a little sick inside for bringing it up. I didn't want to talk about it—whatever it was—anymore. But the way she was looking at me, I could tell I didn't have much choice. "Um, well, um, I found the box of stuff. In his, um, closet," I tried to explain. "I'm staying in his old bedroom?" I added, as if that explained my snooping around in Ty's private stuff. The last thing I wanted was for her to tell Zell on me. I had no business rummaging through Ty's closet. I just got bored sometimes. And I was curious. I heard my mother's voice in my head: *I told you not to snoop in other people's things.*

Jencey leaned forward, looking at me intently. "What box of stuff?" She looked as confused and sick as I felt.

"There's an old shoe box in the back of his closet. I, um, sort of opened it and looked through it one night when I couldn't sleep. And it has pictures of you and, um, poems he wrote about you, and a lot of cut-out hearts with your name on them and stuff?" I looked at Lance, who'd put his hand on her back and looked concerned. "I thought you'd know about it. Like it was something he kept from when y'all went out? Like maybe he just couldn't bear to part with it, or . . . something." I looked down and drew a line in the grass with the toe of my tennis shoe, wishing I'd never walked over, wishing Zell had never made me come outside with her in the first place.

Jencey hopped down from the picnic table. "Can you show it to me?" she asked, her voice sounding like it did when Pilar and Zara were bugging her at the pool, like she was working hard to keep from screaming.

I shrugged. "Sure," I said. I motioned for her to follow me and headed back to Zell's, thinking as we walked how in the world I was going to explain this one to her.

ZELL

It didn't surprise Zell all that much, knowing the truth about Ty. She supposed in hindsight, she'd known there was something . . . off about him, especially in high school. He'd grown quieter and quieter, retreated more to his room. Zell worried about the usual things you saw on TV—drugs, drinking, depression. She'd wondered aloud to John about whether their middle child was having suicidal thoughts, or dealing with secret homosexuality, or involved with the wrong crowd. John told her to stop worrying so much, to leave the boy alone, that it would work out, and to quit inventing trouble where there wasn't any. But deep in her mother's heart she knew something was wrong. And now, all these years later as Jencey Cabot sat at her kitchen table and pored over the disturbing contents of a long-hidden shoe box, she knew she should've listened to that nagging internal voice a little closer.

Now she knew: it was her own son who'd driven Jencey away all those years ago. Ty had been a threat, scaring that poor girl to death with his paper hearts left in the most disturbing places. Once, she'd heard through the neighborhood grapevine, a heart had been left on the bathroom counter when Jencey emerged from the shower, the word *love* scrawled in the steam on the mirror. Zell had known all about it, listening to Lois Cabot lament at the pool that last summer before they finally took Jencey up north to an undisclosed college in an attempt to get her away from whoever it was. Lois wouldn't even tell the other mothers what school, saying it was just too dangerous.

And it *had* gotten dangerous. One night when Jencey had been meeting Everett, someone (her son, Zell knew now) had jumped poor Everett and beaten him up, leaving a heart on his unconscious body. Now Zell tried to think about that time in her mind, wondering if she'd seen marks on her son after the fight, if there'd been signs she'd ignored because—much as she would've said differently—she didn't really want to see. She thought of what had happened next door before Debra left. She thought of her son. And it all made a sickening sort of sense. She had given birth to this child, she had raised him, and he had done something terrible. She saw with horrifying clarity her own influence in who he had become.

"I'm sorry," Zell said over and over to Jencey. "What can I do?" She wrung her hands and paced the kitchen. John and Lance talked in the den, their voices low and serious, like thunder rumbling. Cailey made herself scarce, which was probably a good idea. She hadn't intentionally done anything wrong, but her snooping had opened a can of worms, and Zell didn't really know how to talk to her about it yet.

Lance and Jencey took the shoe box and left. Zell went into the den and sat down. Feeling chilled, she wrapped her arms around herself. She wondered idly where Cailey was, reasoning that the girl was probably fine. Her own child was her concern now. John came into the room after seeing Jencey and Lance out. He had his keys in his hand. "I'm going over to Ty's now," he said. "Gonna have a talk with him, let him know how this is going to play out."

She nodded miserably. "Want me to come with you?"

"No," John said, jingling the keys in his hand. "I think we need to talk, man-to-man." He looked down at the floor, and she refrained from mentioning that she'd once begged him to do exactly that. "I'm gonna stay with him until the police get there," he added, his gaze still on the floor. They'd picked out the wood together years ago when they'd replaced the carpet with hardwoods—visiting showrooms, browsing the samples, debating the different choices, colors, prices. It had seemed so important then. Now they hardly noticed the floor; they just walked across it.

"So they're going to report him to the police?"

John nodded. "Lance is concerned that he might've seen Jencey at his house tonight and . . . might resume his old behaviors. He feels it's best to get the authorities involved just to ward off any possible issues. He's much less likely to try something if he knows people are watching out for him to do just that."

Zell nodded. "I can see that. I just . . ." She found John's eyes with her own. "I just hate it."

He walked toward her, crossing the room with his wide stride in mere steps. He took her hand, pulling her up to him. She buried her face in his neck and let his arms make her feel safe. John would take care of her; he would take care of them all. She'd known that when she'd married him, and she knew it now.

"He's going to be OK. We all are."

She nodded, knowing he could feel the movement of her head against his neck. "You take care of Cailey," he said. "I bet she's feeling kind of bad about what happened. She probably thinks it's her fault. For finding the box."

Zell pulled back and looked at him. "Well, it kind of is," she replied, hearing her own cruel words as she said them. She couldn't blame Cailey for being a normal kid. Normal kids snooped around when they were bored. Even some adults snooped around when they didn't have anything better to do.

He put his finger against her lips. "She doesn't need to hear that. She needs to hear she saved the day. That she found something very important that we all needed to see." He gave her a look. "Because we did. Need to see."

She thought of all the things they'd been avoiding seeing, and for so long. He was right. There was much they needed to see.

LANCE

Lance held her until she fell asleep, this time not bothering to hide that they were in his bed together. They weren't fooling anyone anyway.

The children were playing somewhere in the house. He ignored their loudness, their hunger, their bedtimes. He let them feed themselves, fall asleep where they may. They would not die if they were unattended for one evening. They had food, shelter, TV, one another. Tonight his loyalty, his concern, his heart, was for Jencey.

"You're safe here," he assured her as she lay in bed and shivered, the shoe box sitting ominously on his dresser. He got up and threw a towel over it.

"But what if he saw me? I was right outside, right there in full view. And you know how Zell runs her mouth. I bet you money she told him I was back, just making small talk. I can hear her now, 'Oh, Ty, didn't you know Jencey Cabot? Well, she's in town for the summer with her two little girls.'" Jencey pulled him back into bed, her hands fisting his T-shirt as she looked at him with wide, terrified eyes. "My girls could be in danger!"

He shushed her and pulled her closer, burying her head in his neck as hot, wet tears caught in the folds of his skin. "I'm going to take care of you," he promised. He said it so naturally, as if it were nothing, but he heard the catch in her breathing as she reacted to his words. She was silent for a few minutes, and he feared he'd made a dreadful mistake.

"I'm glad you're here. With me," she said.

He kissed her. "Me, too," he said. "Me, too."

CAILEY

I was sitting in the front yard when I heard Zell come up behind me. I'd just seen Mr. John get in his car and drive away. I knew he was going to see Ty. I knew Lance and Jencey were calling the police about that shoe box. And I knew she was coming outside to tell me she wasn't mad at me, that I'd done nothing wrong. I knew Zell would be concerned about my feelings and come try to make me feel better because that was who she was. She was the kind of person who would take in a total stranger and make her feel like part of the family. She would love me because she was a loving person. And what her son did didn't change that.

But she wasn't going to get a chance to say anything to me. Not this night.

Zell started to speak, but I held up my finger, silencing her. I patted the ground where I was sitting, right by the pond in the front yard that she and I had made together. She tried to talk again, but I shook my head hard and pointed in the direction of Mr. Doyle's house. I put a finger up to my lips, as she finally noticed what I'd been sitting there watching. I felt it was right to be silent as the funeral men in their black suits loaded Mrs. Doyle in the back of the hearse. Neither of us said a word as we watched Mr. Doyle wrestle Jesse back into the house after the hearse drove away. We didn't say anything long after the neighborhood quieted down and the light faded. We just watched the night take over.

AUGUST 2014

BRYTE

Bryte let Christopher go with the girls into the pool, then took her spot with the rest of the group, clustered in their usual area—a hodgepodge of lounge chairs, coolers, towels, and bags forming a base camp. Food and drinks covered the available surfaces, all in various stages of being consumed. Bryte loved being part of the jumble of voices and activity.

But today Zell's chair remained empty. Cailey had come with Jencey and Lance for the last several days. Bryte missed the older woman, always doling out advice and saying funny things, but she sensed something was going on and hoped that, whatever it was, it would blow over and Zell would return. Jencey and Lance had been mute about it. But as of today it was August, and time was running out; their summer was dwindling. She remembered the early June afternoons, how summer had unspooled before them, a bright ribbon of days to come. They'd run out of days far too quickly.

"Is Zell OK?" She broached the subject with Lance when Jencey took the girls to get soda from the machine.

He blanched, nodded curtly, and looked away, pretending to be interested in the children going off the diving board.

"Lance," she said. "What?" Zell was, after all, his next-door neighbor. He was most likely to know if there was a reason she wasn't there.

He glanced over at the clubhouse Jencey had disappeared into with a panicked look. "I'm not sure she wants me talking about it," he said. "She's still pretty upset."

Bryte wrinkled her brow. "Jencey is upset? With Zell?"

He shook his head. "No, not with Zell. But with her son. So it's . . . complicated."

Bryte was thoroughly confused. Jencey'd had very little—if anything—to do with Zell's sons, either of them, then or now. What could she possibly be upset at one of them about? She pressed Lance for more information. "What happened? You have to tell me."

She had a déjà vu feeling, hearkening back to the many afternoons with Everett and Jencey spent at this same pool. Jencey and Everett were the couple then, but she'd talked to Everett every chance she got. She could only dream back then that she'd be the one married to Everett. She thought of her looming meeting with Trent, of risking the very thing she treasured most, if Everett ever found out.

Jencey, done buying the sodas, got stopped by a neighbor, buying them time because the woman was notoriously long-winded. Lance looked over and saw her stop as well. He took a deep breath. "I should let her tell you."

Bryte shook her head, dislodging thoughts of Everett. "She won't tell me. She's pretty . . . guarded. With me." Jencey kept their conversations at surface level—kids, weather, the latest headlines, and celebrity gossip. Bryte liked to believe they would move past it someday.

"She's guarded with everyone," Lance agreed.

Bryte kept her mouth shut, waiting for Lance to go on.

"I'm sure you knew the circumstances that surrounded her leaving here back when you guys were kids?"

Bryte nodded, thinking of going to visit Everett as he recuperated. He had a broken rib, a black eye, stitches in his lip. And Jencey had left him like that. Bryte had sat with him instead, slipped her hand into his as he slept, trying to make sense of her best friend's departure. He and Bryte had grown closer as he recovered; she'd felt those first glimmers of hope that something might happen between them, eventually. She just had to be patient, give him time to forget Jencey. The ugly truth was, despite her fondness for her friend, Bryte was glad to have Jencey out of the way.

"The stalker," she said now, to Lance, who she could see clearly loved Jencey. Bryte recognized the look he wore, the way he watched after her. She looked down at his hand and noticed he was still wearing his wedding ring, too. She'd talked with his wife some in the past, made idle conversation when monitoring children in the pool or passing each other on the street while walking. His wife had gotten into running, lost a lot of weight, and looked terrific when she'd left him.

"Yes, well. We found out a few days ago that the stalker was actually Zell's son."

"John Junior?" she asked, thinking of how large Zell's oldest son had been, how menacing. He used to tell them that there was someone in the woods, chase them around and scare them when they were little.

"No, the other one. Ty." Bryte flashed back to one of the last times Jencey and Everett went to the hideaway. Jencey had been so spooked by then, scared of her own shadow and jumpy all the time. It was Everett who'd asked Bryte to come with them, to stand guard outside and keep an eye out so they could have some alone time. Jencey and Everett were going away to college together; at least that had been the plan. Bryte felt they'd have plenty of alone time then. But Everett had asked, so she'd said yes. She'd sat outside the hideaway with a flashlight, feeling like an idiot. She and Everett had never discussed that night, how ridiculous she'd felt, how jealous she'd been that Jencey was the one inside with Everett and not her.

She remembered, with the shock of realization, the pieces falling into place after all these years. Ty, quiet and unassuming, had happened by as she kept watch. She'd suspected nothing and, desperate for attention from a male, had been receptive to his attempt to strike up a conversation. Jencey had heard the two voices and sent Everett outside to see what was going on. Seeing Ty there, he'd smiled at them and left them to talk, disappearing back inside the copse of trees, but not before giving them a thumbs-up. Ty had kissed her that night, his hands groping and grabbing, growing more urgent. She'd pulled back, shocked at what was happening and how fast. She'd said his name, her voice seeming to break him out of some sort of trance. He'd stood up quickly, stepped away from her, apologizing as he backed farther and farther away, then turned and ran.

Now she tried to remember, had he seemed angry when he'd seen Everett, given any indication of what was to come? Days later, Everett was blitz attacked by someone in a ski mask as he ventured into the woods to meet Jencey. Jencey returned home only to hear what had happened hours later when Everett's mom called her from the hospital. A few days later, Jencey was gone. Leaving, she'd said, was the best thing for all of them.

She'd made out with Jencey's stalker. Had she told Jencey what had happened with Ty? Had they giggled about it afterward, mused over whether something would develop between them? She couldn't remember. Did Jencey remember that? She wanted to excuse herself and go throw up in the pool bathroom. Lance was staring at her.

"I'm just remembering . . . that time," she said.

"I think Zell just feels weird, you know, coming around since what happened."

"She didn't do anything wrong." Bryte felt defensive of Zell, of herself, of everyone who'd been inadvertently involved with the situation.

"Oh, we know that, and there are no hard feelings. It's just . . . awkward. The police are involved, and I just think until it gets resolved, she's keeping her distance."

Bryte nodded. "I can understand that. But it sucks."

He laughed, more out of relief than humor. "That sums it up quite nicely," he said. He looked over at Jencey, who was, it was obvious, trying to get away from the neighbor. "Just don't let on that I told you, OK?"

She made the little sign she and Jencey used to use, swearing their silence to each other. They used to keep each other's secrets. Now they kept secrets from each other. Jencey hadn't told her about this. Jencey had told Everett and not her why she was even back. She drew two fingers across her lips, zipping them shut. "Mum's the word," she said.

JENCEY

Jencey had finally managed to escape the long-winded neighbor, walking quickly away as if the woman might whip out a lasso and yank her back like a cartoon character. She caught Lance's eye, pretended to wrap her hands around her own neck and choke herself. He laughed. As she made her way back over to him, she scanned the pool deck like she always did, accounting for four children instead of two.

She spotted a woman hugging Alec on the other side of the pool, saw the familiar way her whole body inclined toward his, the possessiveness that hung in the air between them. *This one's mine,* the woman's body said. When the woman looked up and Jencey saw her profile, she recognized the face from the photos in Lance's house. Debra. The name bloomed inside her like a poisonous plant, a Venus flytrap opening its leaves, inviting the unsuspecting to fall inside and be consumed.

She'd known this was coming, yet she'd hoped it wouldn't happen, that she and Lance and the rest of them could somehow stay cocooned inside this summer forever. But what had they talked about just today? Summer was ending. The back-to-school commercials were coming on, the spiral notebooks and packages of paper crowding the endcaps in every store. She felt the mounting pressure to make a decision—stay or go, enroll the girls in the local school or find somewhere else to land. With each day that ebbed away, she was that much closer to having to pull the trigger. Watching Debra hug her son, she felt the gun go off inside her, the ricochet resounding in her heart as the trigger got pulled for her.

Lance's eyebrows knitted together as she detoured away from him, her eyes seeking out Bryte instead, who was helping Christopher into the pool. She didn't look back at Lance, didn't want to see him see his wife for the first time in months. She beelined over to Bryte, feeling like the schoolgirl she once was, wanting to talk to her best friend about a crisis. She and Bryte had struggled to connect this summer. It was as if each wanted to say more than they could to the other. As if, once they started talking, they would say too much. So they said very little. Jencey felt regret for not opening up to her friend, for withholding herself. And yet she sensed Bryte had done the same.

She plopped down on the side of the pool just like she'd done that first time they'd talked at the beginning of the summer. Then she'd marveled over the changes in Bryte—the lovely, capable woman she'd blossomed into. She'd envied her, too: the house, the husband, the child, the contentment. But Jencey had felt an increasing uncertainty bubbling under the surface, recognized the discontent that had crept in over the course of the summer. Jencey didn't know what had changed, and she didn't feel she could ask. She sensed she was the last person Bryte would discuss it with, yet she longed to be that person in her friend's life. Mostly because she needed Bryte to be that person in hers. She wondered if they could somehow make their way back, and figured that she could be the one to start carving a path in that direction. Maybe the one who did the leaving had to be the one to make the way back.

"So," she said, getting Bryte's attention, "looks like Lance's wife just showed up." She saw the shock register on Bryte's face and would have enjoyed it if not for the situation. "You should see the look on your face," she said, laughing a little in spite of herself. Bryte scanned the pool until she found the mother-and-child reunion taking place.

She turned back to look at Jencey. "Why aren't you over with Lance, staking your claim?" she asked, a sense of urgency in her voice. She made a little shooing motion in Lance's direction.

Jencey allowed a quick glance in Lance's direction, saw that his eyes had now found what she'd already seen. She measured her words, stating them carefully, emotion free. "Because I don't have a claim."

She hoped she sounded like she meant it. She *wanted* to mean it. She tried not to think of the summer they'd had, the unexpected joy she'd found with him, the nights spent in his arms. He'd brought something back to her, carried it in his hands like a bunch of flowers and laid it at her feet. The word was on the tip of her tongue, but she couldn't say it, not even to herself. One night he'd tried to say it, but she'd laid her finger on his lips. "No," she'd instructed. "Let's not do that to each other."

"Why?" he'd asked, a hurt look on his face.

She hadn't been able to answer him. "Just . . . let's not," was all she said. As she watched Debra walk with Alec toward Lance, she felt all the words she hadn't said come to her.

"It's not too late," Bryte said, sounding exactly like the Bryte she remembered.

"It might need to be," she responded, forcing herself to look away from the sight of Lance standing to greet the woman who'd been in their midst all summer, a ghost that had haunted them as surely as if she'd dragged chains around in his attic.

Bryte continued to watch the scene. "Is he hugging her?" Jencey asked, then quickly said, "No, don't tell me."

Bryte glanced at Christopher, who was perfectly safe in the water with floaties on his arms, then back at Jencey. "He didn't hug her," she said. She raised her eyebrows. "Because he wants to be with you."

"I'm not going to break up a family if there's still a chance for them." She looked at Bryte, willing her to understand. She wouldn't wish what she'd been through on anyone.

Bryte met her eyes. "I know you wouldn't," she said. "You're a good person."

Jencey smiled. "So are you."

Bryte rolled her eyes. "I don't know about that."

"Are you kidding?" Jencey gasped. "You're like the best person I know."

"Well, you don't know everything," Bryte responded.

Jencey heard what her friend wasn't saying. She felt the years and distance between them finally begin to erode. She had no right to know Bryte's secrets. And yet, sitting there with her, talking like old times, it was possible that they could somehow get back to a place where she did.

Her eyes flickered over to Lance and Debra, chatting politely. She wanted him to walk away, or her to leave in a huff. She wanted him to stride over and sweep her into his embrace, give her a kiss like a returning soldier. And yet, Jencey understood, there were the things she *wished* were true, and there was what was *actually* true. She was learning that there was usually a great distance between the two.

LANCE

Lance kept his distance from Debra, wondering how in the hell this was happening. The afternoon had been like so many before it that summer. He'd had a few beers and felt the pleasant buzz he usually got, drinking and chatting the hours away. The group of them had formed a sort of club that summer, united by the near drowning and strengthened by a string of sunny afternoons spent trying to make sense of it. They talked about a variety of things—the latest neighborhood gossip, the weather, the news, the kids' antics.

Sometimes Zell had a "conversation starter," as she called it, some silly question or quote that would lead to deeper conversations. Sometimes they even shared personal stories, but never the ones that mattered. He hadn't, for instance, shared that, while he had no idea when she would come back, he'd felt Debra returning as one felt an oncoming storm, the increasing awareness that something in the air was changing, gathering strength as it barreled forward.

After she sheepishly left, he took his time gathering his things to leave, too, looking at Jencey over at the pool with Bryte, thinking of and dismissing a thousand things to say to her. He settled for a kiss on the forehead, a promise to call her later. She nodded and said very little in response. Eventually he walked away slowly, feeling as if he wasn't coming back even though the pool would be open for several more weeks. Between Zell's absence and Debra's appearance, he felt as if, though the summer wasn't over, something was ending.

He returned home to find Debra at the kitchen table, waiting for him, looking penitent. "Mom!" Alec yelled, shoving from behind him to reach her, hurtling himself into her arms as if he hadn't quite believed she would be there as promised. Debra, to her credit, managed to look humbled by her son's welcome instead of exultant, or worse, expectant.

Lilah, God love her, stayed beside Lance, her arms crossed like his as she took it all in. He gave his daughter a sidelong glance, anticipating her next move. Would she yell? Cry? Give in to her body's longing to reach out? He hadn't known Lilah well when Debra left. He knew her much better now. And yet, he couldn't have said what his child was thinking as she registered her mother's presence in their home after a ten-month absence. He couldn't have told Lilah how to react any more than he could've told himself. His wife was home: this was good news. His wife was home: this was terrible news.

"We have plans tonight," Lilah said suddenly, turning to him. She looked over at Debra. "We're going to Taste of the Town," she explained. "With Jencey and Pilar and Zara."

He rested his hand on top of Lilah's head. "We can go another time," he said, surprised by his words, by how easily he could break plans with Jencey when faced with Debra's very real presence. For so long, her return had been a fantasy played out in his mind in so many different ways. Lately, he'd tried not to think about it at all. Focusing instead on Jencey and the way her eyes crinkled at the corners when she smiled, the highlights in her hair that had grown brighter with each day in the sun, the way she tasted and smelled and felt. They had been careful to avoid the word *love*, and that had been wise. He was a man with obligations that ran beyond his feelings.

"You promised we could go!" Lilah yelled, interrupting his rapid-fire thoughts. Angry tears spilled from the corners of her eyes. "You're going back on a promise!" She turned and bolted from the room, leaving him and Debra and Alec to blink at one another like strangers.

"She's in shock." He offered the excuse for Lilah's behavior to Debra, though he owed her none.

"I know," Debra said. "And I deserve it." She set Alec down on the ground. "Why don't you go get that wet suit off and Daddy and I will talk?" she said to him, falling back into the mother role so easily it was as if she'd never been gone. Lance watched as his son obediently trotted off to his room, thankful at least one of the kids wasn't having a complete meltdown.

"So," he said. "You're back?" Stupid question.

Debra nodded. "I didn't think calling ahead would make it any easier." She gave a little laugh. "I half expected the locks to be changed."

He shook his head. "I wouldn't lock you out of your own house."

"Is it? My house?" He heard the hopeful note in her voice and regretted his choice of words.

He shrugged his shoulders, made his voice sound businesslike. "Legally, at least. I mean, there are no papers drawn up between us. Your stuff is still here. Your mail comes here." He gestured behind him, at a box on the floor he'd taken to throwing anything addressed to her into. It was nearly full of running magazines, catalogs, various solicitations, and a few personal letters. He started to get up and show it to her, but she reached out and stopped him.

"I don't want to know about legally. I want to know about us." She removed her hand from his arm, put it back in her own lap. "I'm sorry. I'm coming on too strong, and I have no right. I know that."

"It's just a shock, seeing you again."

She nodded, thinking this over. "You should keep your plans tonight. They seem to mean a lot to Lilah."

"They're friends of hers," he explained, though an explanation wasn't warranted. "They moved into the neighborhood this summer and . . . we've hung out."

"We?"

"Our families."

She drew back, as if his calling what they were a family even when she wasn't a part of it was somehow hurtful. "And you're friends with the dad?" she asked, pressing. The look on her face told him she already knew there was no dad. Somehow Debra knew, when he still had no clue what had driven her to leave him the way she did. Maybe the difference was that Debra wanted to know and he didn't. It crossed his mind that she wanted to be absolved, but he had no proof of that. All Debra had ever admitted was that she needed time away, to think about what she wanted out of life. He'd suspected there was someone else—that part of her decision making was whether she wanted another man—but she'd refused to give him any more information than that.

"No," he said simply. "The mom."

"I see," Debra said. Which wasn't true, of course. She didn't see at all. She hadn't been there to see.

His legs were growing stiff from standing, but he didn't dare sit. To sit across from her at their kitchen table would be far too intimate. He could not be intimate with her. He did not know, standing there with his aching legs and fickle heart, if he could be intimate with her again. She didn't fit in this room anymore; her presence poisoned the air. And yet, she belonged here. She was his wife, the mother of his children. If she was back and wanted a chance to make things work, he owed his family that chance, didn't he? He'd known this moment would eventually come, and now it was time to do the right thing.

He turned from her and went to look out the window, his gaze falling on Zell's house. He'd missed Zell today, missed her witticisms and cantankerous outlook on life, the way she was always smacking him on the shoulder when he teased her, how she tended to them all, ever the nurturer. She'd grown on him; they all had. Yet this thing with Ty had made things weird, and soon Cailey was going back to her mother. The summer was drawing to a close—hadn't they just been teasing the kids about school starting this afternoon?—and it all felt suddenly very sad. In his heart he was already letting Jencey go, working out how to say goodbye to the best friend he'd had in a long, long time. He glanced over at Debra, looking mournful at the table.

"I'm going to go cancel my plans for tonight. Maybe you should go up and try to talk to your daughter." He grabbed his phone from the counter and trudged outside, his heart aching as he found the last number called and hit "Redial."

CAILEY

Ever since they'd found out about Ty, Zell had stayed inside, refusing to come to the pool and cooking up a storm instead. The house smelled good, and there were always cookies cooling on the counter. More cookies than any of us could eat. She kept sending stuff over to Mr. Doyle's house, making me carry food across the street nearly every day, forgetting all about her warning to stay away from him. He always opened the door with that little smile, told me what a good girl I was for bringing him food. I told him that I wasn't doing much, just delivering. Then one day he asked me if I was ready to earn some money, to finish the pond he'd started for his mother.

I gave him a confused look and almost said, "But she's dead." Then I thought maybe that wasn't the nicest thing to say.

He knew what my confused look was, though. "I'm going to finish it in honor of her. A memorial," he explained. "That way Jesse and I can sit outside by the pond and think about her." I'd never seen Jesse sit still if there wasn't a video game involved, but I didn't say that.

He rested his hand on my head and looked sad. "I was inspired by what you and Zell have done," he said, and pointed across the street at our pond, which had shaped up nicely, if I did say so myself. "You've created something so lovely."

"I better go ask Zell," I said. "She might, um, have something else she needs me to do." The truth was I didn't know how Zell would feel about that. Carrying food over to his house and coming back home was one thing, but working for him for an afternoon might be another.

"OK, well, go on and ask, and if you can, you should change into some work clothes and come back right away." He got this nervous look on his face for about a minute. Then he smiled at me and waved me in the direction of Zell's house. I hurried back across the street, hoping Zell would say yes.

"Zell!" I hollered when I got inside the house. She came limping into the kitchen, looking startled. She'd been so jumpy and weird since everyone had found out about Ty. I guess she thought people would think bad of her because of what her son did. But I didn't ask her about it. I just let her keep on cooking stuff and hoped she'd snap out of it.

"Can I go help Mr. Doyle make a pond in his backyard? He asked me to and said he'd pay me." I raised my eyebrows and gave her my serious look. "I could really use the money," I added.

Zell laughed, but I didn't see that anything was funny. She glanced in the direction of the Doyle house, looking concerned. It was quiet as she thought about it for a few seconds. "He's doing it for his mom." I realized how weird that sounded. "In her memory," I explained. "Isn't that nice?" I gave her my puppy-dog eyes. That's what my mom always called them. I only used the puppy-dog eyes for special occasions. If you used them too much, they didn't work the same. It was better to hold them back for when you really needed them. My mom called it "bringing out the big guns."

Zell walked over to the door that led from the kitchen out onto her driveway. She opened the door and leaned out, looking at Mr. Doyle's house, then back over her shoulder at me. She raised her eyebrows, giving me her serious look. "I'm going to carry my magazine and sit out on the driveway in one of the deck chairs. So I'll be nearby if you need me. I want you to peek your head around the corner and wave at me every so often. OK?" she asked.

I nodded my head really hard. "OK!" I said. Then I ran off to change my clothes before she could change her mind, calling, "Thank you!" over my shoulder on my way up the stairs. In Ty's room, I threw on some work clothes, the same ones I wore all those long, hot days when we worked on Zell's yard.

When I got back to Mr. Doyle's house, he pointed me toward a big pile of flat, jagged, dark-gray rocks he was going to use to border the pond. But what he showed me didn't look a thing like our pond. It only looked like a big old mud pit. He could use some lessons from Zell. But I didn't say that. I just thought about what I was going to buy with the money he gave me. A present for Cutter. A present for my mom.

I carried those heavy rocks back and forth, back and forth, the sun beating down as I worked. Every so often, I kept my promise to Zell and poked my head around the corner to wave at her that I was safe. I was a sweaty mess, and my head hurt from the sun. The work was hard and long, and I was starting to think maybe the money wasn't worth it. Mr. Doyle was trying to install a fancy fountain, but it wasn't going so well. He was cussing and sweating, his frustration growing the hotter it got.

He went inside to get us water bottles and left me out there alone, and I took the opportunity to stop moving for a few minutes. I stared at my reflection in the sliding glass door that led into his basement. I thought of the padlock he'd had to have to keep his mother from falling down those basement stairs. I wondered if he'd taken it off the door yet, seeing as how he didn't need it. I stared at the glass door so long I thought I saw the curtain move, and it spooked me. I thought of his mother, and wondered about a ghost. I took a step away from the door, my reflection growing smaller as I did.

Mr. Doyle came around the corner and called my name. He handed me a water bottle. "Break's over!" he said. "Back to work!" He turned me around and pointed to the rocks. Then he resumed working on the fountain. I sucked down half the bottle and started arranging the rocks. We worked side by side like that for a while. I could smell our sweat in the air, mixing with the heat. I wished I'd never said I would do this. I glanced back at the curtain hanging over the sliding glass door, but I never saw it move again. My mind was playing tricks on me in the heat. And there was no such thing as ghosts.

When we were finally finished, he dug in his pocket for the money and fished it out, holding it up to me. I went to reach for it, but he stopped me. "I get a hug first," he said.

He was sweaty and he stank. I didn't want to hug him. But I wanted that money, and I got the feeling I had to hug him to get it. I couldn't tell how much money was in his hand, but it looked like a lot. I stepped toward him and let him pull me into his arms. He was a lonely man who'd lost his mother. So what if he stank to high heaven? The hug would last a second, and then I could go home and shower.

He pulled back and looked at me, and then he moved his face closer, his mouth closing over mine before I knew what was happening. He used his lips to pry mine open and put his tongue in my mouth. I tried to get away, but he held me in place. Mr. Doyle was surprisingly strong when he wanted to be. He should've been the one carrying those rocks.

He stopped kissing me, and I looked away, toward the direction of Zell's house, longing to run back to it. But he held me in place, one hand on each arm. My mind was racing with a million thoughts about how gross and awful what he'd done was. I expected him to apologize. But all he said was, "Don't ever tell anyone I did that." He didn't have to worry about that. I would never tell anyone. It was too terrible to say out loud. Then he handed me the money and released me. I ran away from him as fast as I could, still feeling his fat eel tongue inside my mouth, unsure whether I would ever outrun what had just happened.

ZELL

Zell sat with her magazine in the driveway, but instead of reading she found herself mostly just staring at James Doyle's house. She caught glimpses of Cailey trudging back and forth, lugging those rocks, and occasionally, as promised, she popped her head around the corner and waved, her wave growing less enthusiastic each time. It was hot as Hades out. Zell decided she needed a spray bottle to spritz water on herself and dashed inside to get it.

She was coming out of her house with the water when she saw Debra walking toward her, emerging from the heat waves like a mirage. Zell nearly turned back to hide inside her house, but Debra had already seen her. She still looked as fabulous as the day she'd left. Zell made her mouth do something that came close to a smile, and waggled the water in Debra's direction.

"Hello," she said, being neighborly. "I didn't realize you were back." That was a lie. She knew everything that went on in Lance's house. (Sometime in the past ten months she'd started thinking of it as his house, not Debra's. This, she felt, was significant.) She'd seen Debra's car pull up just a few afternoons ago, watched from her kitchen window as she let herself in just as pretty as you please. Zell had thought to herself, *Oh no, you don't.*

She paused on the stairs and let Debra come to her, her heart pounding away, knocking against her rib cage more urgently the closer Debra got. She tried to gauge what the other woman would do. Yell? Deny? Apologize? Threaten? She hadn't spoken to her in so long. In that last encounter, there hadn't been much said. This moment had been inevitable, coming as certainly as the end of summer, Cailey's departure, and everything else she'd dreaded.

"It sure is hot out," Zell said, just to talk about something. But she knew Debra hadn't come over to discuss the weather.

"Yes," the other woman responded, her voice hesitant.

"Was it this hot wherever you were?" Zell regretted the question the minute it was out of her mouth. Debra might think she was prying into where she'd gone when the truth was it didn't matter a hill of beans where she'd been. All that mattered was that she'd run away from her family, her home, her responsibilities. A good mother didn't do that. Zell tried to take comfort in the difference between them. No matter what she'd done, she'd never abandoned the people she claimed to love.

And yet, she thought of Ty, how she'd avoided him ever since the truth had come out, the shame she'd taken on over what he'd done. But it was more than that; it was her shame, too. She'd been too ashamed to seek help for her injury, too ashamed to admit what had happened.

"I just wanted to . . . clear the air," Debra said. "Make sure there was nothing we needed to say to each other after . . . what happened."

Zell was quick to reassure her. "No, not at all. Things are fine. It's your business."

Debra's voice was quiet and even. "Well, you kind of made it your business."

"I'm sorry about that," she said. "I really am."

"Yes, well, I also just need to know what you've said about what happened. To Lance, or to anyone else who might say something to Lance."

Zell looked away. "I didn't say anything to anyone," she said softly.

"Good." Debra nodded to herself. "That's good." She looked in her own backyard, right at the spot where it had happened. "We're going to work on our marriage and . . . make a fresh start."

"Are you moving back in?"

"Well, not right away, of course. But in time I expect that to happen."

"Does that mean you're not going to tell him what happened?" Zell couldn't keep the incredulity out of her voice.

Debra swallowed, glanced over at her house. "It's in the past. There's no need."

"I just think secrets can be harmful. They can eat at you, wear away the foundation of—"

Debra's face changed, and she held her hand up. "You're hardly one to lecture me about keeping secrets, aren't you?"

Movement over at the Bryson house caught Zell's eye, and she looked over to see Alec standing on the side porch, watching them inquisitively. She would miss the children. She sensed Debra would do whatever she could to keep them away from her now that she was back. She didn't exactly blame her.

Alec waved at her and hollered, "Miss Zell, we're going to the pool as a family!" Both women heard that last word, his emphasis on the word *family*.

"I think that's my cue," Debra said, taking a step back toward her house. "I'm glad to know you won't do something that would hurt our *family*." She waved at Alec. "I'm coming, honey," she called to him.

Debra hustled back toward Alec just as Cailey came trotting up the drive, running like someone was chasing her. She was caked in dirt and sweat and smelled like it. She came to a stop beside Zell, and together they watched Debra trudge across her own driveway and disappear inside her house.

"Is that Lilah and Alec's mom?" Cailey asked. But instead of watching Debra, she glanced over her shoulder at the Doyle house. She moved closer to Zell.

"Yes," Zell answered idly as the door closed behind Debra. She directed Cailey into the house, still trying to process what had just happened. She might've been the reason Debra had left, but she wasn't the reason she'd stayed away. And now that she'd decided to return, she expected Zell to keep her secret. But Zell was tired of doing that. And yet, could she tell Lance what she knew? Now, after all this time? Did she dare confess what she'd done and what she knew after everything else that had happened?

"I wish she hadn't come back," Cailey said, giving voice to Zell's thoughts.

Zell said the right thing in response, instead of what she wanted to say. "I'm sure Lilah and Alec don't feel that way. Let's let them have their family time," she said, thinking of how Debra had used that word against her. "And you and I will get cleaned up, then go get some ice cream. How does that sound?" She feigned more enthusiasm than she felt. The heat combined with her conversation with Debra had left her winded and exhausted. But this was Cailey's last day with her, and she wanted it to count.

BRYTE

Walking across the hotel lobby, Bryte felt less propelled than pulled by the sight of Trent sitting alone on one of the couches, talking on the phone, holding court even though he had no subjects at the moment. When he turned, saw her, and smiled, she knew she wasn't there about the job.

She paused and let the truth hit her, the force of it surging through the core of her. It had never been about the job, no matter what she'd spent the past weeks telling herself. She swallowed the truth down, let it settle inside of her, and continued toward him, focusing on his face. How uncanny the resemblance to Everett was.

Trent gestured for her to have a seat and held up one finger. She did as she was told and sat down, smoothing her skirt and wondering if she looked OK.

He ended his call and turned his smile on her. He reached across the space between them and rested his hand on her knee. "Wow. It's good to see you." He nodded as if agreeing with himself.

She smiled. "You, too."

He shook his head. "I'm still sort of shocked you wanted to meet. I thought I'd lost you for good."

He's talking about the job, she coached herself. *He's not talking about the two of you.* She willed her smile to stay in place. "No, just been busy."

"You said you've been out of work for a time and are looking to break back in?" His brows drew together in concern. "Everything been OK?"

"Oh, sure, everything's been fine. My husband and I moved, and we, um, had a child, and things have just been crazy. I'm just now able to start thinking about going back."

"Aw, man, you had a kid?" he asked. His face shone. "That's cool! Boy or girl?"

"A little boy." She swallowed. "Christopher." She shifted in her seat and smoothed out her skirt again. She wanted to get up and run out of there.

She knew she wouldn't be going back to work. She would miss her son too much. She would miss his sticky kisses and their walks around the neighborhood. She would miss reading him a story before his nap and the warm, sleepy smell of him when he woke up. She would miss hearing children's programming on the TV in the other room as she made his lunches. She couldn't leave it up to someone else. She closed her eyes for a fraction of a second, erasing the image of her son from her mind so she could focus on the reason she was there.

She looked back at Trent Miller and admitted to herself why she was there. It wasn't about the job. It wasn't about catching up with him. It was about what Everett had been asking for, for months, and the only way she knew to make it happen.

EVERETT

Everett had been relieved when Bryte scheduled her meeting for the same afternoon as his appointment, but dismayed when she told him what she was going to meet about. She wouldn't be home when he got home, which gave him time to think over how he was going to present whatever the doctor said to him. He would have a glass of wine or two, play with his son, and go over the best way to approach her while he waited for her. Trouble was, he now had two challenges: to talk her into whatever the doctor said, and to talk her out of getting a job right now if that meant they would not pursue having a second child. Of course she had the right to go back to work if she wanted. He was just surprised that was what she wanted all of a sudden. Until recently she'd been happy at home. His talk of another child had sent her running in the other direction, and he needed to find out why.

"I'm just covering my bases," she'd assured him that morning. "Seeing what my options are. It could be good for us."

The doctor bustled into his office and sat down at his desk, interrupting his thoughts. Dr. Ferguson opened a file folder and looked it over, then looked up. "I'll say it again that this is quite unusual having a husband come in without his wife." He gave Everett a conspiratorial smile, as if the two of them were in cahoots. He thought inexplicably of the kids he'd grown up with in the neighborhood, their many games of "boys versus girls."

"I'm just covering my bases," Everett said, echoing Bryte. "Seeing what my options are."

Dr. Ferguson looked down at the chart. He kept his eyes on the words and numbers printed there when he spoke again. "Are you here to discuss a donor?" he asked. "I know some men struggle with that, but it's done more often than you might think."

Everett's heart rate picked up, and he stared at the bald spot on the top of the doctor's head, as he processed his words. "I—uh, a donor? For, um, what?" he managed to stammer the words out.

The other man raised his head. "A sperm donor," he said. There was a weariness in his voice, a heaviness that told Everett he hadn't wanted to say it out loud. No man wanted to tell another man he shot blanks, even if it was part of his job.

The doctor flipped through the file in front of him to avoid his eyes. "That's really your only option," he said to the paper.

Everett stood up abruptly, his sudden movement startling the doctor. "You know, you're probably right," he said. "I should probably come back another time. With my wife."

Dr. Ferguson blinked at him a few times. Everett considered just bolting out of the room. In the silence, he was already piecing it together. If he was infertile, if they needed a donor to get pregnant, then where had his son come from?

"You didn't know," the doctor said in realization.

Everett considered lying. But how could he lie about this? *Oh, sure, I knew. I just . . . forgot.* He exhaled loudly. "No," he said. "She never told me and I . . . never asked. When she got pregnant, I was just . . . happy." He looked up at the doctor and decided he never wanted to see this man again. If it meant they never had another child, so be it. "I was just really happy."

He started to walk out of the office, but the doctor's voice stopped him. He stood still but didn't bother to meet the other man's eyes this time. "Mr. Lewis," he said, "you can still be happy."

Everett nodded once, then fled.

BRYTE

Trent still drank gin and tonics. And he still drank a lot of them. She watched him down the second one just as fast as the first, then raise his hand for another. His tolerance had to be incredible. Her own tolerance had dropped off significantly since she'd become a mother, and six a.m. wake-up calls became de rigueur.

It hadn't taken him long to suggest they move from the hotel bar to the hotel couches. She stirred her drink, a weak Crown and ginger, and took a polite, dainty sip. The last time she'd matched him, drink for drink. When she'd stood to her feet and swayed upon standing, he'd been quick to offer to help her to her room, extending his arm gallantly. She'd rested her own hand unsteadily in the crook of his elbow and given him a coquettish smile. Tonight she met his eyes and saw not quite the same look she'd gotten that long-ago evening, but a look that was on the verge of that one.

"Stay for dinner," he said. "We'll talk more. About the job. And where I could use you."

She almost said, "Oh, what the hell," and ordered another drink. For a moment she was tempted to let things go the way they once went. It would work just the way it had before. She knew that in her depths the same way she'd known it back then, the knowledge settling inside her like a stone dropped into water. But Everett's face filled her mind, edging out any possibility she might've been considering. Whatever she'd come here to do wasn't going to happen. Time had passed. Things were different. She wasn't a woman who could do that. She never really had been. Though her son wasn't a mistake, what she'd done had been. She would wrestle with that for the rest of her life.

She smiled without showing any teeth and looked back down at her drink. "Can't," she said.

"Oh, yeah. The kid." He rolled his eyes.

"Yes, there's dinner and bath time and story and . . ." She looked up at him as Christopher's face filled her mind. She held up her hands. "It's quite a production."

He received a fresh drink from the bartender and gave it a vigorous stir. "Sounds like it." He took a greedy gulp and leered at her. "If I were you, I'd welcome a break from it."

The words were on the tip of her tongue: *Well, you're not me.* But there was no point in being contentious. She needed to get out of there, as politely and quickly as she could. He was still a good business contact. Someone she might need someday. No sense making things weird between them. Weirder.

"Actually, I enjoy it, as strange as that sounds." She made a production of checking her phone for the time. "In fact, I better be going." She pulled her wallet from her purse to pay for her drink, but he held up his hand. "I've got this. Business expense." She'd always been business to him, and that was good. That was what she needed him to think. She didn't need his affection, his emotion, his reminiscences of that night. He'd served his purpose when she'd needed him. She cringed internally at the thought of what Trent Miller had been to her.

She put her wallet away and gave him what she hoped passed for a grateful smile. "Thank you," she said. She made sure she looked him in the eye when she thanked him, held his gaze.

She leaned over and kissed his cheek, leaving the faintest imprint of her lips behind as she pulled away. "It was so good to see you again."

He looked at her and raised his eyebrows, his expression reminding her of Christopher. "Call me if you ever need . . . anything," he said. He gave her that captain-of-industry grin and turned back to his drink. She rose from the bar and left him behind.

Bryte slid into her car, pulse racing as though she'd just escaped from a crazed killer instead of a handsome man who'd been interested in more than just her résumé. She closed the car door harder than necessary, the slamming sound reverberating in the mostly empty parking garage.

She turned the key in the ignition, and the radio came on loud, blasting an oldies station she'd played on the drive over. She reached for the knob and turned it down. She just wanted silence.

At the same moment that her hand touched the knob, the sound of the singing voices registered in her head, making a kind of unexpected sense. Heart singing, Ann and Nancy's voices blending. She turned down the volume and leaned back against the seat with a sigh, the fingers of a headache beginning to massage her brain. It had been that damn Heart song that had started everything.

She recalled the image of sliding into the rental car that afternoon nearly four years ago, her heart heavy with what she'd just learned from the doctor. Heart was singing then, too, a "lost hit" that she'd forgotten all about until she heard it that day. As she listened to the words, the kernel of an idea took root in her mind, a vague what-if she never intended to go through with, until that very night, she did.

She shook her head to dislodge the memory and put the car into reverse, easing out of the parking space and pointing herself in the direction of home. She couldn't get there fast enough. Once she got home, she could stop thinking of all this nonsense, immerse herself in her husband and child, in dinner and bath and story and bed, in the familiarity of a home she didn't deserve but was desperate to hang on to. Her mistake was in the past, and with any luck, she would keep it there forever.

◆　◆　◆

The noise of the television playing cartoons was the first thing she heard when she stepped inside the house. Bryte let the sound of normality wash over her as she stepped into the kitchen, already looking toward opening the refrigerator and what she would pull out to cook, just to keep busy.

But when she turned and saw Everett sitting at the kitchen table, she knew instinctively it wasn't going to be that simple. His eyes, as they met hers, told her that something had happened while she was away. Something terrible. "What's wrong?" she asked, her insides turning to jelly. She stepped toward him, but he put up his hand like a traffic cop. Don't come any closer, he was saying. She stopped moving, her hand resting on the kitchen island.

"I saw Dr. Ferguson today," he said.

No, no, no, no, no! her mind screamed. This can't be happening. Not now. She blinked at him and said nothing.

"I'd intended it to be a surprise for you. Instead I got the surprise," Everett added. He gave a little bitter laugh.

She nodded once and closed her eyes to block the vision of his mournful face. Her stomach twisted in on itself, and she gripped the island harder.

"He's not—" His voice gave out, and he swallowed, cleared his throat, a choking sound. He tried his voice again. "He's not mine."

She understood that he wasn't asking a question, that he'd drawn his own conclusion with no help or explanation. She nodded again and looked down, studying her white knuckles. She was hanging on to this island, and suddenly the name of this kitchen fixture had taken on a whole new meaning.

"Who?" he asked. The word felt like a slap, and she felt the impact of it reverberate through her. She'd been waiting for this moment—dreading that one word—for a long time.

She took a deep breath before answering. "Someone from work." She paused. "It doesn't matter."

He narrowed his eyes at her, leaned forward as if he was trying to get a good look at her. "Doesn't matter?" His voice was incredulous. "Of course it does."

She looked toward the den, where Christopher was watching TV. She shushed him, turning to him with fire in her eyes. He leaned back, chastised. "You're his father," she said, keeping her voice even and calm with something inside her she didn't know she possessed.

"Yeah, that's what I thought until this afternoon. And you let me think that. Like an idiot."

"You are his father," she said again. "In every way that counts." She thought of Christopher's biological father tossing back gin and tonics like water, loving the sound of his own voice, reeking of a confidence that—in a weak moment years ago—had seemed like a good quality. She wanted no part of Trent except the part that had been invisible to the naked eye, the part that had enabled her to become a mother. She'd absconded with that part, and he'd never missed it, sleeping oblivious, his arms thrown over his head while she crept out of his hotel room as light dawned in the window over the bed.

Everett sighed, a long exhalation that sounded like it was coming from the huge crack in his chest, a crack she'd created just the same as if she'd swung a hatchet and lodged it there. She crossed over to him and knelt in front of him, her words tumbling out. "The words 'I'm sorry' fall so short, but . . . I was crazed over what I'd learned about you—about us—and I thought, I thought it would be a way that we could still have the family we wanted and—" She stopped, knowing how stupid this would sound but also knowing she had to admit to it. "I thought no one ever had to know and no one would get hurt. I was so, so stupid." She tried to catch his eye, but he wouldn't look back at her. He kept his gaze just over the top of her head, looking instead at the refrigerator just behind her, papered with photos and reminders of the life they had together, their little family of three. He'd wanted nothing but that, and she'd been determined to give it to him.

A long silence passed. Her knees ached from stooping in front of him, but she didn't dare move. She kept her posture penitent, staying as close as he would allow. "Is that who you met today? The 'guy from work.'" He gave a little ironic laugh. "I thought it was weird that you suddenly wanted to go back to work." He shook his finger at her. "But I believed you." He put his hand back in his lap and kept his gaze there. "I always believed you."

Her knees throbbing, she eased out of the position she was in and slumped into the chair next to his. She let the silence stretch between them for a few minutes as she gathered her words. She kept her gaze on the top of his head, willing him to look up even though she knew it was futile. She began to speak.

"You got called into that big meeting that day, and you couldn't go to the doctor with me. You told me to tell you what I found out, and you said it so flippantly as you walked out the door. You said, 'You tell the doc we're up for the challenge.' You kissed my forehead and sauntered out the door, and I so envied you, your ability to always expect the best. I'd lost that more and more with each passing month we didn't get pregnant."

She paused for him to speak, but he didn't, so she continued. "So after the doctor told me what he found, I walked around numb for a while, just trying to figure out how to tell you. And what it meant. And I decided exactly what to say, had this whole rousing speech ready to give you. But when you walked in and asked how it went, I couldn't bring myself to tell you that it was you. That no amount of trying was going to fix what was wrong."

"So you lied to me," he said.

She started to tell him it wasn't a lie, but he was right. It was. "Yes," she said. "I told you that we'd just have to try harder. And that night we did try. And all I could think while it was happening was, I'm probably ovulating and it doesn't even matter." She caught his eye, finally, and held his gaze. "It was never going to matter," she said without flinching.

"So you got back at me?" He gave her a challenging look. "Because I couldn't get you pregnant? Found someone who could?"

She shook her head, leaned toward him imploringly. "No," she said, the word emphatic. "Getting back at you never entered my mind. *Keeping* you did." She tried to catch his eye again, but he wouldn't look at her. "You wanted a child, a family, so much. We were so close to having everything we talked about. I couldn't face what might happen if we couldn't."

"What might happen?" he asked.

Her voice was very quiet, barely more than a whisper. "You might stop loving me."

She watched as the words sank in, hopeful that they might change the direction of the conversation. But when he spoke, it was clear he wanted to keep fighting—if only, she knew, to keep the pain at bay for a bit longer.

"So you just took matters into your own hands." He gestured toward the den and the cartoons and the little boy watching them in rapt attention. She was grateful Christopher loved TV the way he did at that moment.

"The next day I left for a work trip, if you remember. It was a trade show, and while I was there I met this recruiter. He was there to scope out the industry's talent, and he and I talked. We . . ." She didn't know how to finish the sentence. How could she describe what had happened between them? He had looked so much like Everett that it had drawn her to him. He'd been charming, disarming her as they talked and laughed and drank and drank some more. The hours ticked away, and suddenly she was drunk and he was offering,

When she'd woken up the next morning with him beside her, it had been too late to take it back. And when she puked for the first time a month later, she'd known. She'd known that they were having a baby, and she let Everett believe it had happened that same night the doctor told them to just try harder. She'd let him believe it because she wanted to believe it, too. She wanted to pretend.

"You were . . . *with* him," Everett finished for her.

"It was . . ." Again, she fumbled for the right words. How could she say it was a mistake when it had given her a beautiful child she loved with all her heart? She tried again. "It was wrong of me to do, and wrong of me to lie to you about it after. And I'm sorry. I am so, so sorry." She willed him to look at her with understanding and forgiveness, to look at her at all. But he did not. "I've been sorry every day." Her voice, hoarse with emotion, was barely audible.

He kept looking at his hands. "I'd like for you to leave," he said. She leaned back heavily in her chair, thrown by his unexpected request. He looked up suddenly, his gaze angry and hurt. "I'm serious. I need for you to get out of here." She blinked at him a few times but then complied, rising slowly to her feet. She started to walk into the den to collect Christopher, her mind already spinning as to where she could go.

He stopped her. "You can leave Christopher. I'll put him to bed. I just need for you to not be in this house for a few hours. You owe me at least that." She started to go tell her son goodbye, but he stopped her. "Don't stir things up with him. He hasn't even realized you're back, so better just to go." He looked at her, his eyes pleading. "Please."

With the briefest of nods, she scooped up her purse and keys where she'd dropped them earlier. She paused at the door to look at him still sitting at their kitchen table. She started to speak, to apologize one more time, but he rose and walked into the den, turning his back on her as he joined the son he once thought was his own.

EVERETT

Everett listened for Bryte's car to start up and back out of the driveway, but he never heard the sound of the engine. He got up and went to the window to see her walking toward Myrtle Honeycutt's house, her shoulders hunched forward, her head down, her steps deliberate. She was still going to walk that damn dog even with everything else going on. He watched until she disappeared from sight, then went to put the boy to bed. Could he call him his son still? He didn't know if he could stop. The thought of admitting that child wasn't his nearly brought him to his knees. But he forced himself to keep moving.

After Christopher was tucked in with his stuffed elephant and his five kisses (forehead, chin, cheek, other cheek, nose), Everett sat in the darkening house, not bothering to turn on the lights. He thought of his wife, gone for several hours now. In the distance, he heard sirens and wondered idly what might be happening. He wondered if he should worry, but he couldn't consider another tragedy just then.

He wanted to be angry at her. The baser parts of him wanted to divorce her, deny the child, and start over. Declare the Bryte years a false start. He'd get it right the next time. He cataloged in his mind what it would take to separate their lives. He was a math guy, but he could not estimate the cost. He'd always made sense of things, but nothing made sense anymore. He could not be angry at her because she was not the only one who'd kept a damaging secret.

An image came to mind of him and Jencey as inexperienced teenagers, hunkered at a corner table of the town library in late winter of their junior year. He'd said they needed to research sex before they did it so they'd know how, and she'd gone along with his plan. They'd taken books off the shelf and sat side by side, elbows touching at the most remote table, her eyes taking in the words and pictures along with him, two bright spots of color on her cheeks in the too-warm library. Under the table, he'd reached for her hand. She'd taken his, and he'd known that it was as close to real love as he'd ever find.

That one winter afternoon in the overheated recesses of the town library was what had driven him to find Jencey before he could propose to Bryte. He'd tracked her down, living in Connecticut with a husband and two—two!—children. He'd called her, told her he would be in New York and wasn't that close to Connecticut, playing dumb. She'd said she could get away, that it would be nice to see him. He'd met her in a restaurant in the city, and they'd had a long dinner, catching up and drinking stiff drinks until they were both just shy of shit-faced.

At the end of the night, she'd looked at him and asked why he was really there. He'd never lied to her before, and he didn't intend to start. So he said nothing. He signaled the waiter for the check, paid the bill, and reached for her hand. Surprisingly, she didn't argue. She just took his hand and let him lead her to his car, a rental. He turned on the heat in the car, tuning the radio to a decent station.

"Are you ever going to answer my question?" she asked.

He looked at her, and that was all the answer she needed.

"I'm sorry," she said. "For never coming back."

"I had to know it was really over." He laughed at himself. "I mean, of course I know it's over. But . . . seeing you makes it real."

She started to cry, tucking her head into her chest. "Yes," she said. "I have a family now."

"I wanted a family," he said. "With you."

"I know," she said.

"I thought that was what you wanted, too." He hated the way he sounded, whiny and clingy. But it was how he felt. And he would probably never see her again. He needed to say it before he moved on.

"I did." She gripped his arm, trying to catch his eye. "You have to believe I did. But then everything happened, and I just had to get away."

"You said you'd come back." He felt anger building up inside of him—anger at her, anger at the stalker, anger at himself for not stopping her. He thought of the hazy days after the attack, the shame and pain all mixed together. He was weak. He had failed to protect her. And Jencey had left because of it.

"I never meant for this to happen," she said. "It all got away from me. I swear."

It had all gotten away from him, too. He kissed her then, because he believed her and because he thought that the kiss might make a difference. He forgot all about Bryte back at home. Bryte, who thought he was asleep in his hotel room. Bryte, whom he planned to propose to when he got home. Bryte, who didn't deserve to come in second but knew she was.

Jencey pulled away, her hand on the car door. "I should go," she said. On the radio, Death Cab for Cutie sang about peeling freckles from summer skin. He wanted to stop her from leaving, but he sat motionless, listening to the song on the radio and the gentle hiss of the heat from the vents of the rented car. Neither of them said a word. He could feel her wanting him to stop her, to pull her toward him, away from the door. If he asked, she would go with him to his hotel, and he could have her just once more.

"It was good to see you," he made himself say instead.

"You, too," she said, her voice gone stiff.

"I'm going to ask Bryte to marry me," he told her. Because that was what he had come there to say.

She nodded and blinked away tears. "Congratulations," she said.

"So I should?" he asked her. He wanted her permission. He wanted her to stop him.

She turned to him and gave him a resigned, sad smile. "Yes," she said.

He could not recall how the night ended beyond that, beyond her yes that freed him to marry Bryte, to make this life he was living now. If Jencey had said anything different, he would not have come back to Bryte, he would never have proposed. It would've been the worst mistake he'd ever made, but he would've made it willingly if it meant he got another chance with the girl he loved first. In the end, it was Bryte who loved him best. It was Bryte he was meant for. It had taken him far too long to come to terms with that, and he'd made so many mistakes along the way. He saw how his mistakes had led to hers. She'd tried so hard to make their life perfect, to make him happy. And he'd taken it all for granted.

He walked into Christopher's room, thinking of what she'd done, and what he'd done, and finding it hard to distinguish what was worse. He looked down at the boy he could not give her and thought of all the other things he had not given her. He had not loved her the way she deserved, but he could start to. He would not tell her what he'd done in New York; it would be too much for her. But he could forgive her, and maybe in doing so, it would be like she was also forgiving him. He wanted to take her in his arms and absolve all their secrets. He would do anything to make it right with his wife who was, it turned out, the only one for him.

BRYTE

Myrtle Honeycutt was confused when Bryte showed up so late asking for the dog, but thankfully the old woman turned over the leash without too many questions. Rigby gave her an excuse to walk, to move instead of sit, to feel the blood rush through her veins for a reason other than shame and fear. Rigby pranced along beside her, seeming to enjoy the fact that she didn't have the leash so tight today. She didn't care how far he wandered tonight.

Her jaw continued to quiver no matter how much she tried to steel it. She refused to give in to tears and gave herself a good scolding instead, her feet beating out a rhythm in time with the steady stream of harsh words she had for herself. She'd made this mess. She deserved everything that was happening. She'd been a liar and a manipulator. She'd hurt the people she loved most. She had to face the music. She would lose everything, and that was what she deserved. She was a horrible person who'd done a terrible thing.

She reached Zell's house and stopped, looking in at the warm lights glowing in the gathering darkness, the house like a beacon. She moved up the driveway toward it, tugging Rigby along with her, thinking that perhaps Zell would open her door and welcome her in. She might even make her hot chocolate; that seemed like something Zell would do. Bryte could go to the door with the pretense that she was just passing by and wanted to tell her she was sorry she hadn't seen her at the pool recently. When Cutter had nearly drowned, Zell had soothed Cailey when everyone else was too afraid to speak. She'd been the one who knew what to do.

That day felt like a lifetime ago. She'd been a different person then, still believing she could hide the truth forever, and run from it if she had to. She thought of Zell and Cailey, of Jencey and Lance. Not one of them who'd gathered around that crying girl as the ambulance wailed its way out of the pool parking lot were the same people they were then.

She walked slowly toward the door and took a deep breath before raising her hand to knock, tempted in that second to turn around. She thought about what Lance had told her about Ty, how Zell was too ashamed to show her face. She felt a kinship with the older woman. She exhaled and knocked anyway. Rigby watched with a curious look.

It was Cailey who opened the door, her eyes widening when she saw who was there. She peered past Bryte. "Is Christopher with you?" She knelt down and petted Rigby.

Bryte smiled and shook her head. "No, he's at home in bed. But I'll bring him by another time."

Cailey gave a despondent shrug and said, "I'll be gone by then." She dropped her hand from Rigby's head.

"Well, you'll still be in the neighborhood." Bryte gave her a smile that she hoped looked encouraging. She looked past Cailey to see if she could spot Zell.

Cailey noticed her looking and waved her in. Rigby trotted on in with no hesitation, partly because the house smelled so delicious, Bryte guessed. "I'll go get Zell." Bryte watched the girl disappear up the steps, her shoulders stooped and her head down. Bryte took a seat at the kitchen table to wait, wondering idly as she did why Cailey didn't seem happy about going home. Most children, she would guess, would want to go back home. She'd often wondered as Cailey's brief stay stretched into a long one why it had been that way. But looking around at Zell's home, she understood better why she wouldn't want to leave. Rigby flopped at her feet and closed his eyes.

She heard the uneven gait of Zell limping into the room. Zell paused as their eyes met, then proceeded to the table. She pulled out the chair across from Bryte and sat down.

Cailey tromped loudly into the kitchen and retrieved a mason jar from underneath the sink. She held it aloft. "I'm going outside to catch lightning bugs with Lilah and Alec," she informed Zell. She hustled out the door without waiting for the OK from Zell. The two of them watched her go, grateful, Bryte thought, for the distraction.

"So she's really going home?" Bryte asked.

Zell nodded, looking bereft. "Tomorrow."

"I'm sorry for interrupting your last night together," Bryte said.

Zell waved her words away. "I cooked her favorite meal. Later we're going to watch a movie, stay up late." Zell shrugged. "To be honest, I'm glad for the distraction. It was feeling a little maudlin around here." Her grin was just a flash before she narrowed her eyes at Bryte. "So what can I do for you?"

"I was just walking Rigby and saw your lights on and . . . I wanted to say that I've missed seeing you up at the pool. And . . . I hope everything's OK."

"It will be," Zell said. She folded her hands and studied Bryte. "It always is."

"You really believe that?" Bryte asked, hearing the waver in her voice.

"I do. You don't?"

"Not tonight," Bryte said. The two women looked at each other, an understanding passing between them.

"I'm all ears," Zell said, then stood up. "But first I'm going to pour us some wine. And you better start talking." Bryte cleared her throat and began her story, watching her neighbor stump over to the refrigerator to get the wine. She began to speak, letting her words flow like the golden liquid that poured into the glasses, words that had been bottled up for far too long.

CAILEY

I stood outside with the mason jar in my hand and the lightning bugs flying around, uncaught. For a while I just watched them zing past me, their little bellies glowing as they gathered in the cluster of trees toward the back of Zell's yard. From where I stood, I could see inside Zell's house, right into her kitchen. Zell was talking to Christopher's mom at the kitchen table. But they didn't see me. They were drinking wine and looked really serious, nodding a lot, their mouths in straight lines across their faces. I knew better than to go back in and interrupt them.

I looked over at the house next door. Lilah and Alec weren't home. Ever since their mom showed back up, they were always off doing stuff with her. Zell told me to give them time, but I didn't have time. Everyone said I'd still be in the neighborhood and nothing had to change, but I knew that sometimes things just changed and there was nothing you could do to stop it from happening. That was what the whole summer had been about if you thought about it. All around us things had changed, and changed again.

Since there was nothing better to do, I walked toward the front yard just to see something other than lightning bugs. At least in the front yard I could sit in my favorite spot by the pond and watch cars going by, when a car did come by. In this neighborhood it wasn't often that even happened. I put the empty mason jar on the grass and rested my chin on my knees, listening to the sounds of the nighttime all around. I tried to look up at the moon, but it was covered up by clouds.

Mr. Doyle's house was right in front of me, but I couldn't look at it. Since the kiss had happened, I'd thought of little else besides his tongue filling my mouth, about to choke me to death, his coffee breath nearly making me gag. He'd told me not to tell anyone what happened, and I didn't intend to. It was too embarrassing, and there was no one to tell anyway. Zell would overreact, and my mom didn't need anything else to deal with. Sometimes I thought of warning Lilah not to ever go to his house, but I had a feeling Mr. Doyle wouldn't mess with her because he'd be afraid of her dad finding out and kicking his butt.

I watched his house and thought of his mother dead in the ground, and the pond he was building even though she'd never see it now. I thought of how we'd worked to finish his pond and the curtain I saw move, how that nagged at me almost as much as the kiss, though I couldn't say why. No matter how much I told myself it was just my mind playing tricks on me, the heat getting to me, I kept seeing the curtain move and the lock on the basement door—one after the other, like a movie playing in my mind on repeat.

Sitting there thinking about it all, I got an idea. His car wasn't in the driveway, and I knew he'd gone over to play poker at a friend's house because I heard him talk to him on his cell phone when we were working on the pond. I'd seen him whistle his way to the car hours earlier, hating him with all the hate in me. The lights were out except for a faint blue glow coming from Jesse's room. That meant he was playing one of his video games so he would be distracted. If I hurried, I could do some spying before he came back.

Before I knew it, I was up on my feet and heading toward the house, feeling a bravery I'd never felt in the light of day. I crept closer and closer, knowing no one could see me. I know a lot of folks are afraid of the dark, but I learned something important and true that night: sometimes darkness can work to your advantage.

I stood on his patio just looking at the locked sliding glass door I couldn't possibly get into, wondering what had made that curtain move and whether I'd be brave enough to go in there if I could figure out a way to get in. I had no key and no idea how to pick the lock. There was a small rectangular window that led into the basement, but there was no way I was going to fit through it. I looked around for another way to get in, but saw nothing. My body felt cold and hot all at once, my heart had moved into my throat, and I thought about hightailing it back to Zell's. I could run away and not look back. I could leave in the morning and pretend that I'd never gotten this close. I could let whatever was weird about Mr. Doyle's house stay weird and spend the rest of my life trying to forget what he did.

I thought of the way he looked at me after he kissed me, how he gave me that smile at the same time his eyes went flat in his head, like his mouth and eyes weren't connected to the same brain. And I got so angry I wanted to hit him, to pound my fists into him until it hurt. I spied my reflection in that glass door, saw my puny little self that couldn't hurt a grown man no matter how much I wanted to. Then I remembered the river rocks we'd used to make the border of the pond. And I got an idea.

If I got in trouble, well, what did I have to lose? I would only have to deal with the fallout for so long before I went home. Zell didn't like Mr. Doyle anyway. I smiled and walked over to pick up the biggest, heaviest rock I could find. I lugged it over to stand in front of the sliding glass door again, watching the reflection in the glass, someone I wasn't sure I knew anymore. The rock was so heavy I had to hold it like when I used to take granny shots at the basketball goal in gym class. I kept my eye on the glass door and got ready to take a granny shot of a different sort. I was about to let the rock fly when I heard a car on the street. The engine sounded like it was slowing down, maybe even fixing to turn in to Mr. Doyle's driveway.

I laid the rock down and rushed over to peer around the side of the house. I watched as a big SUV pulled up across the street in front of Alec and Lilah's house. I could see that it was Jencey, idling there at the curb just staring at the house. The windows were rolled down, and I could hear her radio playing some sad love song. She kept on sitting there without noticing me at all, so I went back to what I was there to do, hefting the rock back into position, my eyes once again leveled at the intended target.

I imagined how loud the glass would sound as it shattered, the mess it would make. I feared Jesse running out and catching me, Mr. Doyle coming home to find me before I could get away. I tried not to think about what might be behind that curtain—maybe it would be something I didn't want to let loose. But I couldn't let any of that stop me. I was there to do something, and though I didn't really understand it, I had to see it through.

As I went to raise my arms, it felt as if another set of arms came underneath mine, making me ten times stronger and ten times braver than I'd ever been. I looked at the glass, and with every ounce of strength I had, I hurled the rock into the window, these mysterious arms helping it go faster and harder than I ever could've on my own. I covered my ears as the sound of breaking glass drowned out the chorus of crickets, cicadas, and tree frogs I'd just been listening to over in Zell's yard.

When the noise died out, I took in the scene I'd created, my heart going a mile a minute. The glass scattered across the patio looked for all the world like a million diamonds shining in the moonlight. It took my breath away. But not nearly as much as the face that appeared in the hole the rock had made. It was a face I'd seen about a hundred times, the face that had been on TV and posters and billboards nearly everywhere we'd gone that summer. "Have you seen me?" the posters asked.

And now I had.

JENCEY

Jencey hadn't meant to stay outside Lance's house as long as she had. She'd intended to just drive by, to see if his car was in the driveway. The irony wasn't lost on her: the stalked somehow becoming the stalker. But the music on the radio had been perfect, one song lapsing into the next, the night air like a caress on her bare arms through the open window. Her parents had taken the girls out to a movie, and she had nowhere else to be. She'd stopped frequenting the hideout when Lance came into her life.

It had been a normal night in the neighborhood, one like any other, except on this night she'd given in to the urge to venture over to the last place she'd been truly happy in a long time. She didn't blame Debra for returning; she just wished she'd come back sooner, preferably before she'd had the chance to fall in love with the woman's husband. She wondered if this summer had just been a step out of time, if Sycamore Glen had simply been their own version of Camelot. She thought of Lance's stupid joke about being named after Lancelot, how she'd believed him for a moment, how gullible she'd been. She pounded her palm into the steering wheel a few times. She'd been so stupid.

She thought she heard something—a disturbance of some sort—and turned down the radio to listen closer. She needed to get out of there and was about to pull away when the sound of four feet thundering across the road stopped her. She looked toward the noise to see two girls running as fast as their little feet could carry them. Curious, she emerged from her car. "Girls?" she called out, looking back to see where they'd come from. Someone came out of Mr. Doyle's house, a dark figure on the porch. Danger crackled in the air; Jencey started to follow the girls up the driveway. They disappeared into Zell's house, and she looked back to see that the figure was gone.

Lance's car pulled into his driveway, and she stepped into the shadows, hiding uselessly. She knew he'd seen her car parked in front of his house, but the last thing she wanted to do was face him. She didn't want to see the happy, reunited family emerge from the car. She turned away and cursed herself for ending up here in this place she no longer belonged. She would take the job in Virginia. She would start over . . . again. She heard three car doors slam and looked over, waiting for the sound of the fourth door. But only three people stood in the driveway, their eyes turned toward Zell's house. They didn't see Jencey because they were looking at Zell on her stoop, yelling for them to come and help.

ZELL

When Cailey came bursting through the back door, she wasn't alone. Zell looked up from her conversation with Bryte, her mind struggling to process what was happening. She'd been so wrapped up in Bryte's story she'd—and she was ashamed of this—forgotten all about the girl in her care. Now there were two girls in her kitchen, one of them as familiar as her own reflection, the other vaguely so. She rose from her chair and gripped the table, blinking at them, her mouth working to find words as a million questions came to mind. She was trying to place the dirty, disheveled child with Cailey. She'd seen her somewhere before.

The child spoke, her breathing heavy, her eyes confused and darting. "I'm . . . I'm Hannah." She paused. "Sumner. I've been kept in that house for"—she looked to Cailey, who nodded—"ninety-four days." She turned and pointed at James's house, her hand quivering as she lifted it. Zell took in the snarled, matted hair, the hollowed-out eyes, the skinny frame underneath a dirty man's undershirt. Blood dripped from a gash in her arm. Improbably, her nails were painted a garish purple that stood out against her pale, pale skin.

Cailey rushed forward and grabbed Zell's phone from the charger, thrusting it into her hand. "Call the police, Zell!" she hollered. "Call them now before he comes over here!" Next door a car pulled up in the driveway, scaring them all half to death. Bryte leaped up, tugged the girls farther into the kitchen, and slammed the door behind them, twisting the lock. She turned to Zell, panic on her face, the story she'd been telling all but forgotten. There were some things more important than the mess of their own lives.

Zell looked at the house next door, as had been her habit for so long. She saw Lance and his two children standing there, but not Debra. She walked over and unlocked the door, stuck her head out, and waved Lance over. "Hurry!" she yelled. "We need your help!" Then she dialed 911, amazed at how steady her fingers were as she pressed the numbers.

When Zell spotted Lance in the yard after Cailey and Hannah went whizzing away in the ambulance, she figured she should be a few minutes late getting over to the hospital. It'd be best to let Cailey's mom be the first one to arrive, leaving her with a good time to speak to Lance. She walked over to him and tapped him on the shoulder. He turned to her, his eyes still wide with shock. "Thank you," she said. "For your help in there."

Lance shrugged. "I don't know what I did. You were the hero."

"No, Cailey's the hero."

He nodded. "That she is." His eyes strayed back to the scene across the street. "I asked Debra to leave," he said, addressing Debra's absence without provocation. "I tried to make it work, but there was just something . . ." He waved his hand in the air, dismissing it.

"What do you mean? There was something?" she pressed, easing the conversation in the direction she needed it to go.

He gave a little laugh. "Nothing. It's not worth going into."

She raised her eyebrows. "Maybe it is."

Now it was his turn to raise his eyebrows. "Like how?"

She crossed her arms. "Why'd she tell you she left?"

He hung his head, ashamed. "She said that I wasn't supportive. That she lost all this weight and I didn't appreciate it. That she was depressed and I didn't even notice. She said I did emotional damage, and I'm sure I did. She had to go away to work out her feelings about it all, to decide if she wanted to continue in the marriage."

He was a good guy—probably one of the best—and that bitch had convinced him he'd done this. She wanted to wring Debra's neck. Zell shook her head. "She was lying."

His eyes widened, telling her she should press on. She was eager to be done with her confession, to finally get off her chest the weight she'd been carrying for far too long. "Well, you know she and I became running partners." He nodded. "And we ended up becoming . . ." She weighed the next word before saying it. "Friends." She took a deep breath and noticed he'd turned his face away again, watching the house across the street as it became a crime scene.

"She started telling me things, and mostly because she knew I was right next door and would see him coming and going, she told me when she started having an affair. At first I was just looking out for them. And then I just . . . started watching them. Together." His neck jerked as he whipped his head back in her direction. "I'm not proud of it." She made herself meet his eyes when all she wanted to do was look at the ground.

"Wait. You're telling me you . . . spied on my wife and her . . . lover?" She saw the disgust on his face, knew he was thinking about what Ty had done, how maybe voyeurism ran in the family. It was nothing she hadn't thought of herself.

Shame colored her face as she answered him. "I would sneak into your backyard and watch them have lunch at your kitchen table, sit and talk on your couch." She sniffed. "I watched it go from innocent to not so innocent, and I should've walked away, but it became a . . . a compulsion. I was lonely and bored and . . . nosy."

He swallowed, and when he went to speak, his voice was ragged. "And they were . . ." He didn't need to finish the sentence.

She nodded. "One day he happened to look up and he . . . saw me. I tried to duck out of the way, but it was too late. I started to run away, but it had rained earlier and I slipped and fell, and that's when I hurt my knee. Debra came outside, found me rolling around in the mud, holding my knee. She looked at me and . . . she knew. She knew what I'd been doing and what I'd seen." Zell stopped talking for a moment, letting her words sink in. Across the street, police personnel were erecting a large portable floodlight. "She left the next day."

She ducked her head. "I just thought you should know. I talked to her the other day, and she told me she wasn't going to tell you, and that I shouldn't or everyone would know what I'd done." She held her hands up. "But I think she knew I was going to tell you. And it's time I did. I don't care if everyone knows. I wouldn't blame you if you never spoke to me again." They were silent for a few minutes. Lance opened his mouth as if to speak, and then seemed to think better of it. Zell watched him walk away, gave him the space and time to absorb all that she had said. She turned back to watch the action across the street and waited to feel the good feelings she'd imagined her confession would bring.

JENCEY

The police moved like bees around a hive, encircling James Doyle's house. Lance was nearby talking to Zell, who was also standing on her front lawn to watch the scene. She looked around but didn't see Bryte anywhere. One by one the media arrived, leaping from their cars to be the first on the scene, two of them actually sprinting across the yard, racing each other. It would've been comical if there was a different reason for their presence.

Though it was now fully dark, the place was lit up like midday. Jencey had watched several policemen lead a confused and frightened Jesse from the home, looking for all the world like he was the one being arrested, his eyes darting around, taking it all in, or trying to. Alone and terrified, she'd seen him run out of the house after Cailey had smashed the glass, then back inside. She'd felt sorry for him, but kept her distance. She was just another stranger to him, even if once upon a time she'd ridden the school bus with him, never making eye contact, avoiding the weird guy from her neighborhood. Though it was too late, she wished she'd been the kind of girl who would've been nice to Jesse. Maybe if she had been she could've crossed the yard, walked beside him, helped him somehow understand what was happening. She wondered where he'd spend the night. She shook her head. First his mother's loss, now this.

Hannah had also been removed from the scene, taken away in an ambulance moments after the authorities arrived. This time Cailey had been allowed in the ambulance, mostly because Hannah Sumner had flipped out about getting in until they said she could have Cailey with her. Jencey watched as Cailey bravely climbed into the ambulance and perched on the side of the stretcher, taking the girl's hand with a resolute look on her face, looking far older than her years. Hannah was slipping into shock, her mind protecting her from reality. Jencey thought of the times she'd seen that face on TV this summer, the times she'd changed the channel so her girls didn't see it, believing that if you didn't look directly at it you could pretend it wasn't there. She didn't like to think of the many times she'd spent the night at Lance's, steps away from a child's endless nightmare. She tried not to think of Hannah's parents seeing her again, imagining their simultaneous joy and terror. Parents were supposed to be the ones to make the nightmares go away.

So far there'd been no sign of James. Cops were coming and going in their attempt to locate and arrest him. She supposed she was waiting for news of his arrest, hungry for some sense of justice. She hoped some cop got in a few good kidney punches once the cuffs were on. Ordinarily she was opposed to violence, but tonight her blood boiled. She thought of being a frightened young girl herself, never held prisoner except in her own mind. She looked behind her at the house where the person who'd terrified her—who'd made her flee—had lived. It was over now. She never had to worry about someone threatening her, never had to look over her shoulder again.

She glanced over and caught Lance watching her. Slowly, meekly, she raised her hand in greeting, relieved when he said something to Zell, and ambled over in response. She longed to reach out to him, to feel his strong arms make her feel safe like that night after they learned about Ty. Not knowing where Debra was or why Debra wasn't there, she kept silent, kept her distance. For a few minutes, he stood wordlessly beside her as they both took in the scene, disbelief floating in the air between them. Other disbelieving neighbors began trickling out of their houses as word spread, needing to see this with their own eyes. They formed clusters in Lance's and Zell's yards, everyone grappling for a clear view, angling for the latest news.

She needed to call her mom, let her know she was OK. They'd be home from the movies by now, would no doubt hear and be concerned. She thought of her mother's face as she'd said goodbye to her before she'd left for that college so far from home. She could see now that her mother had been terrified but worked to keep her from seeing it. When she got home, she would thank them for making sure she was safe by letting her go. If the tables were turned, she wasn't sure she could've done the same.

Tears began to fall, but she made no motion to wipe them away lest she call attention to herself. This night shouldn't be about sadness. Jencey was free and so was that little girl. Lance stepped closer. He put his arm around her and drew her into him, closing the distance between them. And then, ever so gently, he reached up and wiped her tears away. She hadn't drawn attention to her tears, but he'd seen them anyway. She began to cry harder, and he pulled her in, surrounding her with love.

BRYTE

Thankfully, Myrtle Honeycutt was still up watching a Braves game when Bryte brought Rigby back. "Did you hear all that commotion out there?" the old woman asked as she opened the door, her eyes wide and darting around. "You got any idea what's going on?"

Bryte patted Myrtle's shoulder, assuring her that everything was fine. She helped her settle in for the night and watched to make sure she locked the door behind her. Still keyed up from the events of the night, she came home to a darkened house. She worried that Everett had done exactly what she'd feared he would do since the day they got together. But would he take their son? The word caught in her throat: *their.* He would not take Christopher because he was not his son. And the knowledge of that might've been the final straw. She resumed her internal lecture from before: she'd done this to herself, and she deserved everything that came to her.

Still, she called out into the darkness, "Everett?" her voice a loud, urgent whisper. She wanted to tell him what had happened that night, all that she'd witnessed at Zell's house. She thought of the terrified little girls in Zell's kitchen, the flashing lights of the police cars throwing red-and-blue patterns against the neighboring houses, the onslaught of reporters. She'd snuck away while everyone was distracted. Hannah's discovery was a big story, but she had an unfolding drama of her own to sort out.

Everett didn't answer her, so she moved quickly toward Christopher's room, not bothering to turn on the lights as she went. She knew this house in her sleep, could feel her way through the darkness without bumping into furniture or walls. The knot in her throat grew as she thought about leaving it. There was no way she could afford to keep it on her own. All she'd ever wanted was to live in this neighborhood with her own family one day. Her dreams had been relatively small, yet still too big for her to attain.

Christopher's door was open, the night-light they kept lit for him spilling the tiniest bit of light into the hall. She paused in the doorway when she saw Everett already there, standing beside his toddler bed, Gulliver looking down at the Lilliputian. She stood stone-still, taking in the scene as she waited for the knot in her throat to dissolve. After a few moments, she realized she was holding her breath, and she exhaled. When she did, Everett turned around and saw her. In the darkness, she could barely make out his face, yet she knew instinctively he'd been crying. Just as instinctively, she moved toward him, wanting to hold him, to dry his tears, to make everything OK for him just like she'd always been compelled to do.

But of course that instinct had gotten them where they were today. She kept her arms at her sides and willed herself not to reach for him.

"I thought you were gone," she whispered.

He shook his head, and there was silence for a few more seconds. "I thought about it," he finally said. "I even came in here to . . . say goodbye, to tell him I was sorry."

He went quiet, and she fought the urge to tell him to keep talking. The words were on her lips: "You have nothing to be sorry for." But she held them in, biting on her bottom lip to refrain from speaking.

"But I couldn't say it. I couldn't tell him goodbye." He turned to look at her again, and she could hear the tears in the thickness of his voice. "He's so beautiful."

She nodded as her own eyes filled with tears. "Yes," she said. Below them, Christopher threw his arms over his head, his chin pointed toward the headboard, his little elephant tucked close to him, moonlight highlighting the features she'd searched a thousand times for proof or denial of his parentage. Some days she could see Trent in him as clear as day. Other days she saw Everett, because she wanted to. When he was born, Everett's mother had marched into the hospital room, clasped her hands to her chest, and exclaimed, "He looks just like his daddy!" Bryte had foolishly hoped that meant she was home free. But she had never truly been home free again.

Everett motioned for her to follow him out into the hall, and with one last glance at Christopher, she did. What she'd done was stupid, but her son's existence was the opposite of regrettable. She would spend the rest of her life caught in that paradox. She pulled Christopher's door nearly closed, leaving just a crack between the frame and the door itself, the way she herself had slept as a child.

She followed Everett across the hall and into their bedroom, pausing at the threshold again. He slumped into the overstuffed chair she'd long ago stuck in the corner of the room when her mom was getting rid of it. It had become a repository for discarded items of clothing draped across the back—his and hers—that neither of them ever bothered to look through unless they needed something in particular. She was pretty sure her coat and his thick flannel shirt were still there from winter, waiting to be discovered.

She couldn't look at him sitting there, his head in his hands. Her eyes moved over to their bed just for somewhere else to look. She wished it was like any other night and she could just crawl into it, could feel Everett's steady presence beside her, have him tease her with his ongoing accusation that she snored. The little things were what she'd miss. She heard him inhale and steeled herself for whatever he was going to say.

"Do you have feelings for him? Do you want him in Christopher's life? Is that why you went to see him?"

The words stunned her. "No," she said, the objection ringing in the silent room. "Nothing like that. I—" She was going to say that she truly went there to talk to him about a job. But as she met his eyes, she knew he saw through that, probably faster than she had. Her voice was softer as she went on to explain. "You wanted another baby so much. And I knew it wasn't going to happen. And then I found his business card. I'd kept it because . . ." She made herself look at his eyes. "Well, I kept it just in case there was ever something . . . genetic. That came up."

They blinked at each other for a moment, absorbing the weight of all she'd kept hidden from him.

"And when I saw it again, it just made me think about . . . seeing him again. You kept talking about another baby, and I was feeling pressured to finally tell you the truth, and I guess I wanted to try to remember what could've possibly made me think it was the answer."

There was more silence, more broken gazes. She spoke again to fill the silence, to somehow utter the words that would make him understand.

"I wanted to tell you since the moment it happened. I wanted to look you in the eye and say, 'We are never having children of our own so let's figure out how to deal with it.'" As she spoke, she moved toward him, her steps deliberate and certain. She would wrap her arms around him, and if he pulled away, he would be the one to pull away. But she wasn't going to pull away anymore. She would love him until the last second she had to love him. And if she lost him anyway, well, at least she'd made the most of the time she had with him.

She stopped when she got close to him, her arms hanging limply at her sides. "But then I would see you with him and the two of you would be laughing and talking about what you were going to work on in the yard or what his favorite kind of dinosaur is and I would think, 'How can I possibly wreck this?' Why would anyone want to wreck this?" A tear escaped the corner of her eye and traveled the length of her cheek. She didn't bother to wipe it away. It fell off the edge of her face and disappeared into the carpet.

"I love him," Everett said, his choked voice barely more than a whisper.

"Of course you do."

"He's my son."

She felt some of the tension she'd been holding in her body whoosh out with those three words. "Yes," she said.

"It'll take a long time to let it sink in. That he's not. Technically."

She bristled but kept quiet.

"And he doesn't know? Anything?"

This was a different he, but Bryte knew who Everett meant. She shook her head. "Nothing."

Everett reached up and took her hands, lacing his fingers in hers. She looked at him, surprise evident on her face. But on his face she saw a look she couldn't ever remember seeing. It was a hard look, a determined look, his jaw like steel, pulsing. "Did he make a play for you when you were with him today?"

Her heart picked up speed. She swallowed as she determined how to answer. Truth. She had promised herself she would tell the truth from now on. "S-sort of. I think . . . he thought perhaps what happened before could h-happen again. He wanted me to stay for dinner."

"And it would've happened again, if it had happened." He pointed at her stomach. "I'm right, aren't I?"

She nodded. Of course she'd thought of the timing, how easy it would be—on one level—to let it happen again.

He let go of her hands, and for one desperate moment, she feared she'd given him the wrong answer. But then she saw him glance over at the clock, and she knew. They looked at each other, and for a few moments neither of them spoke as, without words, each took in what was happening.

"I can't give you a child," he said.

"I know."

"Ever." He leaned over as he said it, as if he'd been punched. "It's hard to say that out loud."

She watched as he righted himself to a standing position, trying not to get ahead of what he was saying.

"After you left I thought about it and . . . we can't have any more kids." He exhaled loudly. "We'll have to either adopt or get a donor, and if we do that, then that child will be different from Christopher. It'll be totally obvious. To him. To everyone."

"Yes," she said. She was doing her best to keep her knees from giving out. Her head thrummed, and Everett's face swam a little before her eyes.

He took a deep breath, held it, and exhaled. "I don't want different. I don't want anyone to ever know. Most of all, him. I'd do anything to protect him from ever finding out that I'm not his real father. Because I am."

Her eyes filled with tears, and she closed them briefly, then opened them to find Everett looking back at her. She'd gone to the hotel to see if she could perpetuate the illusion she'd created. But she'd lost her nerve because it would only be another lie piled on top of the festering heap she'd created. She opened her mouth to speak, but no words would come.

"If I could pick out any little boy to be my own, I'd pick him." He reached for her hands again and squeezed them hard. "I want you to know that. I need you to know that."

She willed herself not to cry even as more tears leaked from her eyes. Later she would fall apart. Now something was happening that could not occur if she gave in to her emotions. She remembered the robotic feeling from the night she'd made Christopher, how she'd so easily exchanged her warm flesh for cold metal, her skin barely registering the contact as he moved over and inside her. In her head she heard that damn Heart song playing on an endless loop. What Everett couldn't give her was the one little thing he could.

Everett swallowed, his Adam's apple bobbing inside his throat, and she thought for the millionth time what a tragedy it was that this man—this handsome, charming, kind man—could never reproduce himself. "How drunk do you think he is by now?" he asked. His breathing pattern had changed. He sounded like he did after he'd been lifting weights.

"He was well on his way when I left at five. He might even be passed out by now. Or with someone else. Or . . ."

"Shhh," he said. He rested his finger on her lips for the briefest of seconds, and then reached into the pocket of her shorts to retrieve her cell phone. He held it out to her. "Yes?" He raised his eyebrows, shaking the phone the slightest bit.

She took the phone from his hand, felt his gaze rest on her, and in it his assumption that she would do this thing. But would it be any easier with his complicity? She saw them in her mind, her two beautiful children, a perfect matched set. It was so tempting to perpetuate what she'd created, and guarded, for so long. It was right there if she wanted it, and all it would take is one more meaningless night. But of course, it wasn't meaningless. That one night held more meaning than nearly any other before or since. It divided and defined, haunted and hindered. But no more.

She exhaled, the whoosh of air loud in the silent room. She cupped his chin in her hands and gave him the barest hint of a smile. "No," she said, and handed him back the phone.

ZELL

John honked the horn in the driveway, and Zell hurried outside to see the truck. He climbed out and swept his arm past the bed, loaded down with their surprise for Cailey and her family. She came over to stand beside him, rested her head on his shoulder. "You're a good man, John Boyette," she said.

"You're a persistent wife, Zell Boyette," he quipped. He chuckled and shook his head. "I don't know how you get me into these things."

She elbowed him. "You wanted to do this as much as I did. That child grew on you this summer."

"That she did." He elbowed her back and raised his eyebrows. "She also got you out of going with the Robinsons to Lake Lure."

She waved her hand in the air, refusing to admit just how true that was. "She needed us a lot more than Clay and Althea did."

He touched his finger to her nose, gave her that look that told her he was wise to her ways. "And you needed her."

She smiled, holding her hands up in mock surrender. "Maybe just a little."

"You know," he said, "I've been thinking."

She laughed. "Oh no."

"No, I'm serious. I think you should go back to teaching somehow this fall—Sunday school or maybe substituting again? Something where you can work with kids. You're good at it."

"Yeah, I was thinking about calling around, seeing if there're some schools that might need help with beautifying their grounds or even doing the Wildlife Habitat program. That's how Cailey knew about it— they did it at one of her schools. So, seeing as how I know what to do now, I thought maybe I could put that hard-earned knowledge to use."

He nodded, smiled. "I like it."

"Yeah," she said. "Me, too."

He clapped his hands together. "You ready to go? It's only gonna get hotter, so we might as well get started."

"Sure, I just need to make one quick phone call before we go."

"Whoever it is, you're probably gonna see them there," he groused.

She paused, thought of the promise she'd made to herself. She couldn't go love on someone else's child unless she'd done the same for her own. Her son was hurting, but she'd been too wrapped up in her own shame to reach out to him. She couldn't spend one more day with him thinking he'd failed her, when the truth was he was just like her.

"It's Ty," she said.

His smiled widened. "That's my girl." He pointed at Lance's house. "I'll just go see if Lance remembered his hedge clippers."

She nodded and went back inside. She picked up the phone, dialed the number, and listened as on the other end, it began to ring.

CAILEY

Two days after I got home, they all showed up. Zell and Mr. John, Jencey and Lance with Lilah, Alec, Pilar, and Zara all whooping and hollering as they chased each other around in that terrible bare yard of our eyesore house. Bryte came, too, and brought her husband, Everett, who hadn't been around a whole lot that summer but who was very nice. They left Christopher with his grandmother, though, because they said they didn't want him underfoot. They had work to do, they said. With big smiles on their faces, they pointed to a pickup truck parked in our driveway. It was filled with bushes and flowers and even a small tree.

Zell came and stood beside me as I took it all in. "Every gardener should have a garden of her own," she said.

"Thank you," I said, but I barely had a voice to say it with.

She shrugged. "We all helped." But I knew it was mainly her idea. She was the only one who knew how much this would mean to me.

"The other night," I said, "I never really got to say goodbye with everything that . . . happened."

She shrugged. "We don't really need to say goodbye, do we?" She waggled her finger in my direction. "I mean, we're still neighbors, and that means you better come see me." She pointed at the little tree John was unloading from the truck with help from Everett. "Do you know what kind of tree that is?"

"A sycamore?" I guessed.

Zell laughed. "Well, yes, we thought it would be fitting to get a sycamore. But that's not what I call it."

I raised one eyebrow, something I'd been teaching myself to do. It always made Cutter laugh. "What do you call it?"

"The Miracle tree," she said.

"The Miracle tree?" It made me think about that Miracle-Gro stuff we used in Zell's garden.

"Yep." She nodded. "We're going to plant it in the front yard so that we can all see it as we drive by. It'll be a nice reminder of the miracle that happened here this summer."

I looked at all the people gathered there—Lilah and Alec running around with Pilar and Zara, Jencey and Lance making goo-goo eyes at each other, Bryte looking a lot happier than she had when she showed up at Zell's the other night. We had a lot of miracles going around. We probably needed a whole forest full of trees in my front yard.

Zell put her arm around me and kissed the top of my head. "You were my miracle," she said, her voice so low I didn't know if I'd heard her right. But then I looked up into her eyes, and I knew I had.

I had to change the subject before she made me cry. "Well, you know what I don't want in my garden?" I asked.

"What's that?"

"A pond!" I said, and we both cracked up.

"Hey, Zell!" Jencey hollered. "We need you over here!" Zell gave me a little smile and walked away. As soon as she did, Lilah, Pilar, and Zara came over.

"It's really cool what you did," Pilar said. Beside her, Lilah and Zara nodded their agreement.

I shrugged because I didn't know what else to say. I wasn't quite ready to talk about what I did, or who I found, or how I came to find her.

"Wanna help us plant the flowers?" they asked.

"Sure," I said. They handed me a trowel with a yellow handle, just like the one I used at Zell's house. I looked around me to see Alec and Cutter standing together in the bed of the truck, helping pass out the plants. Lance took a flat of pink geraniums from Alec, then handed them off to Jencey, but made her give him a kiss before he'd let go of them, which made Pilar and Zara giggle. Bryte braided Lilah's hair so it wouldn't be in her face. She did such a good job that we all said we wanted her to do ours.

"You're good at braiding. You should have a little girl someday," Lilah told her.

Everett and Bryte looked at each other. "Actually," Bryte said to Lilah, "we think we might adopt one."

"Cool!" Lilah said, then bounced away to help dig holes for the flowers.

We worked until the sun went down and we couldn't see to work anymore. When we were done, John ordered pizzas and we all sat on blankets in the front yard to eat, dirty and tired and hungry. I don't think pizza ever tasted better. Mom came home from work with Gary the Ambulance Guy. She cried when she saw what they'd done for us, and then Gary went to the store and bought beers for the adults and sodas for the kids. Later, Everett disappeared and then came back with boxes of fresh, warm donuts from Krispy Kreme. And though Zell said, "Oh I couldn't," she did.

We stayed that way past everybody's bedtime—even the adults'—but no one made a move to leave. Alec and Cutter fell asleep on the blankets, tired from chasing each other around in the hot sun all day. I sat with Zell on one side and Mom on the other, and I didn't think about James Doyle or Hannah Sumner or Cutter—quiet and still at the bottom of that pool—even once. We laughed and talked long into the night, and it felt warm, cozy, familiar. To quote that entrance sign, it felt like family, a family I never expected to have.

JENCEY

Jencey motioned for the girls to keep up and made a silly face at them, attempting to lighten the mood. They could be so serious sometimes. She supposed that was her fault, but she was doing what she could to be a different kind of mother.

"Are you sure about this?" Zara asked, her voice quavering slightly.

Jencey smiled. "Yes, I'm sure." She kept her voice light, wanting to put her daughters at ease. Both of them had heard the story of what had happened to poor Hannah Sumner. Though all the parents attempted to keep the details from the kids, Jencey had seen them gathered at the pool in little clusters, parsing what they knew, creating their own narrative that was, Jencey suspected, probably worse than the actual truth.

Hannah Sumner had escaped. She would never be the same again, but she was alive. She had a future ahead of her that was as bright as she chose to make it. Jencey supposed that was all anyone could ask for in this broken, screwed-up world.

She moved branches and brambles from their path, clearing the way for her girls as they ventured deeper into the woods. Neither girl thought this was the best idea, but Jencey insisted. She'd lured them away from the house with the promise of an adventure. The thing about adventure was, it usually required at least a modicum of danger. They pressed forward and finally found the clearing. She tried to see it through their eyes, to remember what it felt like when she'd found it as a child, how it had felt like hers from the moment she saw it.

Now she would bequeath it to her girls, passing it along as if it were hers to give. They looked at the copse of trees with wide eyes, then back at her, the concern on their faces giving way to excited grins. "It's a hideaway," she explained.

"Can we go in?"

"Sure!" she urged, motioning with her hands for them to enter.

For a moment she felt fear creep in, a fist gripping her heart. Maybe it wasn't the best idea to show them this place. Look what she'd done here, after all. She wasn't sure she wanted either girl holing up here with a boy. And yet, that had come much later. In the early days, it had been only about having a place of her own—a place to escape to, a place to dream. Since it looked like they'd be with her parents for a while longer, the girls could use such a place.

She crawled through the branches after them. Pilar hugged herself and looked around, delight etched on her face. "This is so cool," she breathed. Zara turned around and around in circles, her arms outstretched and her face tilted toward the little patch of sky. She stopped and staggered around, dizzy from the spinning. She lurched into the waiting arms of Jencey, who planted a kiss on top of her head. Pilar edged closer to the two of them, and they stood together in silence.

"Can we show this place to Lilah and Alec?" Pilar asked, her voice still laced with a breathy excitement. The thought of Lance's kids made her think of Lance, made her smile. He'd talked her out of Virginia, talked her into seeing what the future held in Sycamore Glen. They were taking it slow, but they were moving forward.

"You can show it to whoever you'd like," she said. "It's yours now."

"I might want to keep it a secret," Zara said, burying her head in the crook of Jencey's arm.

"Well, that's for you girls to discuss."

"And you think we'll be safe here?" Pilar, always the responsible eldest, asked.

Jencey thought about how to answer. "I always was." And as she said it, she realized it was true.

"It's kind of dark in here," Zara said, doubt in her voice.

"Let me show you how to fix that." Jencey grinned and walked over to the border of trees. She looked over her shoulder at the girls as they watched with interest. She beckoned them over and gestured for them to stick their hands into the branches. "OK, now pull," she instructed. "Pull hard!" Together they tugged the branches apart, pulling wider and harder as, together, they let the light in.

ZELL

As she walked to her car, Zell spotted a single yellow leaf on the drive, a harbinger of summer's end. School was starting in a few days, but when she'd asked Cailey if she'd gotten her teacher assignment yet, she'd just said, "Ugh, don't talk about it."

Cailey still turned up at Zell's door quite often, making the trek across the neighborhood with Cutter in tow. His gait was still a bit off, and sometimes he had trouble accessing the right words, but other than that, he was doing well. He was healing.

She looked across the street at James's empty house. It was already starting to show signs of neglect. Some kind soul had found a place for Jesse to live, and of course James would likely never see life outside prison after what he'd done. Someone had graffitied their thoughts about what should become of him across the front door after the press finally went away. John had made noises about going over and painting over it eventually.

He and Lance were trying to keep the grass cut, but they were busy and it didn't always get done in a timely manner. There were still marks where some kids had egged the house late one night. Zell had been awakened in the wee hours of the morning by the rhythmic thunks of the eggs hitting the wood. She'd gone to the window to see figures moving around in the yard, the white projectiles shining in the moonlight as they took flight again and again. She supposed she should've been alarmed, but all she felt was fascination. This was how people healed: they went and did something—anything they could—to redeem the situation.

It was time for her to do something, too. She was starting with the doctor's appointment she had in thirty minutes. She would finally submit her knee for examination. She would perch on a cold, sterile table and answer his questions. She might even tell the whole truth about how it had happened. She would discuss surgery and rehab. She would ask how soon she could start exercising. She would let herself dream of the day she would run again.

CAILEY

Zell gave me a bulletin board to put up in my room for all the news clippings and photos about what happened. People said I was like David the shepherd boy, using a stone to topple a giant. The interviewers always asked the same questions:

How did you know Hannah was there?

What made you throw that rock?

Do you consider yourself a hero?

Will you and Hannah be friends forever?

I even got paid money to come on TV and talk about what happened (even though I'm not supposed to say I did). And I got the reward money for finding Hannah, too. My mom said that made me a double hero. It was enough money to be able to put a down payment on a house of our own—even though moving didn't feel so urgent now that we didn't live in the eyesore of the neighborhood anymore, thanks to all the hard work our neighbors did. Mom and I agreed we would take our time and find the best house, a house of our own, something I never dreamed we'd have. I told my mom my only request was we had to stay in Sycamore Glen.

When people ask me what I think a hero is (which they always do), I tell them about Cutter: how he nearly drowned, but after he got better, he got back in the same pool that nearly killed him. He stood on the edge, his toes curling into the cement as if he was grabbing hold. I could tell from the look on his face that he was thinking about turning away. I wanted to whisper in his ear that no one would blame him if he did, put my arm around him, and walk him over to the drink machine to buy him a Dr Pepper. He could try again next summer, or he could stay out of the water forever.

But then I saw him look at that water like it was his opponent in a wrestling match he wanted to win. I saw his face get that determined look that I think I probably had when I launched that rock into that glass. His eyes found mine, and I nodded that I understood; I nodded that he'd be OK. His feet left the edge, and though his toes remained curled, he flew into the air. As I watched, I imagined that those same arms I'd felt that night were underneath him, holding him close and throwing him up at the same time, helping him fly without letting him fall.

I heard everyone around me inhale as we watched my brother break the water's surface. No one dared to breathe while he was under the water, and when his head popped back up, everyone started to clap, their held breaths all coming out in one relieved rush of air. Someone hugged me and someone else yelled, "Go, Cutter!" At that moment, I thought of the day the spider nearly blocked our entrance to the pool, and how we never knew what message he might've spelled in his web. And I realized that it didn't matter what the spider said. It mattered that we knocked that web down and walked right in.

AUTHOR'S NOTE

Several years ago, a little boy nearly drowned in our neighborhood pool. In the days after this event, I noticed how it united and changed our neighborhood.

I could say that this novel was begun in the ensuing days, but that's not entirely true. Instead, I think the novel began in earnest at our end-of-the-season swim-team banquet several weeks later, when that same little boy went forward to get his swim-team trophy. There wasn't a dry eye in the house as we all witnessed the miracle of him—healthy and whole—going forward to accept a trophy for the thing that had nearly killed him. There was so much hope—so much joy—in that moment, and I knew then I would write about it somehow, some way, if for no other reason than to try to lasso some of what I felt whoosh through the room in that moment.

I hope that in the final scene, when Cutter goes back in that water, you felt a tiny bit of what we all felt at that swim-team banquet. And I hope that maybe whatever you've been scared to dive into won't scare you so much anymore.

ACKNOWLEDGMENTS

Abundant thanks go out to the following people:

Liza Dawson, my agent, who called late one Tuesday night and told me not to give up, and then didn't give up, either.

Tara Parsons, Jodi Warshaw, Nicci Jordan Hubert, and the team at Lake Union. Without your valuable skills, none of this could have happened. Thanks for making this story so much better.

My husband, Curt, and our kids: Jack, Ashleigh, Matt, Rebekah, Brad, and Annaliese. Home is wherever all of you are. I won the family lottery. And specifically to Curt, I am thankful every day I get to do this life with you. Your wisdom, support, and encouragement sustain me. Another twenty-five? Let's do it!

Ariel Lawhon, you're the other half of my brain—which should terrify you but does not. I bless the day our lives converged.

My mom, Sandy Brown. I can only hope to be the mother to my kids that you've been to me.

The local writers who meet to write, brainstorm, gripe, and celebrate this gig. Nobody gets it like you guys do. Erika Marks, Kim Wright Wiley, Kim Boykin, and Joy Callaway—I don't know what I'd do without you!

The friends Curt and I do life with: Tracy and Douglas Graham, Billy and Jill Dean, Lisa and Mike Shea, Dawn and Jamil Massey, Kim and Sam Young, April and Paul Duncan, Terry and Jen Tolbert, Beth and Steve Burton, and Amy and Clay Gilliam. Thanks for asking about my novels and always being willing to raise a glass of champagne when I'm ready to celebrate.

My neighbors. (I'm not even going to attempt to write down all your names!) You share the neighborhood that served as the inspiration for the setting of this novel, so you know better than anyone else how special it is. I'll see you guys at the pool!

Every teacher who ever nudged me in the direction of writing and gave me the tools to do it better.

The Master Storyteller: I trust You to keep telling my story the way You see fit. The pen is in Your capable hand, and I wouldn't have it any other way. I Chronicles 16:8-12

(And Billy Dean, that Death Cab reference was just for you. Jill Dean, in the next book I promise to name a character after you!)

QUESTIONS FOR DISCUSSION

1. What is each character—Zell, Jencey, Cailey, Bryte, Lance—lacking when the story begins? Are they aware of it? Why or why not?

2. Jencey seems to feel a good bit of shame and guilt over Arch's arrest. Is this reasonable? To be expected? Is she complicit, as Arch claims?

3. Why do you think Jencey tells Everett the truth about why she came back before telling anyone else?

4. Why does Jencey go to the hideaway night after night when she first returns? Boredom? Longing? Nostalgia? Something else?

5. Why does Zell keep Cailey long after most people would have sent her back? What does this say about Zell? (Your answer could be positive or negative.)

6. Bryte and Jencey were friends as children. How does that play into their relationship in the novel? Do either of them feel a sense of "claim" on the other? Should they? How important are old friends to you?

7. Were you surprised at the identity of Jencey's stalker? Why or why not?

8. Zell senses something is "off" about James Doyle, but she's the only one in the neighborhood who seems to.

Ultimately, she's right. Have you ever had a sense like this about someone? Did you listen to it? Did it ever prove true?

9. What ultimately makes Everett forgive Bryte? Should he have forgiven her?

10. What makes Bryte hand the phone back to Everett? Would she have done that at the beginning of the book?

11. In the end, Jencey "gives" the hideaway to her daughters. Why do you think she does this? What does the hideaway symbolize?

12. When does the title come into play in the book? What character expresses it? How does it apply to each character? To you?

ABOUT THE AUTHOR

Photo © 2016 Portrait Innovations

Marybeth Mayhew Whalen is the author of five previous novels and speaks to women's groups around the United States. She is the cofounder of the popular women's fiction site She Reads and is active in a local writers' group. Marybeth and her husband, Curt, have been married for twenty-four years and are the parents of six children, ranging from young adult to elementary age. The family lives in North Carolina. Marybeth spends most of her time in the grocery store but occasionally escapes long enough to scribble some words. She is always at work on her next novel. You can find her at www.marybethwhalen.com or www.shereads.org.